"Elizabeth, please. Put down the gun. I mean you no harm."

Ian's gun stayed trained on Patrice.

"Your husband was a friend of mine," he said. "I was in Maryland to watch over you. He asked me to make sure both you and your daughter were safe."

"So to protect us, you find some way to follow us, drug my friend's dog and then hold her at gunpoint."

I heard the van crank outside, and so did he. "Where is your daughter?" he asked.

"I sent Cara to call the police."

Before he could say another word, the side of the building exploded. Wood flew everywhere. When I looked up, I couldn't believe what I was seeing. Patrice's VW van had burst through the side of the old barn.

Cara beckoned to us through the open side door. "Get in!"

I pushed Patrice forward, tumbled in on top of her and slid the door shut.

Then I saw Ian reach for Cara in the driver's seat. That bastard was coming in through the window.

Not if I could help it.

Dear Reader,

The character of Elizabeth Larocca first came to me when I was toying with the idea of what might have happened in my own life if I had married the wrong man but loved him anyway. What would I have done if I'd found myself swept into his dangerous world and I had a twenty-three-year-old daughter who was right in the midst of it? Would I hate him? Could I find a way to forgive him? And to what lengths would I go to protect my child?

I drew on my experiences as a mother with two daughters who have made the transition from children into trusted friends. The give and take of those relationships, the admission that we are all only human and, even as parents, don't always know the right thing to do, are part of what makes this book special to me. I tell my children that we may grow older, but inside we never age. We gather wisdom but we never become infallible, and sometimes the wisest thing we can do is trust our children's decisions.

Elizabeth was scarred by her relationship with her husband, Stephen, and by the loss of her sister. I wanted her whole as I would any dear friend. I loved writing her story. It was a great adventure. I invite you to come along.

Judy Fitzwater

NO SAFE PLACE

JUDY FITZWATER

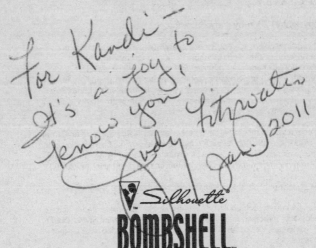

For Kandi—
It's a joy to
know you!
Judy Fitzwater
Jan. 2011

Silhouette®

BOMBSHELL™

Published by Silhouette Books

America's Publisher of Contemporary Romance

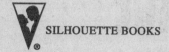 SILHOUETTE BOOKS
®

ISBN 0-373-51405-0

NO SAFE PLACE

Copyright © 2006 by Judy Fitzwater

This edition published by arrangement with Harlequin Books S.A.

www.SilhouetteBombshell.com

Printed in U.S.A.

JUDY FITZWATER

is the author of seven published novels. She loves to weave suspense and mystery with romance to take both herself and her readers into a world full of adventure. She's fascinated by the woman who finds herself in extraordinary circumstances and rises, strong and determined, to confront her situation.

Judy grew up an air force brat before attending high school and college in Kentucky. Her first foray into writing was with a small newspaper in North Carolina where she wrote feature articles, columns and reports of superior court proceedings. She loves to write the sort of books she loves to read: fast-paced, exciting tales about intriguing women. She invites you to contact her by sending an e-mail to judyfitzwater@judyfitzwater.com.

For Miellyn, my Cara

Chapter 1

I should never have married Stephen Michael Larocca. I knew it when he and I were standing in front of the minister, I knew it when I kicked him out of my life and I damned well knew it when his body turned up again—after I'd buried the son of a bitch.

"Did you read this?" Cara asked, waving the piece of paper I'd given her in my face.

"Every word." I took a swig of the scotch I'd poured myself. It stung my throat and I choked. I'd forgotten how nasty it tasted. Scotch was Stephen's drink, not mine.

"It's a request asking if we want Dad reburied at sea. You call me and insist that I leave work, skip lunch and get my butt over here—"

"I didn't use the word *butt*."

"—without a single word of explanation, scaring me half to death. I thought something horrible had happened. This is some stupid bureaucratic mistake. Pick up the phone, call the coast guard and tell them whoever that fisherman snagged in his net isn't Dad."

She came to the kitchen table, took the glass out of my hand and smelled it. "What's wrong with you? You're drinking Dad's scotch."

"Only theoretically. Drinking requires swallowing. I thought..."

Actually that was the whole point: I didn't want to think. For just a little while, I wanted to slip into oblivion and pretend the last six hours hadn't happened. I wanted the phone call from the coroner not to have come. I wanted Stephen not to be dead. I wanted Cara happy like she'd been two weeks ago. Twenty-three was too young to lose her father.

I looked at her again. She was beautiful—thick, dark hair; brown, almost black eyes; olive skin; a saucy, pouty mouth with a hint of mischief—just like her father. But under the skin, she was my daughter, and that meant I was in for trouble.

"This is a mistake," she insisted.

I almost laughed. I retrieved the glass from the sink where she'd put it, and got the scotch out of the cabinet to try it again. I'd heard the first few sips were the worst, that it got better.

This time she took the bottle away and poured its contents down the drain.

"Mom, we buried Dad two weeks ago." The words caught in her throat. "We stood together and watched his casket lowered into the ground. We threw dirt on top of it. This is someone else's body. Do you want *me* to call the coast guard? Is that why you asked me to come over?"

I sat back down, numb, unable to comfort her or focus my thoughts.

Cara opened the blinds behind the small table. I winced at the afternoon sunshine. I wasn't in the mood for light.

"Christ, Mom. Snap out of it. How much did you drink?"

She pulled the coffee can out of the refrigerator and, not bothering to measure, dumped some grounds into the basket of the coffee maker. She never was much good at math. Or cooking. Or dealing with the fact that her father was dead. Her eyes were ringed with red.

She stuck the carafe under the spigot and then poured the water into the reservoir. She needn't have bothered. I wasn't drunk. I just wanted to be. I couldn't get the foul stuff down.

"It's his body," I said evenly, watching carefully for her reaction.

"Now I know you've lost it. It couldn't possibly—"

"I saw it."

That stopped her cold. I wanted to reach out to her, but I felt frozen.

"You mean you identified the corpse they pulled out of the water?" She slid into the chair across from me, the slightest tremble to her hands. She dropped them in her lap where I couldn't see them. Weakness was something we Laroccas hid well.

"An hour and a half ago."

I didn't go into the details of what two weeks in open water does to a corpse. I wish I hadn't seen it. The image was etched in my brain. The body *was* Stephen's, what was left of it. The tattoo of the U.S. Navy SEAL insignia wasn't the only give-away. He'd had his initials added just below. And just below those, mine, two days after I'd agreed to marry him.

"There's more," I added.

I saw her look at the scotch bottle, empty, on the counter. She was about to be sorry she'd poured it out.

"The body had been cut open and sewn back up again."

"Dad was skiing alone when he died. Of course the authorities would order an autopsy."

"Not in Denver. Not before we buried him. When we got him back, his body was whole."

Now my pain was hers. As her horror grew, some of my numbness waned. I moved to put my arms around her, but she shook me off. She had her father's strength, or the illusion of it. I watched her features soften and, for the briefest moment, I glimpsed her panic.

I never spoke ill of Stephen, not in front of her at least. But she knew how I felt. And I think, for the first time in her life, she might have had just an inkling that I had cause when I said there were things concerning him she knew nothing about, things I couldn't live with, things I'd spent a lifetime protecting her from.

She licked her lips, and gave me a long stare. "Are you saying someone stole Dad's body after we buried him?"

And then dumped it like trash in the bay.

"When?" she asked. "Why?"

"I have no idea." At least, none I was willing to share with her.

As to when, my best guess was that the body had been removed from the coffin at the funeral home, between the service and the interment. It would have been so much easier than digging him up.

The why was a much more difficult question. I hadn't spoken with Stephen in months, not since that last visit, before I got the call from the funeral home in Denver saying he was…

I still couldn't get my mind around the word.

"What are we going to do?" Cara asked.

"Have him reburied."

To her credit, she didn't roll her eyes. She just kind of

squinted at me. "I didn't think you were going to keep him for a souvenir. That's not what I meant. What was Dad doing that someone would want to steal his body?"

She was angry with me, and she had every right to be. I hadn't wanted to share any of this with her. But I dared not keep it from her.

"I don't know who stole it," I said, "or when it was stolen. There were rope marks on his ankles. Whoever dumped him in the Chesapeake never intended for him to resurface. And I'm sure they didn't expect me to be notified. When a body like that washes up, autopsied, they assume it was a burial at sea and rebury it without notifying the family. They don't usually take the trouble to identify it."

"So why did they?"

"The tattoo. Remember a few years ago when he went missing for a while on that hiking trip through the Rocky Mountains?"

"As if I could forget. We thought he was dead."

When he showed up two weeks later, he said he'd lost his compass and become disoriented. But his clothes were clean and his beard was neatly trimmed. He was well hydrated and he didn't look to me as if he'd missed a meal.

"That was when they entered a photo of his tattoo in the FBI database, in case his body turned up," I explained. "Someone checked it out. Guess it was still there."

"Terrific."

My thoughts exactly.

"So. We just bury him again and forget it?"

"That's my plan." God, how I wished it could be that simple.

"And let whoever did this get away with it? They desecrated his grave. I take that very personally and you should, too. We've got to call someone," Cara insisted. "The police? The FBI?"

"That wouldn't be wise." I didn't want anyone to know that we knew. It might buy us some time.

"Why?"

"Cara, we don't need to get in the middle of some investigation. I know you're angry, but the best that could happen for you, for me, is to let this pass and go on as though we know nothing about it. Trust me. Please."

"Trust goes both ways, Mom."

"Believe me, I know." I just wish Stephen had known it, too. "That's why I called you."

She nodded. Good. At least that gave me one point.

"Have you gotten his things yet?" she asked. "Wasn't one of his coworkers supposed to be taking care of them?"

I would have flown out to do it myself, but Cara had a fear of my flying and made me promise not to go. She'd already lost one parent and wasn't about to lose another. And to be honest, I didn't want to go through Stephen's clothes, pack his books, his music, the items he touched every day.

"James is having them shipped out here from California," I said. "He had your father's things packed and put in storage. I called him the day before yesterday to say I'd rented a place, so he could go ahead and have them sent directly to that address. By the way, he said to tell you hello."

"Do I know him?"

I nodded. "James Lowell. You met him year before last when we went to California after your graduation."

Stephen had insisted we go, as though we were still a family, to celebrate Cara's milestone, *cum laude* from Georgetown, as if we were still one unit, as if we had never separated.

"Blond, six-two or so, good-looking in a frat-boy-into-lifting-weights kind of way. Three, maybe four years older than me?" she asked.

"That's the one."

"I'm surprised he remembers me," Cara said. "Neat guy. We spoke for fifteen minutes, if that. It's good that he's sending Dad's things out."

Actually I would have preferred to have all of Stephen's belongings burned. I had enough memories. But I knew Cara would never have stood for it.

"I don't suppose he might come out with Dad's things," she said. "He struck me as the dependable sort."

"I doubt it."

I'd only met him a couple of times. The first was several years ago. He'd helped Stephen find an apartment when he moved to California.

James hadn't come for the funeral, which surprised me, considering how involved he'd been in tying up the details of Stephen's life. As for the dependable part, why should he be? Stephen certainly wasn't. I didn't even know who they worked for. Stephen should have chosen a wife who didn't notice inconsistencies, who wouldn't call him on them, who was content not to know where he was when he left for weeks at a time, who didn't give a damn.

Every confrontation I'd had with Stephen had created another layer of lies that eventually caved in on itself. After a while I wouldn't have believed him if he'd told me his own name. Or mine.

Cara glanced at her watch and stood, letting out a mumbled curse. "I've got to go. I'm already twenty minutes over my lunch break. Let me know when Dad's things get here. This conversation isn't over."

She took a good look at me, in my jeans and tailored shirt

with the tail out and the sleeves rolled to my elbows. Heaven only knows what my hair looked like.

"Aren't you going to class?"

"I called Mitch. He's taking my two-o'clock, and I told him to cancel the 3:10."

"An unexpected holiday. Your students will be thrilled."

"Yep. Nothing new happening in ancient Greece. It'll wait."

She shook her head at me. She had no interest in antiquities and couldn't understand my fascination. "Are you going to be all right?"

"Peachy keen."

"Yeah, right. My mom, the would-be alcoholic, trying to swim her way to the bottom of a bottle of scotch, gagging all the way. Maybe you should try Harveys Bristol Cream."

"Maybe I should."

"I was kidding, Mom. Stay off the sauce and remember to call me. You don't want me coming back over here and doing an intervention. If we haven't gotten some answers from the coast guard in the next couple of days—"

"I'll handle it," I promised.

"Good, because I've got a date tonight."

"Who with?"

"No one you know. I'll give you a ring when I get home, to see how you're doing and what you've found out."

"I'll be here."

She stopped at the door and turned back, most likely surprised I hadn't gotten up to give her a hug and see her out, but I was still unsteady on my feet.

"You going to be all right?" she asked.

"Absolutely."

"Love you," she said, and closed the door after her. She would hit the elevator and be out of the condo's parking lot and off down the beltway toward her K Street office in less time than it would take me to strip down and get into the shower, where I could cry and scream and nobody would hear me.

God, Stephen, what were you really doing in Colorado? Was that even where you died?

And why did someone murder you?

Chapter 2

Sometime in the wee hours of the morning, I must have fallen asleep because I was dreaming. We were hiking, and Stephen was just a little way ahead of me on the rock face. I looked up to see his tanned calves between his khaki shorts and rolled socks. Then he was on top of the cliff, looking down, calling to me, smiling, flashing white, even teeth. His dark hair had blown wild with the wind, and his skin was creased from too much sun. Black sunglasses hid his eyes. He motioned for me to catch up.

I felt myself being drawn toward him. He stood there beckoning like a huge piece of chocolate cake tempting a highly allergic addict, looking oh, so delicious. Until I took a bite, and then I was always so sorry I gave in because the pain that followed could never be worth the momentary thrill.

I have no idea how long the phone had been ringing before I finally forced myself awake. The clock read 4:17 a.m., and all I could think was that something had happened to Cara.

I fumbled for the receiver and managed a feeble, "Are you all right?"

"Elizabeth?"

"James?" I pushed myself up, totally awake, and switched on the light. The caller ID showed a number with California written above it. A quick calculation put the time on the west coast at 1:17 a.m. "What's wrong?"

"I heard about Stephen's body."

My chest heaved, and silently I cursed James, Stephen, even myself. If I'd had any idea James would find out, I would have called him. All my instincts told me it'd be best for everyone if the person or persons who slipped that body into the bay thought it was still there. Now James knew. And that meant other people did, as well.

"Who told you?" I demanded.

"One of the guys Stephen and I worked with a few years back is now with the FBI. He was there when the ID came through. He called me. I wanted you to know Stephen's belongings are in transit. They should be delivered to the unit you rented sometime Friday. But, Elizabeth..."

I closed my eyes. I should have known there was more. "Just tell me."

"The storage area I had them in was broken into tonight. There may be something in his belongings.... Look, I'm booking a flight first thing in the morning. I should be there by afternoon, your time."

I ran my hand through the tangled mass that was my hair. I'd let it dry naturally, too exhausted to blow it straight before I went to bed. Now it was a mess.

Pushing the panic out of my voice, I tried to sound natural, all the while knowing the firestorm that had always surrounded Stephen was about to envelope me again. It was not a place I wanted to be, not a place I wanted my daughter anywhere near.

"I'd really rather you didn't," I said.

"I'll call you from Reagan National." *Click.*

"No," I shouted to the dial tone. I dropped the receiver back into the cradle.

Damn, damn, damn! This man, whom I knew so little about, was coming here, to my home, into my life, into my daughter's life, and there was little, if anything, I could do to stop him.

I grabbed my terry cloth robe off the foot of the bed and wrapped it around me. My anger was giving me a chill. I needed to redirect it, to get busy. I liked to be at my office in plenty of time to prepare for class, so I might as well get up. It wasn't as if I was going to be able to go back to sleep. And I had plans to make. The sooner I got Stephen—and James—out of our lives again, the better.

The first thing I had to do was to get Stephen's body back into the ground. Cremation would be better, and it was what he'd wanted in the first place, but Cara had been so upset. She'd wanted a place to grieve. If I hadn't given in… No. They still would have stolen the body. And none of this was her fault. I would never have her thinking it was.

My first call would be to the morgue. I'd have him picked up by a different funeral home. Have him cremated this time. I'd watch it done if that was what it took.

Then I'd need to call Cara and let her know James was flying in.

And I should go to the insurance company and pick up the cashier's check for Stephen's insurance. Go by the bank. Distribute the money among my accounts. Finalize Stephen's death. And I'd have to do it all before my ten-thirty class.

It had surprised me to discover I was still his beneficiary.

We were still legally married, but I don't know why. We hadn't lived together in more than six years, except for the occasional weekend when he flew east to visit Cara. I moved out of our house the month that Cara went away to college. I don't know why I called it ours; he was so seldom there. He'd sold it two years ago, once he'd finally accepted the fact I wasn't coming back. I would have thought he'd sign everything over to Cara then. Two million dollars. *God, just let it be enough.*

Light streamed through stone archways, dappling the covered walkway. As I headed in the direction of my office on the first floor of Pearson Hall, Ian Payne fell into step next to me. I really did not feel like talking, not to him, not to anyone.

"Rough night? You look as though you've been conversing with the dead," he said in that clipped English accent of his.

I stopped cold and turned to stare at him as the blood drained from my face.

"Sorry. Just a figure of speech. Are you all right? I certainly didn't mean to offend you."

I'd be lying if I said I didn't find Ian intriguing. He was new to campus this spring semester and had caught the eye of almost every unattached female from student to dowager.

But, as attractive as he might be, the uncanniness of some of his comments—like the one he'd just made—and the boldness of his eyes made me uncomfortable. I had no use for flirtation, or even casual conversation.

"It's a beautiful day," Ian added, cocking his head and offering an impish grin. "I thought we might grab a cup of coffee."

Despite the clear, sunny skies, it was cold, even for early April. I'd thrown a short coat over a turtleneck and jeans and pulled my hair back at the nape of my neck. It would have to be curly today. I hadn't had the energy to wash it again and straighten it, and, frankly, I didn't give a damn. At least, I hadn't until Ian approached me.

"I've got papers to grade," I told him.

He lost his grin. This was his third offer; I'd probably not get another.

"You sure?"

No, I wasn't sure, and I didn't think he was just talking about coffee. Ian was tall, athletic, academic, with a worldly kind of charm, and I hadn't had a man other than Stephen interested in me for some time. He had just enough of an accent to make almost everything he said sound a bit more astute than it would have coming from someone else. And he had an endearing way of lifting one eyebrow that had almost the same effect as a wink.

I shook my head.

"Maybe some other time," he offered as he began to turn away.

"No, I mean, I think some coffee might be nice." I looked at my watch. It was close to noon. I'd done everything I'd needed to do this morning, and I needed a distraction. James would be here all too soon.

After all, wasn't opening myself to new experiences the reason I'd gone back to school to get my doctorate in the first place? I'd wanted to find an environment where I'd have some control, one as far away as I could get from the "real" world Stephen had lived in.

Died in.

I tried to smile. "Could we add a sandwich to that coffee? I didn't have breakfast." Or lunch or dinner the day before, but he didn't need to know that.

Ian raised his eyebrow, obviously pleased, and a smile again tugged at his lips. "Certainly. Shall we take my car?"

He really was a charming man. A man with light-blue eyes, longish dark hair and skin as pale as my own. Physically, nothing at all like Stephen. There was no harm going with him. Besides, I needed to eat.

He steered me across the grassy common area toward the faculty portion of the parking lot. His car was a red BMW. He opened the door for me, and I felt as if I were climbing into someone's midlife crisis.

I didn't know much about his personal life, just that he wasn't married, and that he taught in the philosophy department housed down the hall from mine. One thing I did know: someone was paying him a lot more than they were me. Or he had some other source of income. The seats were leather and the dash had all the bells and whistles room would allow.

He moved around to his side of the car. Lean and smooth, he was in good physical condition, surprising for a professor of philosophy. I had no idea how old he was. He'd entered that ageless phase that many men slip into. He could have been thirty-five. Or forty-nine. I wondered if he realized I was forty-four. But why should it matter? This was not a date.

"There's a place not far from campus," I told him as he slid behind the steering wheel. "The menu's a minefield and the service is lousy, but it has one thing that makes it irresistible— no student would be caught dead inside."

He nodded his approval, and I gave him directions. He maneuvered onto the beltway with a confident and deliberate driving style that defied my midlife-crisis theory. In less than fifteen minutes, we were seated in a back booth, away from most of the noise of the little diner. Ian slid to the end of his bench, his back against the wall, and took a quick survey of the place. It had the requisite amount of chrome, pink Formica and gray tile, all of which were better if not examined too closely. Early sixties music played on the oldies station.

"The ambiance of this place…"

"Is dreadful," I finished. "Order the tuna salad. The shrimp salad is excellent, too, but only on a Monday."

"Like leftovers, do they?"

"You don't want to know."

Our waitress handed Ian a menu and then looked at me. "Tuna salad on unseeded rye, dill pickle, tap water with ice. You want slaw today?"

I did a quick calculation. It was Thursday. Monday and Thursday were slaw days. "Sure."

"I'll have what she's having," he said, without opening the menu. "Do you have iced tea?"

"I think we may have some mint somewhere in the back of the fridge. Want me to look?"

I gave a slight shake of my head.

"Maybe some coffee…"

Again, I shook my head. "Tell you what, do you have hot water and a tea bag?"

The waitress nodded and disappeared.

"So, Elizabeth…" Ian began, studying my face, his eyes kind. "One more month of classes before we bump this crop of glassy-eyed malcontents up to the next level. Another year of ungodly tuition in exchange for a C average and one more column of credits on the transcript."

"Not all of them are like that," I defended. "I have three this year who are enthralled with the *Metamorphoses*."

"Tales of transformation. Do you really think a nineteen-year-old will find any of it relevant?"

"We're all in the process of changing, becoming, evolving. Or we should be," I insisted.

"Your idealism is admirable."

"Your skepticism isn't."

"Spare me. You're teaching Ovid to a roomful of—"

"It's a seminar class."

"Of course it is. Can't fill a whole room with Ovid fans, but you say you've got three. And the other seven or so?"

"I like to think I'm planting a spark that may someday catch fire."

"But will most likely go out. This is, what? Your second year teaching? Most of the students here major in beer and minor in pot. Yet the powers that be expect us to pretend we're a Mecca for culture and knowledge."

"You're awfully cynical for a philosopher."

"A professor of philosophy, a considerable difference."

"So what was it that made you turn?" I asked.

"Pardon me?"

"A handful of students out of a hundred a semester finding the beauty in Ovid or Homer is enough for me, as long as only a dozen or so who finish the course actually consider it rubbish. The ones in between can fend for themselves. So what happened? When did you lose it? When did you no longer care what your students were thinking? Did one of them somehow let you down?"

I'd hit a nerve. It showed in his face, a slight sag to his jaw and a turn of his head so he was looking at me only out of the corner of his eye.

"Actually, one of them did," he said. "A particularly talented young man whom I'd prefer not to discuss." He faced me. "But I'm afraid my current attitude is more of an adjustment problem. Most of my experience has been at large universities. This is my first time at a private school filled with the privileged elite. I'm certain I'll find some redeeming qualities in the little beggars given time. But enough of this nonsense. Tell me about your summer plans. Are you heading off to Greece or Rome? Joining up with some archeological dig?"

Summer plans. I couldn't see past this evening, let alone to the summer. The thought hit me like a blow to the stomach. What did I think I was doing? Just about now, what was left of Stephen's body was being picked up for delivery to the funeral home I'd called this morning, and I was out having lunch with some man.

I grabbed my purse and got out my wallet. "Maybe this wasn't such a good idea."

"Of course it was. What are you doing?"

"I'm leaving." I scooted toward the end of the booth, a ten-dollar bill in my fist.

"If it was something I said, allow me to apologize."

"It wasn't. I just don't want to be here anymore."

"Please…"

I reached forward to lay the money on the table. Ian grabbed my hand.

"I know about Stephen."

Chapter 3

I jerked back my hand, along with the money, my heart pounding in my chest.

"What is this?" I demanded.

There was a back exit not twelve feet away at the end of the narrow row of booths. I tried to stand, but Ian was already on his feet, blocking the end of the booth. He was a big man. Funny how that quality, so attractive a few moments earlier, had suddenly become ominous. I plunged my hand to the bottom of my purse. It tightened around a canister of pepper spray.

I could scream. But surely if Ian meant me harm he wouldn't be so stupid as to try something in a public restaurant, especially when students had to have seen us leave campus together.

"What I meant is, I know that your husband just died," he said softly. "You must be under considerable stress. You don't have to talk about it. You don't have to talk about anything. Please stay, let me buy you lunch. You need to eat."

I hadn't told anyone at work about Stephen. When I moved out, I took off my wedding ring. For all anyone at Gilman College knew, I was divorced, or a spinster with an out-of-wedlock child. I didn't care what they thought.

I looked at him. His posture was relaxed, not at all threatening. He seemed sincere. Of course, so had Stephen when I met him.

"Who told you?" I asked.

"Nobody. I read the obituary. Stephen Larocca."

"I wasn't listed."

"No, but you carry his name, and I saw you leave campus the afternoon before with your daughter. She was crying. You seemed distracted."

Actually, I'd been in shock.

"Then you were on leave for two days," he continued. "It had to be your husband. Or your brother. Frankly, you don't look Italian. Your daughter does.

"I would have sent you flowers," he added, "but I didn't want to intrude. And if I'd been wrong, think how embarrassed I would have been."

I wasn't about to be taken in by the lift of that eyebrow or by the softness of his tone, not, at least, without a few more answers.

"Why were you reading the *Washington Post* obituaries if you just moved here?"

He smiled. "I know this is going to sound morbid, but it's an old habit. It's a way for me to get to know the names of the families who populate a place, the old guard. It makes me feel more at home. I've moved around a lot."

I wasn't really buying the "old habit" thing, but professors could be quirky. If this was his quirk, I'd known stranger.

"You're from England originally," I said.

"A long time ago. My mother was English. My father was

in the U.S. Diplomatic Corps. Once his tour was up, he stayed in London as an expatriate for a while until he came to his senses and moved the lot of us back here."

The waitress came up, and Ian slid back into his seat.

"Two tunas with coleslaw and two ice waters. Darn. Forgot your hot water and your tea." She set down the plates and glasses and disappeared again.

"I'm sorry," Ian said. "I shouldn't have intruded into your personal life. I just didn't want you to leave. Don't you ever feel like you'd give almost anything to have an intelligent conversation with somebody—anybody—over the age of twenty-five?"

I understood about the over-twenty-five deal. I also understood about the over-twenty-five-opposite-sex deal. What I didn't understand was why Ian had chosen me for his discussion partner when there were others more willing than I.

There were three possible explanations for Ian's behavior, and I didn't like any of them. Somehow he knew Stephen, or knew of him or was mixed up—damn, I really was paranoid—with whatever Stephen had been mixed up in. Or, he was far more interested in my life than was healthy for either of us. Then again, maybe he had simply heard gossip about me in a small college where talk and speculation were the answer to everyday boredom. Like it or not, I needed to know what motivated him.

I looked at my watch. James couldn't possibly get into town for hours yet. In the meantime, Ian and I could talk. We could eat. I knew exactly where my pepper spray was. And I knew how to handle the small pistol that was also in my purse. I knew it was illegal to carry it, but I also knew, with Stephen's body turning back up as it had, I didn't have a choice.

* * *

I checked the phone again. The dial tone was definitely there. Cara had called a few hours ago to see if Janes had arrived, so I knew it had to be working. I carefully seated the receiver back into its charger. It was almost eight o'clock in the evening. What had happened to James? He had my phone number; he'd called me last night.

The phone rang with my hand still on it and I jumped.

"Mom."

"Cara?"

"Turn on the news."

"I'm waiting for a call from—"

"Turn on Channel 4. Now."

I found the remote for the TV under a cushion and hit the button.

"…unknown if the victim knew his assailant or whether the assault was a random act of violence. No one else was harmed in the bizarre attack against an unidentified passenger at Reagan National Airport, which occurred in one of the tunnels leading to the upper level of the parking deck."

The announcer paused and pressed her ear. "We're just getting word… It has now been confirmed that the victim is dead. The attack appears to have occurred at close range, and the wound is believed to have been made with a sharp instrument which most likely punctured the heart. Again, at approximately three-twenty this afternoon a man was severely injured, now confirmed dead, at Reagan National Airport shortly after disembarking from his flight from California. The perpetrator is at large and no description is currently available. We will continue to update you with news of this breaking story as it develops."

For a moment I couldn't breathe. I hit the off button.

"Mom, it's James, isn't it?" There was a catch in Cara's voice.

I managed to say, "I don't know." I didn't want to hear what I knew she was about to say.

"Mom, was Dad murdered?"

"Have you eaten?"

"You didn't answer my question."

"I want you to put a few items into a backpack or whatever you have handy. Toothbrush, lipstick, deodorant, underwear, a couple of changes of clothes—whatever you can't live without for two or three days. I'll be there in twenty minutes to pick you up."

"You can't. I'm still at work."

"But you're watching TV."

"We had it on in the lounge. Two of the kids we've sent to camp for the past couple of years are here. Their dad started beating the hell out of their mom, so they came here. I called the police. He's in custody. She's at the hospital. And I'm trying to locate a family member to take them."

"Let Social Services take care of that."

"They're scared, Mom. That's why they came to me. They trust me. I can't just leave them."

"Listen to me," I said with as much strength as I could summon. "There has to be someone else there that can help. Go home now and—"

"No," she said, cutting me off. "I told you, I can't. Besides, I have work tomorrow."

"Tell your boss you need a few personal days. Tell them you're sick. Hell, tell them I died."

"You're kidding, right?"

"I wish I were."

"Mom, is this really that serious?" she asked.

"Yes," I said, praying I was wrong.

I could hear her sigh.

"I should be able to make it to your place in a few hours."

"Now," I insisted. "I'll pick you up now."

"A few hours," she repeated firmly. "I'm not going to bail on these kids. And I'll have to call Phillip to explain what's going on."

I hadn't yet met Phillip, but Cara seemed to be crazy about him.

"No! You can't tell him anything about your father," I warned. "I don't want him involved."

"I'll tell him whatever I want."

"Not until I've had a chance to talk to you. Promise me, Cara."

She paused for several seconds.

"Cara…" I repeated.

"All right. I won't tell Phillip anything, and I'll come to your place as soon as I find the kids' aunt. I promise."

I swallowed back the fear that insisted we leave now, without another second of delay. Surely a few hours would make no difference. Cara would never abandon those children, and I wouldn't leave without Cara.

Maybe I was overreacting. Maybe seeing Stephen's body had put me so on edge I'd lost all reason.

Or maybe it had alerted me to a real danger I'd been trying to deny ever since Stephen's death.

"When you get here," I said, "don't bring your car inside the security fence. Park behind the building and walk around through the gate."

"All right."

"If you can get away earlier—" I began.

Cara hung up without letting me get in one more plea.

I dropped the receiver in its cradle. I had my own packing to do and some phone calls to make.

I didn't want Cara near me, but I didn't want her out of my sight, either. I could only hope whoever did this, whoever murdered James, was certain I knew nothing about Stephen's life. All I could offer Cara was the little I knew. I prayed that it would be enough to keep her safe.

Chapter 4

Cara didn't make it to the house until after two in the morning. I'd nearly worn a path in the carpet working off my worry.

She'd brought her bag with her, but she wasn't quite ready to go. She also wanted answers about what had happened to James and what it had to do with us. Unfortunately, everything I said only led to more questions.

"Dad was a geologist," Cara stated evenly. "When he was away, he was on expeditions. Are you saying he wasn't?"

"I'm saying I don't know what he was or where he went. He told *me* he was a geologist." That was his first story, the one he'd kept publicly, and the one I used when people asked and I had no better answer to give them.

Cara drummed her fingers on my kitchen table. She was pale and exhausted. I hoped she'd had some dinner.

"But you knew otherwise and you're only now telling me?" she said.

"I *suspected* otherwise," I said. "What was I supposed to do? Tell you your father was lying? Have *you* confront him?"

"No, Mom. I'd say that was your job," she snapped, putting me squarely in my place.

"What should I have said to him?" I asked. "That no matter what story he came up with I knew he was working for the government or some secret agency? Besides, I didn't know. Hell, he could have been working for some madman in the Middle East."

"Don't say that." Now she was angry. "He may have lied to you and to me, but don't say things out of bitterness. My father was a good man. I know that and so do you. Whatever he was doing, he was doing it for the right reasons."

I threw up my hands. How could I make her understand? "It doesn't matter if he was good. It wouldn't have mattered if he were working for God Himself. It's…" I couldn't get out another word.

"It's that he lied to you about it."

"Yes, and I hated him for it." She had cut right through to it. The pain was evident in her face, but I wanted to give her the gift that Stephen had denied me, the only gift I couldn't live without—honesty.

The muscles in my throat were so constricted it actually hurt to speak. "When you want to share your soul with another person, like I did with your father, when you're willing to share every part of your being, how is it that that person whom you care so much about can keep a huge part of who they are from you? I would have kept any secret he had. I would have done whatever he asked. But I had to know."

"And he never told you."

"Never. Even before we married, he'd become aloof, distant. Foolishly, I believed things would change between us because I was convinced your father really loved me. Even later, after I realized that whatever Stephen was involved in was dangerous, too dangerous, he thought, for me to know about, I had to have answers."

"That's why you left him."

"Physically I left him. Mentally, he'd left me years before. My one concern was you. Somehow Stephen managed to keep us safe. I know this is going to sound crazy, but I felt you were in less danger with him knowing exactly where you were. But I was always terrified that whatever he was involved in would spill into our lives. I wanted you to have a father. I wanted you to have *Stephen* for a father, but…"

"You loved him."

It'd been so long since I'd put a label on my feelings.

When I didn't answer, she said, "Mom, you did love him. That's why you never divorced him, why you still went on vacation with him, why you let him sleep over. Did you not even listen to what you just said about him?"

"I don't know what I felt for him. Maybe I loved him. When I wasn't hating him."

I didn't cry. I'd spilled so many tears when I'd lost my sister Josie all those years ago—and with Stephen. Tears changed nothing.

Cara came to my side, her anger gone. She folded me into her arms and lay her head on my shoulder. Then she cried for both of us, like she used to when she was a little girl and I would hold her tight.

But we only had so much time. I hugged her to me. "I want you to go to West Virginia now. Tonight. It shouldn't take you more than four hours. I've already called your great-aunt Rachel. She's expecting you. It's better that you be there than with your grandparents. They're too easy to trace. The difference between my maiden name and Rachel's married name puts you one step further from discovery. We can reevaluate tomorrow."

She pulled back from me and frowned. I wiped her tears with my fingers and tried to smooth the wrinkles between her eyes.

"Why are you so certain we're in danger?"

I'd never planned to tell her any of this. If she'd been younger, I might have gotten away with it, but now she gave me no choice.

"Do you remember when you were five and your father picked you up from kindergarten?"

"Yes. We met you at work and he took us on a surprise vacation to Disney World? Sure. Why?"

"He packed your clothes and he packed mine, and he ordered me into the car. I had no idea where we were going or why. I almost lost my job over it. But I saw the fear in his eyes and I dared not refuse.

"On the way to Florida, your dad told me a man had been seen talking to you on the playground of your school. He had you by the hand when a teacher saw him. She got you inside the building and called your father as well as the police. But the man was gone by the time they got there."

She paled. "It was probably some random—"

"There was nothing random about it. It was a warning. I was furious with your father."

"But you went to Florida, anyway."

"Yes. I went. I had no other options. We were gone two weeks, three days of which you and I were by ourselves. I have no idea where he was."

"He never offered you an explanation?"

I shook my head. "Only that there'd been a security breach, and he'd taken care of it. He promised it would never happen again, and it didn't. Not until now. It was after that incident that he started training me."

"Training you? What are you talking about?"

"He made sure I knew how to use a gun, showed me how to canvass a room, plan an escape, secure phony ID."

"Crap, Mom. What the hell was going on?"

"I told you. I don't know. All I know is that it was dangerous to be with him—and to be away from him. One time he came home with a wound to his calf. You remember. You must have been about nine."

"Sure. He'd been hurt on a hike."

"He'd been shot."

"He told you he'd been shot?"

"No. He said a pick had gone through his leg in an accident on a climb. He'd been treated, but he never went to the doctor for any follow-up visits. When I dressed the wound, I knew he was lying. The entry and exit wounds from a pick would have been neater. This had a small hole on one side and a large tear on the other.

"You already know about the times he simply left on his 'expeditions,' and we had no idea when he'd be back," I continued. "Did you know he carried a copy of your high school schedule with him? He knew every class you ever took, when it started and when it ended, the name of the teacher and the number of the room it was held in. He carried a small book with the names and addresses of your friends."

Her face was ashen. There was too much to absorb. Her pain was evident in her eyes. She'd always known how much he loved her, but she'd never known how much he feared for her.

"Cara, we really don't have time for this. Your great-aunt Rachel—"

"Will have to wait. I'm not going."

"I know you don't want to do this—"

"You know I *won't* do it."

Damn. Why did she have to be so much like me? And like her father.

"I don't intend to make the same mistakes that you and Dad did. I have to tell Phillip what's going on. He deserves an explanation."

"You don't have a choice," I insisted.

"You mean like Dad might not have had a choice?"

"Cara…"

She reached for the phone.

"If you make that call, you may be putting Phillip in danger, as well."

That stopped her.

"What are you going to do?" she asked. "If it's not safe for me to be here, it's certainly not safe for you."

"I have a plan."

She nodded. "How long have you had this plan?"

"As long as I've known this day might come."

"It used to include me," she reminded me. "I know you would never have left me with anyone else when I was a child. And I'm not about to let you leave me out now. If we have to do this, we do it together."

"All right, then," I agreed. "We leave together."

Cara stood and immediately sat back down. Both of her hands were trembling.

"I think I'm going to be sick." She closed her eyes and swallowed hard.

"You didn't eat, did you?" I asked.

She shook her head. Then she dashed for the bathroom. It was all too much for her system—her father's body turning back up, James's murder, no food, no sleep and two children who were counting on her to watch out for them. I could hear her retching through the closed door. After several minutes the toilet flushed and she opened the door. She had to steady herself against the frame. She'd always had a weak stomach.

"I need some time. I can't get into a car like this."

"How long?" I asked.

"A few minutes. Please. Just let me lie down. Then we can go."

She saw me look at my watch. It was already a few minutes after 3:00 a.m. I'd give her half an hour, no more.

"If no one's come for us yet, it's unlikely they'll come to-night," she reasoned.

I didn't like it, but she was probably right. I nodded. If we left soon, surely we'd be fine. I could gather my energy while Cara rested.

I tucked her into bed, lay down in the dark in my own room, and convinced myself we'd be safe for a few more minutes. The dead bolt was on. It was a secure building with a guard station and a fence around it, and my condo was on the fifteenth floor.

The sound of Cara's breathing drifted through the open door. I would have asked her to lie next to me, but she didn't need to know how scared I really was. One crazed woman was enough for what lay ahead of us.

My eyes drifted shut, and somehow, despite my best efforts, I fell asleep.

Breath tickled my neck and brought me totally aware, a cold sweat prickling my body. Someone was bending over me, checking to see if I was awake, and it wasn't Cara. He had a distinctly masculine scent.

I didn't dare open my eyes. Any movement, even to reach for the gun lying next to me, would be too late. It was probably already too late, but that didn't stop me. My daughter, I prayed, was still asleep in the next room.

In one quick move, I rolled to my back and drew my knees to my chest. I felt my feet connect with something solid as I straightened my legs, shoving with all the force in my body. I heard an oomph coincide with a loud thump against the wall, as I grabbed the gun and rolled off the other side of the bed and onto the floor.

"Christ, Elizabeth! Are you trying to kill me?"

"James?" I reared up, still on my knees, the mattress protecting all but my head and arms, the gun pointed into the dark in the direction of his voice. "I thought someone else had saved me the trouble."

"So did I, at least for a while." His voice sounded strained.

"How the hell did you get in here?"

"Tricks of the trade."

With my free hand, I fumbled for the bedside light and switched it on. James was standing between the wall and the bed, hunched, with an ugly expression on his handsome face. One arm under his black jacket cradled his abdomen. I must have hurt him more than I thought I could.

Cara stood in the doorway, holding the biggest damn baseball bat the Sports Authority carried. She must have found it where I kept it under her bed. Her cheeks were pink, her hands steady.

"Who died at the airport?" she demanded.

He turned and shook his head at her. "Damn it, Cara! You gonna beat up on me, too? You can put that thing down. Your mom's pretty much incapacitated me."

She set the bat in the corner, folded her arms across her chest, leaned back against the wall and offered him a smile. "You could have tried the doorbell."

"If I'd known the reception you had waiting for me, I would have. I didn't expect to find you here."

Cara opened her mouth, but I cut her off. "I asked her to spend the night with me."

He looked back at me. "You might want to put that gun away."

I had it pointed straight at his head. I sat down on the bed and lowered the gun onto my lap. That's when I saw the blood seeping into his shirt. I hadn't been the only one who'd hurt him.

"I don't know who jumped me at the airport," James said. "But he obviously wasn't thrilled about my coming here."

"I see." Even I couldn't help but smile at him, this ghost back from the dead. In his late twenties, he looked like the image of a surfer—blond, broad-shouldered, tanned. There had been a time when I thought that was exactly what he was—before I knew he worked with Stephen and wasn't just some guy Stephen had befriended playing Frisbee on the beach.

I'd first met James when Stephen and I were in California for what I thought was a vacation. Cara was doing her study abroad in Italy and I was missing her terribly.

How many times did I need to be taught that the first story someone tells isn't always the truth?

"How bad are you hurt?" I asked James.

"I'm all right." He came around the bed and offered me his hand. "It's great to see you both again."

I saw how he looked at Cara. "They're still in the D.C. area, the ones who took Stephen's body," I said.

"Yes, apparently they are."

"They know about me. And Cara," I reminded him.

He nodded. "They know you buried him."

"And now I know about them. But you're going to have to tell us more," I said, with a sidelong glance at the gun. "We have to know what Stephen was doing, because they didn't find what they were looking for on his body or in his things and they may think he told me something. I can't protect Cara from something I know nothing about."

Or people I knew nothing about. If James hadn't died at the airport, someone else had. And that someone had been killed by the man standing in front of me.

Chapter 5

Cara loudly took exception to the idea of my protecting her from anything—known or unknown. I ignored her and made us all some coffee. It was almost 3:40 in the morning, and I needed a clear head.

She found gauze, tape and hydrogen peroxide in the medicine cabinet and dressed James's wound. It was a long, deep scratch that bled easily. Painful but, fortunately, nothing serious.

When she finished, James caught her hand and thanked her. Then he saw me watching and let her go.

"What really happened at the airport?" I asked, pouring a cup of coffee and setting it in front of him at my kitchen table.

"Some guy jumped me from behind," James explained. "I didn't have a choice. I had to defend myself."

"Who was he?" Cara asked, bringing her own mug and sitting next to him.

"I don't know. I checked for ID, but he didn't have any on him. No ticket, either."

"Apparently he knew you," I suggested. "They said he was coming from California."

"I tore my ticket, the part with my name on it, and planted the rest in his pocket."

I didn't ask whose weapon had done the killing or what he'd done with it afterward. With the security at the airports, it was a good assumption that James had indeed been jumped since he'd just come off a plane. I doubted he could have gotten a weapon through the security at National.

"Why didn't you wait for the police?" Cara's eyes were narrowed. She didn't have patience for foolishness, even when it came from someone who looked like James. "Maybe the guy was a mugger."

"Gloves, well-groomed, expensive leather coat. And what idiot would choose to mug someone at the most secure airport in the United States?"

"It can get pretty lonely in those tunnels, and you were well away from the secure area," she pointed out.

"True, but this guy wasn't after my wallet. Besides, if I'd let myself get involved with a police investigation, it would have left the two of you vulnerable. I couldn't let that happen. Your dad made me promise to watch after you."

"When?" I demanded.

"The week he died."

"Then he knew…" Cara began.

James shook his head. "If he'd known, he wouldn't have let it happen."

"We need to call the police," Cara insisted again.

"They can't protect you, Cara. Or your mother. I can't tell

them what we're up against. Hell, I don't know what we're up against."

"What was Stephen really doing in Colorado?" I asked.

"I don't know."

I sighed. I was so tired of the lies that it didn't matter if James was one of the good guys or not. Hell, he might not be. I'd always hoped Stephen was, but I had no guarantee.

"If you can't tell me that, tell me who Stephen was working for."

"I'll tell you what I know on the way. It's too complicated to get into right now. I want us out of here within the next fifteen minutes." He drained his coffee and checked his watch.

"To where?" I'd been taking care of myself so long, I didn't like the idea of putting myself in someone else's hands, especially a man I barely knew and had no particular reason to trust.

"Someplace safe. I don't want anyone questioning you. I know a woman who has a cabin in the Shenandoah Valley," James said. "That's our first stop."

A safe house. Run by whom? Safe for whom?

"And after that?" I was asking the question while Cara sat silently. The frown I'd rubbed from between her brows was back in place, and she hadn't touched her coffee.

"We'll see," James said. "I'll have to come back here, go through Stephen's personal items. See if I can figure out what it is they're after. But my first priority is to get the two of you away from here."

The way his eyes shifted I wondered if he was mentally kicking himself for not going through them more carefully before he sent them on. Or if he had and had simply missed something.

"I don't suppose you have any idea…" he asked. "Did Stephen send you anything? Leave anything with you?"

I shook my head.

"Okay. We can talk about all this on the way," he said. "Cara, you're already packed?"

Her bags were sitting by the door. He couldn't have missed them when he came in.

"For a weekend, not for a week," she protested.

"It'll have to do. Elizabeth, can you get your things together?"

"It'll only take me a few minutes." I'd packed yesterday evening, but he didn't have to know that.

Cara threw me a surprised look, but she had the sense not to say anything.

"If you need to leave messages at work, do it now. From this phone." He pointed to the one hanging on the wall next to the refrigerator.

"I've already taken care of that," Cara assured him.

"Really? Why?" James asked.

"We're in mourning," I reminded him. "For the second time."

I took up the phone and dialed the classics department even though I'd already told everyone I was going out of town. "Jeannie, it's Elizabeth. I've been called out of town on an emergency for a few days. Get Mitch to cover as many of my classes as you can. Thanks." Then I hung up, not taking my eyes off James. If he felt compelled to give me orders, I thought it best that he think I was following them.

"Okay. Let's go." He was on his feet.

"We'll get our things," I promised. I grabbed Cara's hand, pulled her into the bedroom and shut the door.

"What's up?" she asked. "You're already packed."

"I know. You trust me, don't you?"

"With my life."

"Good. Don't let me out of your sight. If I move, you follow me. Understand? No talk, no questions. We're not to be separated."

"Mom—"

"Understand?"

"You're scaring me." Her eyes were huge.

"That's what I mean to do. James got in here. We don't know who might have followed him here from the airport. They could be inside the building. In the parking lot. On the street. Do we understand each other?"

Cara nodded and swallowed hard.

"Good." I pulled up my shirt and tucked the gun that was still lying on my pillow into the back waistband of my jeans. Then I took the canister of pepper spray out of my purse. "Do you have one of these?" I asked.

"Not with me."

I shook my head at her. I'd told her never to go out without it. I handed mine to her, then opened the top drawer on my bedside table, scooped up another canister and wedged it into the front pocket of my jeans. I pulled the backpack out from under the bed and stuffed my soft leather purse into it.

"Cara…"

"Yes?"

I almost apologized. For getting her into this situation. For choosing Stephen for her father. For screwing things up with her job and with Phillip. But I didn't. She needed to be strong and so did I. I hefted the backpack onto my shoulder and gave her a quick hug. "I love you. Now let's get out of here."

James was smoking a cigarette when we came out. He took the dead bolt off the door. The security chain had been sliced in two. Looking up and down the corridor, he shuffled us outside. Then we hurried to the elevators, and he pushed the down button, dropping the lit butt onto the hardwood floor and stepping on it. Seconds later, the doors opened and we stepped inside.

The building was quiet and so was the parking lot.

"This way," he said, leading us to a light-colored SUV shining silver in the lights illuminating the lot. It had tinted windows. I'd thought we'd be taking my car. How had he gotten it into my condo's parking lot without my being notified?

I had assumed James had ridden the Metro from Reagan National to Bethesda and then walked the two blocks to my place and found a way over the fence or past the guard. When had he rented this vehicle? After he killed the guy at the airport? If so, what had he been doing in a tunnel that led to a parking lot at National Airport? Did he have a car parked there? Why would he? He lived in California.

I looked at the car's license plate, and I could feel the blood drain from my face. That car wasn't rented. It had Colorado tags.

I glanced toward the gatehouse but saw nothing, not even the shadow of a movement. Where was Abe, the night guard?

And James's phone call from California... Caller ID shows the place of registration of a cell phone, not the origin of the call. It could have come from anywhere. Even Maryland or D.C. Even the street outside my condo.

My mind was swamped with questions, and not a one of them did I dare to utter. What was it that Stephen had once called James? I pulled it from the recesses of my memory. A young turk.

I stared at James and then at the open car door. Ringing in my ears was the most important safety lesson I could remember ever being told: once they get you in their car, it's all over.

I balked. "Cara, I forgot something."

"Whatever you need, we can get on the way," James said. He put out a hand for Cara's bag. She let him take it and he tossed it inside. Then he reached for mine.

"No. I'll be right back."

James stuffed another cigarette into his mouth. "Get in, Elizabeth."

"It'll only take me a minute. I feel a migraine coming on, and I forgot my medication. It's prescription and you don't want to be around me if I don't have my pills." I tried to smile, to look casual.

"You don't…" Cara began.

I stared at her hard. I'd never had a migraine in my life.

"You don't want to go back into that building by yourself," she said. "I'll go with you."

James slammed the door. He looked none too pleased. "Is this really necessary?"

"Mom's a terror without her medication. Gets sick to her stomach, and riding makes it worse. Believe me, you don't want to have to stop every five miles for her to hurl." Cara flashed him one of her dazzlers.

"We won't be a minute," I promised.

"Okay, I'll go with you," James said.

"No. You start the car and bring it around to the door. We'll be right out," I said.

My legs were shaking so hard I didn't think I'd make it across the parking lot. I hardly breathed until we slipped through the glass doors.

"What the hell was that all about?" she demanded.

"Where'd you park?" I asked her.

"Where you told me to. Outside the fence, in the Burger King lot on the back side of the building."

I punched the button for the elevator, but once inside I hit the B instead of 15.

"He'll give us no more than five minutes," she warned.

"That's all we'll need."

Chapter 6

We took the back roads across Montgomery County, through Potomac. I drove. It was easier than giving directions, and it gave me an excuse to keep my eyes on the road while I explained to Cara why I'd suddenly become so suspicious of James.

"I just hope you're right," was all she said. Then she added, "I'm sorry, Mom. If we'd left when you'd wanted to—"

"It wouldn't have made any difference," I told her.

My guess was James had been watching the condo, maybe for hours, waiting for us either to go to bed or to come down before he made his move. When the lights went out and we didn't show, he waited a little while and then came up.

A wispy fog turned the road a glossy black in the headlights. There was no one behind us. No headlights as far back as I could see in the Cherokee's rearview mirror. I was on my home territory, and James wasn't. We wouldn't hit a major highway until we got to Frederick, and he had no reason to believe we'd be heading north.

I began to breathe again.

It wasn't like Cara to be quiet. I knew the conflict was coming, but first she had a battle or two to resolve in her own mind, one that I suspected centered around James Lowell.

"What would James or anyone else want with us?" she finally asked. "What do we know that could be of value to anyone?"

"I'm not sure, but I'm not about to let anyone ask us face-to-face."

She'd ask again, I knew that for certain, but for now she let it go.

"How'd you find that exit in the basement?" she asked.

"Your dad," I told her. "When I moved in, he went over every inch of that building, dragging me along."

It was a maintenance exit, a solid door with a bar-activated latch, always locked from the outside, never from the inside. It opened beyond the fence, on the back side of the building.

"He wanted you to be safe, Mom."

Then he should have occupied his time with safe activities.

"Damn," she said for probably the fifth time and shifted in her seat. "I shouldn't have let James take my bag. I don't even have anything to put my contacts in. No eyeliner. Crap. He got my cell phone."

"You did exactly the right thing. If you hadn't left the bag, he wouldn't have let us go. Put your seat back. Sleep if you can," I told her.

"Not bloody likely. Want to fill me in on where we're going? Please tell me you have a plan, one that doesn't include Great-Aunt Rachel and Wild and Wonderful West Virginia."

"We're heading for York, Pennsylvania. I've got directions

in my purse, but we won't need them for another hour. I can get us to the outskirts." I pushed my hair off my forehead. The humidity had made it frizz out of control.

"Why there?"

"Because I've known Patrice Hudson more than half my life, and I haven't seen her but twice in the past ten years. What's more, she's the only one I know who will understand."

"You must be high on something if you think anybody's going to understand what's going on. I was at your condo, and I sure as hell don't understand. Who is this Patrice? Wasn't she a friend of yours from college?" Cara asked.

I nodded, keeping my eyes on the road. Driving was horrendous. "It will take them a long time to find her, and by the time they do—if they do—we'll be gone and all trace that we were ever there will be gone, too."

"What about her family? Won't they resent us barging in on them?"

"Patrice is twice divorced. Her only son died in a boating accident in New York Harbor. His boat capsized. His body was never found."

"No." The word was uttered so low, I almost didn't catch it. I stole a glance at Cara. For all her bravado, she was tender-hearted, moved to tears at even the thought of another person's pain.

"After it happened, Patrice moved to York from Manhattan. She withdrew from the world. No TV. No newspaper. No computer. She actually writes letters."

"Does she have a telephone?"

"If that's your not-too-subtle way of suggesting I call her, I'm not going to. We can't risk a trace on my cell phone."

Her only answer was a sigh, her signal she'd had more than enough of my "precautions."

"You'll like Patrice," I offered.

"Mom, I have a life. Friends. A job. Maybe not the most prestigious job, but one that includes children who need my help. And a cat who depends on me to feed it and change its water and its litter. Tickets to see Pearl Jam next Friday night. Oh, damn! They were in my bag. I should have let Kristi hold them. She's going to have one super hissy fit. We've waited over a year for them to play in D.C."

I threw her a sidelong glance and found her hand with my own. "I'll make it up to you," I promised. I didn't believe my words any more than she did. She drew back her hand.

I was doing one heck of a good job screwing up my kid's life.

"You'll get your life back. Pearl Jam will be back, too," I promised.

She slumped down in her seat, turned away and stared out the window into the darkness. I'd had years to adjust to the idea that our lives were fragile, that they could change at any moment. She'd had less than a day to consider it. I suspected she was crying, not sleeping.

For the next hour and a half she didn't speak.

The yard was lit up with security lights. I drove the Jeep past a mailbox marked with a large 913 and into a gravel driveway. An old VW Vanagon was parked under the carport.

The house was a modest little rancher, probably fifty or so years old with a siding-and-brick front, located off a two-lane road eight miles west of York. It had belonged to Patrice's parents. They'd died and she'd held on to the property. When her world had fallen apart, she'd come home.

I counted two outbuildings. The one not far to the left of the drive had a large door and looked like a garage of sorts. Good. We could put the Cherokee in that. I pulled past it and around to its side so that no one could see the Jeep from the road.

The other building, which looked like a converted small barn and stood a good twenty yards to the back, must be Patrice's pottery studio. I wondered if she missed the glamor of the city, the art shows, the noise. As far as I knew, she'd never been back.

I put on the brake and cut the engine.

"She has no idea we're coming," Cara stated.

"Nope."

Cara shook her head at me.

The sky was brightening in the east, spreading a thin patch of pink through the budding trees as we stepped onto the wet grass. If we were lucky, Patrice had become an early riser with her move to the country, because it was damned early. Somehow I doubted it. When we were in school, her days had started a little before noon and stretched until two each morning.

My knock rattled the old screen door. It seemed a gentler way to wake someone than the doorbell, but there was nothing gentle about the response. The ferocious barking that ensued made me glad the dog was inside and not guarding the yard.

"Maybe this wasn't such a hot idea," Cara commented, stepping slightly behind me. When she was seven, she'd had an unfortunate incident with a neighbor's dog that required three stitches in her ankle. She'd never forgiven the species.

The barking continued for what felt like several minutes before I saw the curtain flutter in the window. I made sure we were well exposed under the porch light.

"Who is it?" a woman's voice called through the door.

"Patrice, it's Elizabeth. Elizabeth Larocca. I've got my daughter, Cara, with me."

The door opened and Patrice stood there, a puzzled frown

on her face. I wouldn't have recognized her. Her skin was as smooth as it'd ever been, but her dark hair had gone completely white since the last time I'd seen her, that beautiful brilliant white that happens to people who go prematurely gray. It hung in complete disarray to her shoulders. She had on an old chenille robe that had lost a good bit of its tufting.

Then she smiled, taking years off her face, and she was the Patrice I knew and loved. And trusted.

"You'd better have one damned good story. Not for coming, but for coming before noon," she said, holding open the screen. "You know I'm not a morning person."

She spoke to the dog in what sounded like German or Dutch and then ushered us inside, enveloping me in a hug. Cara hung back, taking in the dog's muscled frame. He looked like a smaller version of a German shepherd, but his coat was a fawn color. He wore a harness across his shoulders and back.

"Oh, don't you worry about Odin. He's well trained," Patrice promised, letting me go and taking a good look at Cara. "I adopted him out of the canine unit. Bad hip, but it doesn't slow him down much. He won't hurt you. Not unless I tell him to."

I could see from Cara's expression that wasn't much reassurance.

"You're Cara." Patrice took her hand. "You look so much like your father, I would have known you anywhere. Elizabeth, she's gorgeous."

Cara's cheeks colored as Patrice pulled her into a gentle hug. "Come on in and get yourselves out of the doorway. She flipped on the lights in the living room. The hardwood floors were bare, and the couch and chairs were brown leather strung on metal frames. The wall behind the couch was splotched with earth tones. Three original oils hung there, and pottery sculpture, glazed in hues from teal to a golden chartreuse, stood on pedestals, tables, even the floor.

Patrice led us into the kitchen. She pointed toward an oak table with inset ceramic tiles and chairs tucked underneath it. She went straight to the gas stove, scooped up a teakettle, took it to the sink and ran water into it. We obediently sat down, and I realized exactly how exhausted I was.

"You didn't bring Stephen with you."

Cara shot me a look and I could see her jaw tighten.

"Stephen's dead," I said.

Patrice turned toward us, setting the kettle on the counter, the water still spewing in the sink. "Elizabeth…I'm sorry… I…"

"It's all right."

"It's not all right," Cara said.

"She's right," I agreed. "It's not all right."

Patrice cut off the water. "You're in trouble."

Cara bit her lip. She was angry but at least she had enough sense not to take it out on Patrice.

"How long is this story?"

"Long," I told her.

"Then it can wait another four or five hours. Have you had any sleep tonight?"

"Not enough to count."

"I thought not. We'll skip the tea. I'll throw some fresh sheets on the beds. The two of you are going to rest before you say another word."

I didn't argue. She put Cara in one bedroom and me in another. Once my head hit the pillow, I was out. It was the first real sleep I'd had since Stephen died.

Chapter 7

I smelled bacon. I dragged my left wrist in front of my face and forced open my eyes. My watch read one o'clock. The bright sunlight streaming through the gauzy curtains assured me it was p.m., not a.m. I blinked twice. I was lying in a white iron bed with a hand-pieced quilt pulled up to my chin in a room painted a bright sunshine yellow. That's right. I was at Patrice's, and everything I'd hoped was only a dream wasn't.

I'd pulled off my jeans and crawled into the bed, not bothering to put on the nightgown Patrice had laid out for me. Or wash my face. Or brush my teeth. Yuck.

The door was open and I could hear voices. Cara was laughing. I couldn't help but smile. I hadn't heard her laugh like that since before her father died. Patrice. She was a jewel.

A quick shower was mandatory. So were fresh clothes. I'd leave the hair-washing for later. I didn't want to miss that bacon.

* * *

"You're kidding. He didn't!" Cara insisted, as I came through the door into the kitchen.

"He didn't what?"

"Oh, Patrice was just telling me about how you met Dad. How the two of you caught him and a friend in the middle of the night using a rappelling rig to hoist a motorcycle onto the roof of the University of Maryland's admin building, so Dad could ride it off."

"Good thing we caught them, too," I said, "or you most likely would never have been born. It was a long drop to the ground."

"Are you kidding? They would have killed themselves long before they got the blasted thing up there," Patrice assured us.

"The other guy was Peter. Did she tell you that?" I asked.

Cara looked back and forth between us.

"Peter was my first," Patrice said.

"Husband or—" Cara began.

"Both," we answered together and then giggled.

"Your dad was extremely drunk the night he and Peter had their episode with the motorcycle," I said.

"Duh, Mom. That was pretty much a given."

"Evidently Peter had tried to talk him out of it," Patrice said, breaking eggs into a bowl.

"Until another six-pack convinced him it wasn't such a bad idea," I finished.

"Yes, well, that was back when Peter was more fun."

"He's now a federal judge," I explained to Cara. "Back then Patrice thought he was pretty darned hot."

"Yeah, well, he cooled off."

"No fair interrupting the story," Cara protested.

"Your daughter's absolutely right. I have a story to tell.

Your father was so hungover the next day he couldn't remember your mother's last name when he came looking for her," Patrice went on, attacking the eggs with a whisk.

"He was lucky he could remember his own," I added.

"He went to the registrar and gave them some idiotic story about needing your mother's address so he could interview her as a witness to a crime. He was posing as an insurance investigator or something equally ridiculous."

"How could he get away with that? He was a student," Cara said.

"Remember he was older than me. He was in graduate school and he'd already spent several years in the military," I pointed out. "He had a presence about him."

"Anyway," Patrice went on, "he told them two male students had been seen on campus in a potential act of vandalism—"

"And would they please give him my address—"

"I thought you said he didn't know your name," Cara interrupted.

"Only my first name. He actually expected them to go through the entire roster and pull out all the Elizabeths who were freshmen that year."

"So that's how he found you?" Cara suggested.

"Are you kidding?" Patrice asked, pouring the eggs into a frying pan. "Ever try to get an employee at a registrar's office to give out information? You'd think they had national secrets locked up in there. They threw him out. He finally remembered she was an English major, so he waited on the steps of the humanities building for her to show up for class. He was so embarrassed. Terribly cute and thoroughly ashamed that she had witnessed his behavior but willing to suffer any humiliation to find her."

I flung a napkin at her. "You have no room to talk. Peter was smitten with you."

"Sounds like love at first sight," Cara said with an impish grin.

"For your dad? Absolutely," Patrice agreed.

"And for Peter?" she asked.

Patrice shrugged, her smile slipping away. "Peter is complex."

"He was in law school at the time. I think he may be the most moral person I've ever met," I added, "and, yes, he was very much in love with Patrice."

"He was in love with justice and ethics. Under other circumstances, I think he might have gone to seminary," she said.

"Why didn't he?" Cara asked.

"Pressure from his family," I said. "Peter's family had money. We're talking swimming-in-it money. His dad wanted him in a more lucrative profession."

"He showed them." Patrice laughed. "He became a public defender, then a D.A., and, with his first opportunity, a judge. But you don't want to hear about Peter. He could be way too serious."

"Sounds like he could be talked out of that seriousness at times." Cara winked.

"Ah, that was your dad's influence. Stephen was so much fun and so sure of himself," Patrice began.

"Full of himself," I corrected.

"Yeah, that, too," Patrice agreed. "He was a man who knew what he wanted and went after it."

"You mean Mom."

"Right, but their courtship was a little more complicated than that. Your mom was dating Jerry at the time. Now he was something else. You are so lucky you didn't wind up with him for your father."

"I'm not feeling at all comfortable with this conversation," I admitted.

Cara was finding all of this far too interesting. She had one eyebrow raised and was looking at me with that you-could-never-have-been-that-young look of hers.

"I don't know," Patrice said. "She looks like a big girl. I think she can handle it."

"I wasn't thinking about her. Besides, college roommates are not allowed to tell tales to offspring. Didn't you get the memo?" I asked Patrice.

"Too late, Mom. You've been exposed. Now, who was this Jerry character?"

"Where should I begin? I can tell you he was no match for your dad. Once Stephen came on the scene—"

"Patrice," I warned.

"Oh, lighten up. Some stories are too good to die with our generation." Patrice immediately realized what she'd said, and we all fell silent. She dropped her gaze and stirred the already-done scrambled eggs.

"Sit," she commanded, pointing to a chair at the table where orange juice and fresh coffee in a hand-thrown ceramic mug awaited.

Odin, who was lying next to the back door, sat up.

She shook her head at the dog. "Not you, boy. He's learning English. He was trained in Belgium and then sent over here."

I did as I was told, and she brought the skillet to the table, dividing the eggs into threes and scooping them right onto our plates. "That's so I can be sure you eat your share." The bacon and whole wheat toast were already on the table. "I made three slices of bacon for each of us, and there's more in the fridge if we need it."

"Man, this looks good," Cara said.

Patrice sat down opposite me and shoved a bottle of homemade strawberry preserves in Cara's direction. Her white hair was caught in a barrette at her neck. She wore no makeup, but she had that gorgeous radiance that strong, active women have. She was dressed in corduroy slacks, a tank top and a thick, hand-knit cardigan sweater.

Cara was wearing the same jeans and top she'd had on the day before. Now that we were safe, we'd have to do something about her clothing situation.

I helped myself to the bacon and toast.

"Why'd you come here?" Patrice asked. "You know you're welcome, but we haven't seen each other in years."

"Because I trust you. And because you knew Stephen and Peter, and the only trace to you is in my address book, which I have with me. No e-mail, no phone records. My current friends and colleagues have never heard me mention your name. I shred your letters."

Patrice cocked her head. "Whatever possessed you to shred my letters? What could I have written to you—"

"Nothing. It's nothing you did, nothing you wrote. I didn't want your name linked to mine in any way in case we had to come here."

"Are you really in that much danger?" Patrice searched my face.

I dropped my gaze. "I don't know."

Patrice had tried so hard to remove herself from the world in which her son had died. It was a vain attempt to take control of her environment, but I couldn't fault her for it. Heaven knows I'd tried hard enough to do it myself. Now I was threatening what peace she might have found.

"Maybe we shouldn't have—" I began.

"Don't be ridiculous. I didn't say I wasn't up for a little adventure." Patrice winked at me. "You should be all right here. You've covered your tracks, and Cara and I put the Cherokee in the shed."

Cara finished a big bite of toast. "Once they go through Dad's things and find whatever it is they want, surely they'll leave us alone."

"They won't find it," I told her. She'd finished her eggs and bacon. She only had half a piece of toast left, which was good, because after I'd said what I was about to, breakfast would be over.

She shook her head at me. "How could you know that?"

"Because they're right. I have it."

Cara dropped the toast. It wasn't anger exactly that I saw in her eyes. Maybe a combination of fear, intense interest and a bit of resentment.

"Stephen sent it to me," I told them.

"So this—the danger you're in—has to do with Stephen's death," Patrice said.

"Show me what Dad sent you," Cara demanded.

I wiped my hands, went to the bedroom, and drew a padded manila envelope from my bag. When I got back to the kitchen, Patrice had cleared the dishes to the sink and wiped the table. Odin was happily munching on what was left of the bacon. She poured us a third cup of coffee while Cara sat on the edge of her chair.

I placed the envelope in the middle of the table. It was still sealed. It bore no return address, only a Denver postmark and my name and address scrawled in Stephen's almost illegible handwriting.

"I received this a month ago."

"And you haven't opened it?" Cara asked. This from the

girl who still had to unwrap at least one package every Christmas Eve.

"Your father sent me envelopes on occasion, usually shortly before or after he dropped out of sight. He asked me to keep them for him. When he got back from wherever he'd been—"

"He was still going off without your knowing where he was?" Patrice asked.

"He never stopped. When he'd get back, he'd retrieve the envelopes. Unopened. Of course, this time…"

"Was different. I don't know how you stood it all these years. I know I couldn't."

Cara eyed Patrice. "Did Peter go off, too?"

"No. It was nothing like that. With him it was silence. There's nothing lonelier than silence."

Patrice offered me a forced smile as she handed me a pair of kitchen shears. "Shall we?"

I snipped the end off the envelope and shook it. A slip of folded paper, a battered copy of a pocket atlas and two wallet-sized photos fell out. I turned the photos over. Studio shots. One was of a handsome, rakish looking young man with brown hair so thick it wouldn't stay put even for a photo. The other was of a thin, distinguished-looking, middle-aged man. Nothing was written on the back of either, but I knew who they were from photos in the newspapers.

I flipped through the atlas. No notations, nothing circled, no pages dog-eared. Nothing. It looked perfectly ordinary. Cara took it as soon as I laid it down.

Then I opened the piece of paper.

Elizabeth, if you're reading this, I must have screwed up pretty badly. Sorry. I never intended to involve you in my business. James will come to pick up this infor-

*mation. He'll know what to do with it. I do love you. I
always have. Tell Cara I love her. Take care of her. Take
care of yourself. Stephen*

I felt my eyes sting, but I was not about to let Stephen
seduce me yet again. Not from the grave. Not when I had Cara
to think about.

Cara dropped the atlas, took the paper from me and read
it. "Mom," she said, "he wanted you to give the envelope to
James." She handed the note to Patrice.

"Your father made a mistake," I reminded her. "He trusted
the wrong person." I wasn't about to repeat his mistake.

"Who's this James?" Patrice interrupted.

"One of Stephen's associates," I explained.

"The one we ran from last night," Cara added, examining
the photos.

I shot her a look.

"You can't ask Patrice to help us and not tell her what's
going on," Cara insisted. "You'd be doing exactly the same
thing that Dad did."

Cara was right. It wasn't as though not telling Patrice would
offer her some kind of protection. So I related everything that
had happened since Stephen's body had turned back up.

"Tell me again why you don't trust this James," Patrice said
when I'd finished.

Cara crossed her arms. "I'd like to hear this, too."

"He broke into my home. He was standing over me in my
bedroom. I have no idea what he intended to do."

"Mom, that's ridiculous."

"Is it? Cara, he did not come in on that airplane at National—the car with Colorado tags convinced me of that. For
all I know, he's been in the Washington area since we buried

your father. He may have been the one who stole his body. Somebody close to your father murdered him, someone he thought he could trust."

"Still, if that's all James wanted," Cara began, pointing to the envelope, "why not give it to him and be done with it? Then we'd be out of it."

"Would we? And what will happen if the person who killed Stephen gets this information?"

"You think James killed Daddy?"

"I'm saying I don't know who killed him."

"Do you know what these photos are all about?" Patrice asked.

I shook my head.

"What about the book?" Patrice asked.

Cara picked it up and flipped through it again. "I don't see any writing or marks on any of the pages. It looks like an ordinary collection of maps. Why would he send it to you?"

I shrugged. They expected answers and I had none to give them.

"So, if you're not going to give these photos and this book to this James, just what do you plan to *do* with them?" Patrice asked.

Again, I shook my head.

"Who are they?" Patrice asked as I rose to leave the table. "The men in the photos. You know them. I saw the recognition in your eyes."

I did. So did Cara. And so would Patrice if she owned a television set or subscribed to a newspaper.

"Edward and Will Donovan," I told her, sitting back down. "Will's the young one." I tapped my finger on his image.

"Is that supposed to mean something to me?"

"Are you serious?" Cara asked. "Three months ago the entire D.C. police force tore the city apart looking for him. *Dateline, 20/20*—you name it—all had profiles on him."

Patrice's eyes narrowed. "A fugitive, then."

"No," I said. "Just a young man who went missing."

"What makes him so special?" she asked. She swallowed hard. They'd tried to find her son, Marc, too.

"His father is Edward Donovan." Cara drew out the syllables of Donovan's name.

Patrice still looked blank.

"He's a judge in Denver. He's presiding over a huge witness intimidation and bribery trial out there. It's on every newscast."

"No TV," I reminded Cara.

"The young man's dead, then," Patrice said. "With that kind of clout, surely they would have found him if he were alive."

"The family refuses to give up hope." I touched Patrice's hand but she shook it off. I could see the pain in her eyes. She knew all about hope and how cruel it could be. So did I and I had no idea how to comfort her.

"What could Donovan have to do with Dad?" Cara asked.

"I have no idea."

"I'd say we've had more than enough missing persons in our lives," Patrice stated. "I don't think your mother wants to take on another. All it leads to is questions that never get answered." She threw me that look of hers, the one that pierced right through me.

"If you're referring to my sister Josie's disappearance, I have no more questions. Josie's dead," I said. I'd spent so much time, all those years ago, insisting she wasn't. If Patrice needed to hear me say it, there it was.

"Aunt Josie died in an accident before I was born," Cara interrupted.

Patrice turned to me. "Is that what you told her?"

I didn't need this. Not now. I'd tucked Josie away in some dark part of my heart and built a wall around her. I had more than enough to deal with at the moment without adding Josie to the mix.

"She has a right to know. We all have a right to the truth," Patrice insisted.

"Ah, but there's the rub." There was a catch in my voice. "We don't know what happened to Josie."

"What are you two talking about?" Cara asked.

"Your mother's sister, Josie, was two years ahead of us in college," Patrice said. "A year or so before your mom and dad married, Josie married a man named Nicholas Ackerman."

"Ackerman? *The* Nicholas Ackerman?" Cara asked.

Patrice frowned at me.

"It's his trial Edward Donovan is presiding over," I explained.

"You mean they finally got that bastard on something?"

"Not yet," I said, "but they're working on it. He's got his finger in every pie in Denver—car dealerships, restaurants, theaters, hotels, you name it. He's been brought up on charges before, but nothing's stuck. Drug trafficking, money laundering—"

"Murder?" Patrice suggested.

I felt my heart stop.

"Would one of you please let me in on this conversation?" Cara demanded.

Patrice swallowed. "On a bright summer's day, a few months before your mom and dad married, Nicholas Ackerman's wife, your aunt Josie, disappeared."

Cara's eyes flared and then narrowed. "You said—"

"What I thought you could handle. Hell, what I could handle when you were young," I said.

"When, exactly, did you plan to tell me?"

"It hasn't come up," I insisted.

"Well, it's come up now. First Dad and now Aunt Josie. How many other family secrets are you keeping from me?"

"None," I said evenly. "That's my whole inventory."

"Okay, you two," Patrice said. "None of us is the bad guy here. Cara, no one knows for sure what happened to Josie."

"Says you. That son-of-a-bitch husband of hers murdered her," I stated flatly.

"There was never any proof of foul play," Patrice explained. "The police did a thorough investigation."

"Did they look into Ackerman as a suspect?" Cara asked.

"He reported her missing the next morning, after he got back from some binge with his friends," Patrice said. "He had eyewitnesses who accounted for most of his time that night."

"I don't care," I insisted. "Josie was afraid of Nick. He was the last one to see her alive. He got away with her murder and everyone knows it. That's why he moved back to Denver."

"Daddy must have hated him, too," Cara said.

"Almost as much as I do," I agreed.

"That's our link," Cara said. "Ackerman connects Daddy to Donovan."

Chapter 8

It took us all a while to calm down. I felt drained, but having something to focus on had reenergized Cara. She was intent on discovering how Stephen was involved with Ackerman's trial. He'd given us a lead. Right or wrong, we had our connection: Stephen's hatred of Ackerman and Stephen's death in Denver. How that related to Ackerman's trial and what the judge's son had to do with anything was still a matter of speculation. There had to be something that linked Stephen to Will, as well. We needed that link. All we had available to us in York was the public record and we intended to use it.

We found the public library exactly where Patrice said it would be, in the heart of downtown. It was the only place she knew where I could get on the Internet with no questions from anybody.

I logged on to a computer in a back corner of the main room, and Cara pulled up a chair next to mine. I typed Will

Donovan's name into the search engine and pressed enter. It came back with dozens of hits, most of them accompanied by his photogenic image.

"Hot!" she declared.

"He's dead," I reminded her.

"Can't help it, Mom. Look at his hair! And that smile! It's just that much off center. You gotta love it. Besides, I'd prefer to think otherwise—that he's alive and well somewhere, maybe the victim of amnesia."

I threw her a sidelong glance. She'd seen the news coverage just as I had. Will Donovan was a Georgetown law student who'd made a splash in Washington. He'd been featured in *The Washingtonian* magazine as an up-and-coming young bachelor. Smart, quick-witted and gracious when it suited him. If he hadn't been so appealing, would they have cared so much when he vanished? Charm. It was a dangerous, seductive thing.

"They say that when the camera wasn't on him, he was arrogant," I told her.

"Bad-boy charm. Why do you think I like him? Besides, most of that can be fixed," she assured me.

If he had lived long enough. And if he'd found a woman willing to devote herself to his salvation. Why were some women—like Josie—so naive?

"Why are you so certain he's dead?" she asked.

"They say—"

"I don't care about 'they.' Why do *you* think he's dead?"

"His belongings—his clothes, his furnishings—they were all left behind."

"Yeah, but you and I walked out of our houses last night and what did we take with us?"

"Our driver's licenses. Our wallets. Some clothes. His were still in his apartment. So were his keys. So were his cornflakes swimming in milk."

"Maybe we had more time than he did," she said.

"There were no bank withdrawals. He left his car."

"So he had help and the food was staged. Would his father have helped him?"

"Possibly. But why, and if he did, do you think the family would have insisted on the kind of manhunt the city launched?"

"Okay, so it wasn't his family. Mom, he's only two years older than I am."

"I know." I looked back at the screen. I didn't want her to see the fear in my eyes. Death had an equal-opportunity policy. And if it was easier for her to think of Donovan as alive, I had no right to discourage her. I'd willed Josie to be alive when I was Cara's age.

We scanned as many of the shorter articles as we could before I hit the print button. I wanted copies of the three longest ones that had appeared in the *Washington Post*.

Cara pulled them from the printer, then put them in front of me. "Look. January 21."

"So?"

"That's the date Will disappeared. When was Dad last in town?"

It had been about three months ago, shortly after the spring semester started.

"I got back from that trip to Virginia Beach, remember?" Cara said. "I missed him by one day."

"Do you remember the date?"

"January 20."

It couldn't be coincidence. I knew it in my gut. But which side of this did Stephen come down on?

"Mom, do you think—"

"Yes." I grabbed the pages from the printer and stuffed them into my bag. We could look at them later when we had more time, not that I expected them to be of much help. As far as the police could tell, Will Donovan had walked out of his upscale apartment in Cleveland Park and vanished off the face of the earth.

But I knew something the police didn't know. I knew Stephen Larocca. I knew that, whatever else he might have been and whatever I might have said about him in anger, he wasn't a killer. Had he tried to save Donovan? Did he know who had killed him? Had he gone after his killer? And if so, why?

"Cara, let's check the atlas again." I handed it to her from my bag. "See if there's anything at all marked on either the D.C. or the Denver maps."

She flipped through the pages, lingering first on one and then the other. "Unless it's in some kind of invisible ink, there's nothing."

Frustrated, I slipped the book back into my bag with the printouts.

We'd get no more answers today. Cara and I needed to get back to Patrice. We'd been gone far longer than I'd intended. Maybe she'd have some insight into Stephen that had escaped me. Maybe she had some idea as to who might have recruited him. When he graduated, he'd gone to work for the forestry service. He was also in the reserves, doing one weekend a month. Or was he? Did it go back that far? Stephen and Peter had served in the navy together before going back to school. Had Peter said something to Patrice? Could he have known what Stephen was involved with?

Patrice was just about the most intuitive person I have ever met. I remembered her looking at me on our wedding day while she helped me fix my veil. She'd brushed back the netting and taken my face in her hands and asked me if I was sure I wanted to marry Stephen. She told me I didn't have to go through with it. I'd laughed at her, but some part of me knew she wasn't teasing.

She'd been married to Peter for six months by the time Stephen and I wed. What had she known?

We stopped at a mall we passed on the way home. Cara insisted that two days of the same underwear was one day too many. A third was unthinkable. I gave her fifteen minutes in the Express so she could get what she needed, including some jeans and a couple of tops. She took thirty. Then we picked up a pepperoni pizza so Patrice wouldn't have to cook.

It was almost eight by the time we turned into the driveway. I was thankful I hadn't hit anything on our outing. When we'd left the house, Patrice had suggested we take the van and leave the Jeep in the shed, just in case someone might be watching for us in town. Not likely. I was certain we hadn't been followed last night.

Driving the van was like driving a semi. I pulled it under the carport. Cara continued chatting as though yesterday and this morning had never happened, as though we were on holiday visiting an old friend, as though I didn't have a bag full of articles about a young man who had disappeared, as though she'd actually forgiven me for not telling her about Josie. As if I didn't know all her forced perkiness was for my benefit. Cara wasn't the perky type.

I noticed immediately that the house was dark and the security lights that had bathed the yard so brightly when we'd rolled in during the wee hours of the morning had not been turned on. A single pole light with a sensor illuminated a section of lawn beyond the drive. The only other light shone from the windows of Patrice's studio out back. Was she working late, making up for the disruption we'd caused?

Cara opened the door and hopped to the ground, grabbing up the pizza in one hand and her bags in the other. I was out of my door just as quickly, blocking her path. It was obvious she was on her way around back. "Let's go into the house first," I suggested.

"But there's no—" she began.

I grabbed her elbow and pulled her across in front of the large living room windows. The drapes were open, but I saw no movement inside, not even a glimmer from the kitchen.

I opened the screen and my sleeve caught on a tear in the mesh. I ran my hand over it. It was a ragged hole. I hadn't noticed it earlier and I would have. I tugged at the door, but it was locked and I didn't have a key.

Odin wasn't barking. He could be out back with Patrice. If I were her, I'd keep him with me. But wouldn't he have heard the van drive up? Shouldn't we hear him barking, even from that distance?

"Mom, Patrice isn't—"

"You're right," I said, cutting her off. "Let's go around back."

I took the pizza from her, jerked open the passenger door of the van and dropped the box onto the seat. Then I stuffed her bags onto the floorboard. We headed to the corner of the house and stopped. From that angle we could see Patrice and a good part of the center of the room through the large windows of her studio. She sat facing us at her potter's wheel, her head down, her hands cupped around a spinning mound of wet clay. She looked fine.

Then I heard it. A soft, distant whimper, coming from the

shadows near the shed that housed the Jeep. I grabbed Cara's arm and practically dragged her across the grass.

"What are you doing?" she demanded, trying to struggle out of my grip. "I'm not two years old."

I shushed her and, closer now, she heard it, too.

"What is that?"

I pulled her down as I knelt. In the tall grass at the shed's corner, I felt something warm and furry. It whimpered.

Cara jerked back. "What the hell..."

"Odin," I explained, stroking the dog's fur. "Something's wrong with him." My fingers explored his fur. I found something lodged near his shoulder. A dart. I pulled it out and tossed it on the ground. "He's been drugged. They must have dumped him here."

"What are you saying?" Cara whispered.

I didn't have time to answer questions. "They've been here for hours or Odin would still be out of it." The dog whined and I rubbed his neck. "It's all right, boy. You just hang in there."

I turned back to Cara. "They heard us drive up. We need to make them think everything's all right."

"Who are *they?*" she asked. "You think it's James, don't you? Mom, he wouldn't do something like this."

"I don't know that and neither do you," I said evenly.

"Do you think Patrice knows they're here?"

"Yes. The tear in the screen. There must have been a confrontation at the front door."

"But she looks—"

"I know. They can't see us in the dark, but they'll get antsy if we don't show up at the studio soon."

"They may have night-vision glasses. Jeez, I sound as paranoid as you."

She couldn't see my smile in the darkness. "No. There's only one or two of them."

"How do you know?" she asked.

"Because if there were more, we wouldn't be here talking," I assured her.

"Get back into the van." I thrust the keys into her hand and forced her fingers around them. "Wait until I'm within a couple of yards of the studio window and they can see me before you crank the engine. Then get the hell out of here. Call the police. Do you understand?"

"Mom, I can't—"

"Yes, you can," I assured her.

"Come with me," she begged.

"If Patrice is in danger, it's for only one reason—me. I can't leave her." I hugged Cara to me, but just for a moment. We didn't have time to dally. I didn't want whoever was in that shed to come looking for us. I was afraid of what he'd do to Patrice before he did. And what he'd do to Cara when he found us.

"I'm not going anywhere," she insisted.

I grabbed her chin in my hand. "This is not up for negotiation. Promise me you'll get yourself somewhere safe and call the police. It's the only way that you can help me."

She didn't answer.

"We don't have time for this. You're the one chance we've got," I told her.

"Okay, okay! I promise."

"Now get out of here. I love you."

I didn't wait for her to say it back. I simply took off walking fast for the shed, drawing the gun from the back of my jeans as I went. I tucked it into the front of my waistband and let my shirt and coat cover it.

I walked directly to the window and into the light. Patrice had been watching my every move as soon as I'd come close enough for her to see my approach, but she didn't acknowledge me until I tapped my knuckles against the glass. She hesitated, then smiled and motioned with a gooey hand for me to come in. Her eyes, looking directly at me, darted to her left and then back.

So that's where he was, in my right-hand corner, as far away from the door as the studio would allow. I assumed he wanted me alive, or he would have already shot me through the window. I doubted that he'd brought tranquilizer darts just in case there was a dog.

James would probably only kill me as a last resort. He could have easily slit my throat that night in my condo. The prospects of being grilled about something I knew little about did not particularly appeal to me. And exactly what might follow that discussion—after he'd taken the photos and the book—was something I'd just as soon not think about.

Of course, it might not be James.

I took a good look through the window. The only other window was directly across from the one where I stood. A sink and counter ran most of the length of the wall between them. Behind Patrice was a large worktable and to the right were drying shelves. A door, ajar, led to an area that must house her kiln. He would be in there.

What the hell did I think I was doing?

I circled around to the door on the left side of the building and took the gun from my waistband. With my free hand I unlatched the door and shoved it inward.

He wasn't in the closet. In the far right corner, well out of the way of the windows, was a lone man in dark clothing. I couldn't see his face in the shadow but he had one hell of a big pistol in his gloved hand. It was right out in front of him, and it was pointed directly at Patrice.

Chapter 9

"You're armed," the man said. His voice, giving a hint of surprised amusement, sounded familiar, but I couldn't quite place it. All I knew was that it wasn't James.

My little .38 was no match for his cannon, but then, it only took one good shot to fell a man if it was well placed. I was a good shot—Stephen had seen to that—and I was pointing my gun straight at his head. He was sure to be wearing a Kevlar vest. I wouldn't have minded having one of my own.

"Why don't you just put that down," he suggested, "and we'll talk." So civilized and with the faintest hint of an English accent. Blood pounded in my ears. I knew that voice.

"Ian?"

He stepped from behind the shelves, and I felt my trigger finger tense. "Read any good obituaries lately?"

"Elizabeth, please. Put down the gun. I mean you no harm."

His gun, I noticed, stayed trained on Patrice, who had wiped her hands and stood to remove her apron.

"I'd rather you'd sit back down," he told Patrice, who did exactly that.

"Stephen was a friend of mine," he added to me.

"And that's supposed to be a recommendation?"

He took another step closer.

"That's far enough," I warned, and he stopped.

"I was in Maryland to watch over you. Stephen knew that what he was involved in was becoming more dangerous. He asked me to make sure both you and your daughter were safe. I offered my services as an adjunct professor at Gilman and they accepted."

I heard the van crank, and obviously, so did he. "Where's Cara?" he asked.

"I sent her to call the police."

He nodded. "I'd have preferred you not done that."

I eyed Patrice. I wanted her next to me, but I wasn't about to make things easier for him. If he shot her, it'd take him a second to swing the gun in my direction. In that second, I planned to take him down.

"So to protect us, you find some way to follow us, shoot my friend's dog, and then hold her at gunpoint."

"Only long enough to convince you to allow me to help you. If Patrice had been cooperative, there would have been no need for guns."

"Right. So convince me, Ian. What was Stephen involved with? Who was he working for?"

"I can't tell you that."

"Wrong answer."

"I believe he left something with you—"

Before he could say another word, the side of the building

exploded. Wood flew everywhere. I closed my eyes and shielded my face as best I could with my arms. A splinter ripped through my sleeve. When I looked up, I couldn't believe what I was seeing. Patrice's VW van had burst through the door side of the old barn and was heading straight for us. I dove toward Patrice. The van swerved and plowed between the three of us to stop abruptly, leaving Ian on one side, scrambling for cover as the worktable flew toward him, and Patrice and me on the other side.

Cara beckoned to us through the side door, which stood wide open. "Get in!"

I pushed Patrice forward and tumbled in on top of her, slid the door shut and tripped the lock.

I heard something slam against the door frame of the driver's side. Glass shattered. Then I saw Ian reach for Cara in the driver's seat. That son of a bitch was coming in through the window.

It wasn't much of a growl, just a soft warning, and then Odin reared up from between the seats and sank his teeth into Ian's wrist. Ian yelled and disappeared down the side of the van.

Cara wasted no time. She threw the van into Reverse and peeled out of the shed, taking what little was left of that side of the barn with it. I lay on the floor, my hand wrapped around the steel support of the middle seat, trying hard not to add to the bruises I knew would soon cover most of my body.

I could hear the gravel of the driveway spewing as we flew over it, and then I was thrown forward as we braked.

"Which way?" Cara demanded.

"Right," Patrice called. She had crawled between the middle and front seats where Odin lay.

"I need a turn down a back road that will take us out of

here," Cara insisted as the van lurched onto the road. "No dead ends. *Now.*"

"Second mailbox on the right, the dirt road. We'll cut across the Russells' farm. We can head toward Gettysburg and pick up the highway there."

Fine. Just as long as the van held together long enough to get us there. And Ian—God help us—didn't find us.

Chapter 10

The van died going up a hill on a narrow country road not ten miles from Patrice's home and about a mile from the interstate, leaving us stranded in the dark. It was Cara's sheer will that had kept it going as long as it had, considering the damage she'd done to it taking down the studio.

We got out, helping a none-too-enthusiastic Odin onto the grass.

"Thank you for bringing Odin with you," Patrice said as she pulled two flashlights and a couple of tarps from the back of the van.

"I thought I wasn't going to be able to get him into the van at first. Good thing you keep a harness on him. I've seen frat boys at all-night beer parties who were steadier on their feet. He weighs almost as much as I do."

Cara scooped up the first-aid supplies. I handed her a couple of screwdrivers from the toolbox and grinned at her.

She wasn't an animal lover, but she would never abandon any living thing in distress. Her act of kindness had been rewarded. I doubt we would have made it out of the studio without Odin's help.

I grabbed the tire iron, just in case, and retrieved my backpack and Cara's bags. Then Cara rescued the pizza before she took off the brake and shifted the transmission out of gear. Patrice took charge of Odin, who was still groggy from the drugs.

Somehow the three of us summoned enough strength to steer the van around and push it off the road toward some trees in the ravine below. We shone a flashlight after it. It didn't quite make the undergrowth, but it would be hard to see. Someone looking for it, even if they had a notion as to which road we'd taken, would waste a lot of time before finding it.

A short distance away, on the lee side of the hill, we found a sheltered place among the trees near an outcropping of rock that blocked the view from the road. Odin wasn't able to walk well yet, and we were all exhausted. We had no choice but to stop and rest. We needed strength for tomorrow.

We spread a tarp and lay down together, the dog in the middle. I took off my coat and shared it as best I could with Patrice. We pulled the second tarp over all four of us, to pass what was left of the night. Thank goodness it was warm for an April evening, or we would have been forced to find actual shelter.

"You promised me you'd leave," I whispered to Cara. I could hear her chuckle in the darkness.

"I hate to burst your bubble, Mom, but that's not the first promise to you I've broken."

That brought me fully alert. "What do you mean?"

She answered with little snoring sounds.

I felt Patrice's hand on my arm. "We don't always know

best," she said softly. "And God knows you lied enough times
to your parents."

And to Cara. But guilt was a burden I didn't need to carry
that night.

"What could Stephen have been doing?" I asked Patrice,
desperate to make some sense out of what was happening.
"Do you know? Would Peter know?"

"Peter and I don't talk. I haven't seen him since Marc's
funeral. Our son's death broke the last strand between us.
Would he know? Maybe. Would he tell you? I have no idea.
You're not the only one who was lied to."

"Peter?" I asked.

"That's why I divorced him."

"You never told me."

"I never told anyone. We loved each other, Elizabeth, but
not the way you and Stephen were in love. It wasn't enough
for me, not enough to make up for the deceit. He was involved
in something sometime after he became a D.A., but I never
knew what it was."

"I'm sorry." I really was. Patrice was a special person and
she deserved more than life had offered her so far. "What do
you think—"

"I don't. Not since our son died. Peter and Stephen served
in the SEALs together, you know. Did Stephen ever talk to
you about it?"

"No. He always changed the subject when I brought up his
military service."

"Secrets. You know what you get when you press someone
about a secret?" she asked. "Lies. Now get to sleep. I don't
even want to think what tomorrow's going to be like."

Even drugged, Odin, I was sure, would alert us if anyone
approached. I cradled my gun and my pepper spray against

my chest. My left hand found the dog's neck, and I wrapped my fingers in his fur. I fell asleep before I finished my prayer.

Dawn woke us, and we got a good look at what a mess we all were. We examined our wounds, all minor, thank goodness, and applied Band-Aids where necessary.

Having slept off the tranquilizers, Odin was ready to take on the world. He was, however, hungry. We shared the cold pizza with him, but we had no water to offer him. We folded the tarps, tucked them behind the rocks and weighed them down with stones. We took with us the flashlights, the tire iron, the first-aid kit and, of course, our bags.

"What happened?" I asked Patrice. "Yesterday, when Ian came to the house."

Cara and Odin were a few steps ahead on the narrow country road that looked as though it saw little traffic. We'd be able to hear any vehicle that approached in plenty of time to duck into the underbrush. I saw her look back at us and then turn forward.

"He knocked on the door, and, like an idiot, I opened it," she said. "He looked…"

"Friendly, clean-shaven, intelligent—"

"Attractive," Patrice added.

I nodded, shuddering to think how I'd actually gotten into a car with him. Somehow, I should have known. But why had he let me go then?

"He had a map. I noticed the gloves, but I didn't think anything about it. He said he'd taken a wrong turn," Patrice went on. "It was broad daylight. He made no move to come inside. He just stood there, pointing to the map. He seemed so…"

"Engaging," I suggested.

"Yes. I joined him on the steps. That's when Odin started to growl, but he was still inside the screen."

"He must have known Ian was armed," I suggested, "smelled the gun oil."

"I don't know. He grabbed my wrist and pulled a gun from his pocket. Elizabeth, I swear to God I thought he was going to kill me, but instead he shot Odin."

"Through the screen."

She nodded. "Then he jerked the screen open and Odin lunged, even with the dart in his shoulder. But then Odin fell like a stone. I thought he was dead, and there wasn't a damned thing I could do about it. I was so angry, but I was terrified, too. He made me help him carry Odin around behind the car shed. Then he forced me back to the house, locked the front door and took me out the kitchen door and around to the studio. He seemed to know about me, what I do. He didn't talk much. Quite polite, despite his forcefulness. He had a real gun, not just the tranquilizer gun. He told me to work at the wheel. Then we waited for what seemed like forever, until you got home. Elizabeth, I'm so sorry. I should never have opened that door."

"He would have gotten in. You know that," I assured her. "And if you hadn't cooperated…"

"You know him," Patrice said. "You called him by name."

"He's a professor at Gilman, but anything I thought I knew about him obviously isn't true. If it were, he'd be busy preparing to teach class, not threatening us."

"Maybe he moonlights on the weekends," Cara called over her shoulder.

It was a good try—to lighten the mood—but it didn't work. We fell silent. Everyone examining their own guilt, most likely even Odin.

A little before seven we made it to a main road near an exit where we found a Cracker Barrel and its accompanying lot full of cars. We were lucky it was a warm morning. I casually strode up and down between cars in an area at the far end of the lot, trying the doors. One car had its windows slightly open, a Pontiac Grand Prix, at least three years old with in-state tags and its hood still hot to the touch. Careless. The front doors were locked, but one of the back doors wasn't.

"What do you think it'd cost to rent a car like this?" I asked Patrice.

"Maybe two hundred a day," Cara supplied.

I reached inside my bag and pulled out a twenty dollar bill. "You look the most presentable of the three of us," I told Cara. She'd actually changed her clothes in the woods. I licked my thumb and dabbed at a smudge on her cheek. She squealed and drew out of my reach, just like she used to when she was five. "Go inside and buy some stationery and some kind of tape."

"Why?"

"Just do it. Please."

Patrice collapsed on the grass several yards from the Pontiac, her legs dangling down the slope toward the inter-state. I sat next to her and Odin and a small tree that was tethered to cables to force it to grow straight.

"We're in some kind of hellish trouble," she said. Her face held no hint of accusation, only exhaustion, and a rather feeble attempt at a smile.

"Oh, yeah," I agreed.

"How'd he find us?" she asked.

"My guess is Ian put a tracking device on Cara's Jeep. I thought they'd only focus on me."

"You think Ian is working with James?"

I shrugged. "Maybe, but if he is, where's James?"

Cara joined us and set two bags on the ground. One contained the items I'd asked for plus several bottles of water and a small bowl. The other, three large cups of coffee. "The place is packed," she reported, pulling out the bowl and pouring Odin a drink. "All the same, I suggest we move it along. So what's your brilliant plan?"

I took two big gulps of coffee and then pulled the screw drivers from my bag and handed them to Cara. "I don't know how brilliant it is, but you and Patrice need to steal a set of license plates. Look for plastic screws. They're easier to get off. And make sure it's another Pennsylvania plate. Take the ones off the Grand Prix and put them on the other car. We'll do the rest down the road."

"You're going to steal a car?" Cara demanded, her eyes huge.

"Technically, no." I dumped out the stationery and sighed. The paper was printed with bees and flowers.

"What? It was either that or bunnies," she said.

"Right."

"Technically, what are you doing?"

"Renting a car. Now scoot."

I dug farther into my backpack and pulled out three bills from a padded envelope. Three hundred dollars. Hopefully it would be enough, although "renting" a car without permission certainly was a major inconvenience for the owner. I wrote a note on the bee stationery: "You should have your car back no later than tomorrow evening. Please accept my apologies for the inconvenience. Please do not call the police."

Hey, it was worth a try. Then I wrapped the money in the note and stuffed it all in the envelope. I taped it shut and wrote across it: "For the Owners of Pontiac Grand Prix" and then listed the license plate number. By the time I finished, Cara and Patrice were back.

"We almost got busted," Cara said, her face flushed a bright red. "I started to unscrew a plate and then Patrice whistled at me. Someone pulled into the parking space right next to me."

"What'd you do?" I asked

"Dropped down on all fours and pretended to be looking for a contact."

"She was great," Patrice declared.

"Right. *Now* we discover my true talents."

"I'm glad to hear you say that because I've got one more thing for you to do." I handed Cara the envelope along with a twenty-dollar bill.

"Mom…"

"We'll be out of here in less than ten minutes. Give the envelope to the person working the cash register. Ask her not to announce it over the PA system, but to check with people as they pay their bills. The twenty is for her trouble."

Cara shook her head at me. "I'd better not go to hell for this."

"If you do," I assured her, "it won't be the only reason."

She stuck out her tongue at me but went back into the restaurant. We'd already wasted too much time. Patrice climbed into the backseat of the Pontiac with Odin, reached into the front seat and released the latch to the driver's side door. I slid behind the wheel.

"It'd be nice if we had keys."

"True," I agreed, pulling wires down from the steering column, "but we don't." It took two tries before I got the engine running.

"How'd you learn to do that?" Patrice asked.

"From Stephen," I told her.

"Any particular reason why you thought you might need to know how to hotwire a car?"

"Just in case." I backed out of the space.

"In case of what?"

"In case my daughter, my friend and her dog needed a ride."

Cara came out of the restaurant's door, head down, walking fast. I swung the car around, and she jumped into the passenger seat.

"Go. Now!" she insisted. "I don't know what that woman's going to do."

Chapter 11

We headed north on Highway 15 and then west on the Pennsylvania Turnpike.

Concrete barriers separated us from oncoming traffic on our left and a steep mountainside on our right, much like a pinball spinning down a chute. My hands were shaking so hard I could barely keep the car on the road. I never would have attempted that highway except for two reasons: I didn't want to take the Pontiac across state lines, and at Breezewood there was a truck stop that offered hot showers.

Thank God it was still early enough on a Saturday morning that traffic was relatively light. The only thing that saved what little nerves I had left was my conviction that the stolen license plate on the Grand Prix would prevent our being pulled over, at least for a while. We found the truckers' plaza some seventy or so miles down the road. I pulled to the far end of the lot and backed into a space.

The showers, as the sign promised, were indeed hot. So was the food at the Burger King. So was the car we were driving.

When I got out of my shower, Patrice greeted me with a sweatshirt she'd purchased in the gift area. She'd turned it inside out and clipped the tag, which left it a nice gray color with light-blue thread accenting the seams.

"No need to advertise where we're coming from," she said. On the inside was a Pennsylvania logo. Not exactly my style, but it was clean and it was warm and I would have put on most anything not to have to don the sweater I'd slept in the night before. I threw it away in the restroom's trash bin.

By then it was almost nine o'clock. Odin needed one more walk before we took off again, but first he had to have a second hamburger. I'd bent over to unwrap it for him in the grassy area near a picnic table when Cara knelt down next to me. "Smoky at three o'clock."

Out of the corner of my eye I watched as a state highway patrol car turned into the parking area and started past us, cruising at an especially low speed. We watched as he stopped directly in front of the Grand Prix and got out.

"Damned car owners," Cara cursed.

"Hush," I told her. "It *is* their car."

"I suppose you think they told the police about the money you gave them. Hah! I say they pocketed it and *then* turned us in."

"Stay focused, you two, and follow my lead," Patrice directed, shortening Odin's leash, another addition from the gift shop. "Don't talk and don't look back."

If she intended to walk out cross-country, I wasn't sure but what I'd be willing to turn us in. We'd been wise enough to keep our bags with us, but the maps, the flashlights and the tarps were all in the car.

But she didn't lead us into the trees. Instead she headed

across the pavement toward the big rigs. It took every ounce of control I had not to break into a run. She pulled us up short at a white tractor trailer, with the word SUNRISE written in all caps, and banged on the door.

"What the…" I started.

"Yeah?" A huge, shaggy-bearded creature stuck his head out the window.

"Big Mac, meet my friends. You said you could use some company…."

"When the heck did you meet him?" I whispered.

"Coming out of the showers," she whispered back. "He thinks I have a nice ass." Then in a normal voice, "Got room for the lot of us? We could sure use a ride about now."

The beard lifted into a smile. "Hell, yeah."

He got out and helped us up, and I could tell where he got his name. He was huge. Cara and I crawled into the sleeper, leaving Patrice and Odin to deal with Big Mac. We swung out of the parking area toward the road, and I heard Odin let out a low growl and then settle back down. Good for him. He'd keep Mac in line.

Cara snuggled down at one end of the mattress and was out as soon as her head hit Mac's spare pillow, but I couldn't help playing scenarios in my head about what might have happened if that patrol officer had spotted us. Or Big Mac turned out to be half as sinister as he looked. I listened in on a little of the conversation up front as the big rig looped back around onto the turnpike.

"Where you folks headed?" Big Mac asked, slurping coffee from an oversize Dunkin' Donuts mug. He was a smoker. I could tell by the rasp in his voice.

"West," Patrice offered. He could assume that much since that was the direction he was driving. "Ohio," she added.

Ohio was as good a place as any right now. But we couldn't keep running forever. We needed a plan, a goal that would eventually allow us to make our way back to our real lives. I'd promised Cara.

"You in trouble?" Big Mac asked, taking another slurp of coffee.

Patrice let out a titter of a laugh. "No. Just broke."

I heard him grunt. "If you need help, I'm offerin'. No strings. You don't owe me an explanation, but you didn't walk to that rest area and you don't strike me as the sort of dame that's wantin' for money."

"Our car broke down. Actually, my friend's husband's car. She left him and he threatened to come after us. He's probably reported his car stolen by now."

"That your car Smoky was all over back there?" he asked.

Patrice must have nodded.

"Why not call the police yourself?"

"She's tried that before...."

I didn't hear the rest. My mind wandered off to that place where exhaustion dulls all senses. Patrice was telling Big Mac some convoluted story of domestic abuse and it was rolling off her tongue as though it were the truth.

Was that how it had started with Stephen? After those first few words he'd spoken to me that were untrue, did the rest simply flow? Had it become so easy that he would just as soon tell a lie? Or did he hate them as much as I did? What had chased him?

At that point I didn't care, at least not enough to keep myself awake. I burrowed into Big Mac's down-stuffed pillow, ignoring the stale smell of cigarettes and cheap cologne, and allowed myself the luxury of sleep. Cara's head was at the other end of the cab. Her foot stretched and caught against my shoulder. I grabbed it and hugged it to me. We were safe, if only for the moment. No one could see her or me hidden in that cab, and anyone looking for us would be expecting to see three women together.

"Elizabeth, listen!" Patrice rattled the partition between the cab and the sleeper. I sat up to see thick fog shrouding the truck. We must be well into the mountains.

She turned the radio up, and it suddenly blared through the truck.

Cara pulled the pillow tighter around her head and snuggled deeper into the covers.

"—report finding drug paraphernalia near the body. An autopsy will be performed later today. The dead woman had been identified as Jayne Donovan, wife of Judge Edward Donovan, who is presiding over the Nicholas Ackerman witness intimidation and bribery case, and the mother of missing law student Will Donovan. She was found this morning in the Denver mansion she shared with her husband, an apparent suicide."

I closed my eyes. I felt nauseous. First the son, now the wife. How many more people were going to die? What kind of hellish world were we living in?

Patrice snapped off the radio and turned her eyes back toward the road.

"Did you know—" Big Mac began.

"Me? Heavens, no. It's just horrible that a woman like that would do such a thing, but I guess with her son missing… Grief causes people to lose all reason."

"I pass through Denver sometimes, taking a load on down to Albuquerque." He drew a card out of his pocket and handed it to Patrice. "Here's my cell phone number, just in case. Maybe we could have a drink."

"That would be nice. But we're not going to Denver," Patrice insisted.

I noticed she stuck the card in her pocket all the same.

And it occurred to me to wonder if maybe we should be going to Denver. That was near where Stephen had died. Now Jayne Donovan was dead, too. Edward Donovan was a judge. Surely we could trust him. He'd lost both his son and his wife. Maybe he'd known Stephen. Maybe he knew what I should do with the packet Stephen had sent me.

The fog continued to thicken, but for once it seemed more a blessing than a curse. I didn't sleep anymore. Once we got to Ohio, we would have little time to lose. We'd catch a bus and head for Denver. If whoever had killed Stephen was there, maybe he'd killed Jayne Donovan, as well. No matter how careful the killer had been, he had to have left a trail.

Chapter 12

The air in Denver was thinner than we were used to. It took its toll, especially on Patrice. So did the two-hour time difference, the all-night and all-day bus ride from Columbus and caring for Odin, who was more stoic than any animal should have been.

They don't allow dogs on buses or in most hotel or motel rooms, but seeing-eye dogs are an exception. Odin's harness wasn't regulation—it had no handle—but fortunately no one seemed to notice—at least, they didn't question us. Wearing the sunglasses, all day and all night, that Patrice had bought at the bus terminal to complete the ruse added to her misery. So Patrice had one royal headache by the time we got off the bus in Denver and walked to the trolley that carries passengers up and down the main street.

It was almost ten o'clock at night by the time I checked us into the Hyatt under the name of Marie Whitcomb. Cara and Patrice waited for me near the gift shop. The name matched one of my IDs, and the credit card in that name was linked to an account with sufficient funds to carry us for a number of months.

The tightness in my chest began to ease as I unlocked the door to our room. I was confident we were safe, at least for the moment. Of course, I couldn't forget that I had thought we were safe at Patrice's home, too. We collapsed into bed, thankful to be anywhere on solid ground.

The next morning, after Patrice and I had our showers, and Cara finally finished her hour-long bath, I gave Patrice the Marie Whitcomb credit card and sent her and Cara shopping for themselves and for me. I requested something dark and somber, a dress, not slacks, and a pair of black hose. Something that befitted a widow. As soon as the door closed behind them, I began flipping through the yellow pages.

The place started with an *F.* That was about all I could remember. Frawley's Funeral Home was the only *F* in the book. On Kalamath Street. That had to be it. I intended to get to Donovan, but that would be more difficult. So I'd start where it was easier, with the people who'd shipped Stephen's body home. I called and made an appointment for early in the afternoon.

Patrice and Cara woke me when they got back—that is, Odin woke me from my nap with a big sloppy lick across my cheek. "Get him off me," I wailed before I was sufficiently awake to realize what was happening.

"Dogs' mouths are far cleaner than humans'," Cara insisted, dumping her bags next to the captain's chair she collapsed into.

"That's a myth perpetuated by dog lovers," I told her. "Which we all are," I added, hoping not to offend Patrice. "I just prefer being awakened—"

"By a more disciplined animal," Patrice finished.

She said something to him in Dutch and he immediately went to her side, lay down and looked thoroughly ashamed of himself.

"Found you the perfect dress," Cara said. She pulled off the bag that went over it. It was black, with a bodice that wrapped to form a low V in front, a flared, mid-calf skirt and elbow-length sleeves. It had a matching scarf. Some kind of crepe fabric.

I pushed myself up on the bed. "You think a widow would wear that?"

"I told her you wouldn't like it," Patrice stated, "but we did, and we were the ones doing the buying."

For once I was the one rolling my eyes. With a little makeup help from Cara, I was transformed into a grieving widow, which, I suppose, on some level I actually was.

"Mrs. Larocca." He seemed properly sympathetic—a short, slight man with thinning hair and bony hands that tended to rest one inside the other. He looked more like a mortician than I would have liked. And the old Victorian home with its antique hearse on the wide porch was the perfect image of a funeral parlor. Death had been in business for a long time in Denver.

I'd wrapped the scarf around my neck to make the dress a bit more modest, but I saw his gaze drift to the low point of the V, anyway. I pulled the scarf over it.

"My assistant said you had some questions about the handling of your husband's body. I assume it made its journey intact."

Intact. I'm not sure but what any word that came out of that mouth would offend me. "Yes."

"Then how may I help you?" He pulled out a chair and settled next to me. For a moment I thought he was going to touch me with those skeletonlike hands. I drew back.

"Mr. Frawley, I need to know the specifics of my husband's death."

"Oh, my. I thought my assistant had made that plain to you when she called. He died in a skiing accident at a resort in the mountains."

"Yes, I understand that. How exactly did you obtain his body? Was it brought to you? Did you pick it up? Who authorized you to handle it?"

He squinted at me and then excused himself. In less than three minutes he was back with an open file in his hands.

"We were called to the scene of death. I'm afraid he'd been lying exposed in the snow overnight."

Frozen and alone.

Stephen, I'm so sorry. Whatever you were doing, you didn't deserve that.

"The coroner didn't order an autopsy?" I asked.

Frawley shook his head. "Apparently not, although, now that you mention it, that would be highly unusual. Unattended deaths, as a rule, are investigated by a medical examiner. But we do have a signed death certificate, and I see here that the charge for embalming was the standard fee. It would have been more if the body had been autopsied. Of course the angle at which the head…related to the torso made the cause of death obvious. He died of a broken neck."

"So it was the coroner who phoned you."

"No, the coroner has no authority to select a funeral home. It was Mr. Larocca's brother."

"His brother," I said evenly. Stephen had no brother.

"Yes. He identified the body and then called us to pick it up. He asked that you be notified and that we take care of the cremation. He even paid in cash for our services." He checked his notes. "We notified you of the arrangements and you agreed, but then you called back shortly and asked that we ship the body to Maryland instead."

I'd talked to Cara, and, through her tears, she'd asked that I have her father brought back, not just his ashes. I'd been in such shock, it hadn't even occurred to me to ask who had made the arrangements.

Again, the birdlike man looked at his files. "I see here that we have yet to refund that money." His face reddened. "That should have been done immediately. I'll have a check cut for Mr. Larocca's brother right away. Of course that's why you're here. I'm quite embarrassed."

"Don't be," I assured him. "I'd like to know the name of the person who found him. I'd like to thank him."

"Oh, that would, again, be his brother. But surely you've spoken with him."

"My husband and I were separated." That much was true. "His family and I don't speak. I'm dealing with my husband's death without any support from his siblings. Any information you can provide me would be most appreciated. I have a daughter who would like to know what happened to her father."

Mr. Frawley cleared his throat. "Yes, of course. Family situations can make these matters most difficult. My understanding is the brothers were on a skiing trip together. Apparently Mr. Larocca went out for a late-night ski alone, and his brother found him missing the next morning. When he discovered the body, it was too late."

"I see. I'd like a copy of the arrangements that were made, please, and any other information you might have. And, Mr. Frawley, Stephen's brother—he has two. They were all together on the trip. Which one came in? Tall, blond, tan, young? Or the one with dark hair and the hint of an English accent? He spent some time in London, a Rhodes Scholar."

"Now that you mention it, I believe Mr. Larocca did have a bit of an English accent. His hair was definitely dark."

Ian.

Chapter 13

When I got back to the hotel, I tore off that wretched dress and spread out the copies of Frawley's files on the bed.

"Somehow Ian Payne managed to bypass the authorities and have Stephen's body taken directly to Frawley's Funeral Home," I announced. "How? Why?"

"I'd say the why is because he killed him," Patrice suggested.

"Or because he knew who killed him and he didn't want it to come out," Cara added. "As to how…"

"He must have some in with the authorities," I stated.

"Makes sense," Cara agreed. "We knew something was screwed up as soon as that fisherman snared Dad's body in the bay. That's when we realized he should have been autopsied in the first place."

The newscast of Jayne Donovan's death blared in the background. Patrice seemed fascinated by the reporters' continuous ramblings, while all I wanted was to get the noise of death out of my head. Still, I couldn't help watching. The D.A. in Ackerman's trial was speaking.

"...most difficult situation."

He nodded at a reporter in the crowd before him who said something that wasn't caught by the microphone. "No. The trial of Nicholas Ackerman will proceed. Court is scheduled to resume Thursday morning with Edward Donovan presiding. Mrs. Donovan will be buried Wednesday afternoon."

Another inaudible question from the press.

"Judge Donovan is firm. There will be no mistrial."

Donovan had lost his son shortly after Ackerman's trial started. Now his wife was dead. So was Stephen. My heart ached for Donovan even as I felt rage surge through me. Ackerman. I hated him with every atom in my body. He wouldn't have done the killings himself. He was too much the coward, but he was behind it. I knew it. I wanted my pound of flesh, and not just his. James's or Ian's or whatever thug had killed Will Donovan and Stephen. And Jayne, if not by his own hand, then by driving her to suicide.

The screen cut back to the anchorwoman in the newsroom, and I forced myself to let my anger go. I needed a level head.

I glanced over at Cara. She sat curled up in the upholstered chair, munching on a bag of Cheetos she'd gotten from the vending machine, and going through all the pages of newspaper articles about Will Donovan's disappearance that we had copied at the library.

I turned my attention back to the pages in front of me and pored over every scribbling, every typed word on the forms from Frawley's. "Immediate cremation. Effects to be returned to widow." Stephen's wedding ring. His wallet. The clothes he was wearing. I had examined each item when I received them. Sterile. As though Stephen had never touched them, never worn them. They weren't torn in any way.

There'd been no luggage. There should have been luggage. I was so lost in my anger I hadn't once thought about it at the time.

The home address "brother" Larocca gave Frawley was bogus. There was no Sussex, Maryland, at least none that I'd ever heard of. Lucky Mr. Frawley would be getting his check back by return mail.

Ian had gotten my address and my unlisted phone number correct, which made me shudder. What else did he know about me? Did he know enough to guess I'd come to Denver? Possibly. But this time he had no tracking device.

And what about James? My visit to the funeral home had convinced me of one thing, if nothing else: there were at least two opposing forces at work. Ian wasn't the one who had stolen Stephen's body. He'd seen to it that Stephen was set for cremation, and then he'd left, thinking everything was in order. I'd disrupted that order when I canceled the cremation and had his body shipped back to Maryland.

That was when the other force stepped in and stole the body. Did that mean Ian was Stephen's killer? A chill swept through me. How could I have ever thought him attractive?

But if James was the friend he pretended to be, why had he stolen Stephen's body? Why hadn't he simply contacted me and asked to examine the body? Surely he would have known I'd do whatever I could to bring Stephen's murderer to justice.

Or were James and Ian working together?

There was one more troubling matter about James: he'd killed a man at Reagan National Airport.

The TV went quiet and, for a moment, I thought I'd gone deaf.

"If you still want to talk to Edward Donovan, Donovan's holding a news conference in front of his home at seven o'clock this evening to confirm what the D.A. is saying, that there'll be only a three-day recess in the trial. Today may be our only chance to get to him."

"I wonder if he'll question his wife's death," I said. "If I were him, I'd insist on a full investigation. Jayne was the one pushing the investigation into what happened to her son, Will. She was a real go-getter. Impulsive, intuitive, compassionate, into all sorts of charity work. The people of Denver loved her."

Cara held up a copy of a *Washington Post* article we'd gotten at the library. "She said in this article she wouldn't rest until her son was found. She insisted Will's alive."

"But she could have changed her mind," I suggested. "She could have given up. I can only imagine the kind of stress—"

"I don't think so," Patrice stated. "It takes more than two months to give up on a missing child."

I didn't argue. Patrice would know.

"So how do we get him to see us?" Cara asked, crunching a handful of Cheetos.

Flowers. They were my first thought, and I honestly didn't have time to come up with a better ruse. Edward Donovan's house had to be inundated with them, so the arrival of one more spray wouldn't seem unusual. The Donovans had been a prominent Denver family for generations.

The house, an old family home which was also a historical landmark, was north a few blocks, within walking distance of the state capitol, according to the concierge. I was counting on Donovan being there if he planned a news conference in just a few hours.

I pulled on the long-sleeved T-shirt and jeans Cara had

selected for me—studs across both pockets, her little way of telling me to buy my own clothes in the future. Then Cara and I, along with Patrice, her sunglasses and Odin in tow, all headed for the drugstore I'd spotted on the corner. The ads pasted to the window had promised a photo center. They had exactly what I needed: a photo-duplicating machine. I laid the photos Stephen had sent me, plus his note, against the glass, inserted a credit card and pressed the copy button. It spit out two duplicates. Across the bottom of one, I wrote, "These photos and this note were mailed to me. My husband, Stephen, was murdered, too. Please see us." I bought a pack of manila envelopes and some more stationery, plain this time.

Then we found a florist two blocks up. I ordered a huge spray, an arrangement of white mums with lots of greenery, something substantial enough to hide behind. We spent the next hour in a coffee shop, nursing lattes and watching the clock.

When it was time to pick up the flowers, I sent Patrice back to the hotel with Odin. If things went bad it'd be good to have a contact on the outside, and I was sure we'd never get Odin inside the Donovan mansion. Cara, as much as I would have liked to leave her with Patrice, was determined to go with me. It was just as well. A man who'd lost his son could probably relate to the fear I felt for my daughter.

"You're this Stephen's wife?" Edward stated, holding the opened manila envelope in his hand. I'd given the maid who answered the door the envelope along with the flowers. I'd asked her to please hand it to the judge with the message that I was here about his son.

Donovan had come down personally and taken us upstairs to a small library with no windows, just lots of wood, books and a heavy wool rug. I felt claustrophobic. His bodyguard stood just outside the door.

"Yes, I'm Stephen Larocca's wife, Elizabeth."

He was distinguished looking to the point of being unapproachable. As a judge, he was used to hiding his emotions, and he did it admirably. His bearing made it clear that questioning his authority would be a mistake.

"If he's who I believe him to be, that's not the name he used when I met him."

"I'm not surprised."

His gaze came to rest on Cara, and I could see a chink in his armor. He looked haunted, like sleep was a friend who had long ago deserted him.

He looked back at me, his facade back in place, and stared at me with half-lidded eyes. "You said you were here about my son."

"My husband's death is somehow linked to the disappearance of your son."

"I see. What is it you want?"

"To keep my daughter safe. Ackerman's men are after us, so you and I have something in common."

He almost smiled, but it wasn't out of humor.

"This is…" He gestured at Cara.

"My daughter, Cara. Stephen's daughter."

"Stephen's daughter. Yes. I see the resemblance."

"I don't believe your wife took her life," I said. "I believe the man who's behind all of this—Nicholas Ackerman—had her killed in an attempt to prejudice his trial."

I could tell from his expression I wasn't telling him anything he didn't already know.

"He also killed my husband and your son."

His eyebrows arched. "You believe my son is dead."

"Yes," I whispered.

"Why? Do you have new information?"

His breathing seemed to cease.

"No."

And then it resumed.

"I'm sorry. Please, Judge Donovan. Someone wants something Stephen left with me."

He crossed his arms over his chest and narrowed his eyes. "What would that be?"

"Stephen sent me an envelope with the photos of you and your son and the note I photocopied, and a pocket atlas."

"An atlas," he repeated. "Where is it?"

"At the hotel where we're staying."

"That was all he sent you—the photos, the note and the atlas?"

"Yes," I assured him. "Two men seem intent on obtaining those items. I'm afraid one or both of them are working for Nicholas Ackerman."

He nodded, and I saw a hint of kindness in the weariness of his face.

"You have reason for concern," he told me. The dart of his eyes in Cara's direction sent a chill up my spine. "I'll need everything you have as soon as you can get it to me. I'll take care of it from here." He touched my hand, and I could almost see the man behind the judge.

"We're being pursued," I said.

"I'll need that atlas as soon as possible. Have you spoken to Peter Hirsch?"

"Peter? No, I—"

A rap on the door interrupted us. Donovan opened the door of his library. A young man stood outside.

"What is it?" Donovan demanded.

The man leaned over and whispered something in Donovan's ear. "Here?" he asked.

The other man nodded.

"You are not to leave. There's someone downstairs I must speak with. We'll talk when I return." Then he pulled the door shut behind him.

"He knows Peter," Cara declared, perching herself on the edge of Donovan's desk.

I leaned back against the bookcase, wondering how Peter Hirsch fit into all of this.

"I hope it'll be as easy as Judge Donovan seems to think it will," Cara said, making snow fly in a winterscape paperweight she'd lifted from the desk. "So what do we do now? Rid ourselves of Dad's little gift package, and go back home to our lives?"

If only it were that easy.

"We're missing the obvious question here," I said, as Cara put down the snow globe. "If Ackerman wanted to put leverage on the judge in his trial, why would he kill *both* his son *and* his wife? What's the judge got to lose now? He'd be free to nail Ackerman's hide to the wall."

"You're right," Cara said. "Ackerman's not stupid. Something else is going on here. Can we trust Judge Donovan?"

Quietly I opened the library door and stepped into the hall. The bodyguard had followed the judge back downstairs. I could hear Donovan in the hall below, speaking to someone. A second voice repeated a single word, "Upstairs." It was said with a slight English accent, just enough to send dread through my body.

The bastard had found us.

Chapter 14

I grabbed Cara's hand. "We've got to get out of here. Now!" I pulled her into the hallway.

"What's wrong?" Cara asked.

I shushed her. Explanations would have to wait. It was a big, old house designed to have servants. At the end of the hallway we found a narrow door to another set of stairs. They led down to the kitchen, where two Hispanic women were skinning chickens.

"So sorry to bother you," I offered, smiling.

They replied in Spanish.

"Go, go, go!" I insisted, shooing Cara out the back door.

The cooks said something to each other. One started toward us with her knife tight in her hand, but we were already out the back door. She shut it and stood there watching after us through the window as we crossed the tiny backyard, passed through the neighbor's lawn and came out on the street beyond. She'd be able to tell them which direction we'd fled in.

* * *

"What was Ian doing there?" Patrice demanded, her face flushed, as she stuffed clothes into a bag resting on the hotel bed. "Do you think he followed us to Denver?"

I rolled the black dress and slipped it into my backpack. "How could he? Maybe his being here had nothing to do with us. Maybe he's working with Donovan."

"That would be good, wouldn't it?" Cara asked. "That would mean he's on our side, right?"

"I don't know," I said. "Ian may have duped him. Whoever killed Jayne had to have gained access to that house."

"Ian can't possibly know we're here, at this hotel, can he?" Patrice asked, dropping a shirt on the floor. I scooped it up and handed it back to her. We were all shaken.

"I don't think so. But he'll be looking for us. Donovan told him we're here. Hurry up," I insisted. "I wanted us out of here ten minutes ago."

"We didn't get back here ten minutes ago," Cara protested.

"I know." I wished we hadn't had to come back at all.

"Do you think you were followed?" Patrice asked.

I'd watched carefully. We'd taken a long, circuitous route down past the U.S. Mint. "I don't think anyone was behind us, but we have to assume they may have been."

We shoved the rest of our belongings into a plastic bag meant for laundry that I snatched from the closet. "Let's go." I pushed Patrice and Cara into the hallway. Odin whined, but then went quietly forward. We had to get out of the hotel. I wanted Cara and Patrice away from Denver before nightfall.

"We don't even have wheels," Cara whispered.

"I'm going to rent a car."

Cara cocked an eyebrow at me.

"From a legitimate rental agency," I added. "I want you two

someplace safer than that room while I do it." I pushed open the stairwell door, and we took off for the lobby, our footsteps echoing. "Stay in a public area but out of view while I fill out the paperwork. Don't leave with anyone, no matter what they say or how they threaten you."

"Sort of like when I was five years old and anyone picking me up had to say, 'Koalas eat eucalyptus'?" Cara asked.

"Exactly like that. Only this time there is no secret code. Don't leave."

"We'll get a table at the restaurant," Patrice suggested.

Just past the check-in desk was one of the hotel's three restaurants. It was open to the lobby, but there were a few tables tucked around to the left. They offered a panoramic view of people entering the dining area and seclusion at the same time. Anyone coming in would have to pass across the lobby to get there, in full view of the clerks and bellmen and guests.

"Okay," I agreed, pushing open the door to the lobby. I went right; they went left. The car rental desk was directly across from the gift shop.

The woman was busy with a customer when I got there. Smiling, charming, using far more words than were necessary. She finally finished, handed him keys and gave him instructions as to where to pick up the car. He shook her hand and, as soon as he left, she immediately held up one finger at me, picked up the phone and barked instructions about a new Town Car. Then she hung up and offered me that charming smile.

I produced my fake driver's license. "I'd like an SUV if you have one available. If not, something with four-wheel drive."

"I'll see what I have, Ms. Whitcomb." She typed something into her computer and shoved a stack of forms over to me.

I scribbled across the form, remembering to use the fake

address on my driver's license, and agreed to pay for the rental car's insurance.

"I have a nice Subaru for you. Give me just a moment to check on it. That vehicle was brought in this morning and was being washed. Excuse me."

The woman stood. I wanted to yank her back down. To tell her to give me anything with wheels as long as I could have it now, this minute. "I'm really in a hurry."

"Of course you are. There's nothing wrong, is there, Ms. Whitcomb?" Her tone was irritatingly condescending.

I shook my head.

"Good then. I'll be right back." She left.

I raced through the rest of the paperwork. By the time she came back I had finished.

She took the papers. "How will you be paying for this?"

"In cash."

"We'll also need a credit card."

I produced the one I'd taken out in the name of Whitcomb. "And will this be a local or cross-country?"

"Local," I lied. I wasn't about to give a destination.

"For what duration?"

"Two weeks."

"Give us ten minutes. I'll have it brought around front."

"No," I said evenly. "Have them take it to the back entrance."

"But we prefer—"

"I prefer the back entrance," I repeated. "I'm not used to driving in Denver, but I know my way from there. We're heading into the mountains."

She smiled. "It is easier to avoid downtown traffic that way." She ripped off a copy of my rental agreement and handed it to me. "The back entrance, fifteen minutes."

I found Patrice and Cara tucked in a far back booth, right up against the wall.

"Finish your coffee," I told Patrice, who promptly drained her cup. She laid down a five to take care of the two cups of coffee and the tip. Cara hadn't touched hers.

We gathered our bags and ducked through the lobby, past the bank of elevators, down the hall and to the back entrance. A few minutes later, a white Subaru pulled up, and a young Hispanic man hopped out of the driver's seat.

"Ms. Whitcomb?" He flashed a smile as we came through the doors.

"Yes," I answered, showing him my receipt. He helped us load our bags, and I tipped him well, but not enough to remember us, I hoped. Cara, though, he'd remember. He was staring a hole right through her. And the blind lady with the dog.

I drove away, cut over a few blocks and pulled onto a side street and into a parking space a couple of blocks down from the Denver Art Museum. I turned to Cara, who was sitting in the passenger seat. Patrice was in the backseat with Odin.

"There's a hotel in Taos, New Mexico—the Wind Whistler's Inn. I've been there before. It's as secure as any place you could find, and they allow pets. It shouldn't take you more than about five hours to get there. It's straight south from here."

"What are you talking about?" Cara demanded.

I handed Patrice one of my charge cards. "Check in under the name on this card, Evelyn Garrett. Get to a computer. I'm sure they have them at the hotel, maybe even to rent. They hold conventions and seminars there. But if not there, then the library. Cara, you set up a new Hotmail account and e-mail me right away through my Hotmail account. Don't use the college account. Give me your room number but don't mention the inn's name. I want to hear from you as soon as possible, tomorrow morning at the latest, so I'll know you're all right."

"Mom—"

"If for some reason you can't do e-mail," I rushed on, "leave a message for Ms. Whitcomb at the check-in desk of the Hyatt. Tell them you realize I'm no longer registered, but I will be stopping by for messages. If you have absolutely no other choice, drive to the next town and call me on my cell phone from a pay phone using a phone card."

I reached into my bag, pulled out an envelope and handed it to Patrice. It contained enough money to keep them for a good while.

"Taos is a wonderful place. Be sure to visit the galleries."

Cara grabbed hold of my arm. "Just where do you think you're going?"

"Back," I told her. "Not to the Hyatt, but to a hotel downtown."

"You are not staying," she said evenly. "We stick together or—"

"She's right, Cara," Patrice said. "Odin's a liability. He draws attention to us. And you're your mother's Achilles' heel. She needs free rein."

"To do what? Get herself killed?" Cara demanded.

"That's not going to happen," I assured her.

My main goal had always been to keep Cara safe. Sending her to Taos, I hoped, would do exactly that. But it was only a temporary solution. If we were to ever put all this behind us and Cara was to have back the life she'd worked so hard to build, I had to see this through. I still had business in Denver. I had to see for myself where Stephen died. I had to know exactly what had happened to him. It wouldn't be easy to kill someone like him. Whoever had managed it was going to pay.

"I won't take long," I promised. "I'll join you before you've had time to miss me."

Cara let out an exasperated growl.

"Your mother can do more without us," Patrice agreed. "The four of us stand out like a flag. Who wouldn't remember a beautiful young woman and a blind woman with her dog?"

"You're both nuts!" Cara threw up her hands.

I could understand Cara's frustration. Besides, I pretty much agreed with her. I must be nuts. "They don't want me dead. I have the photos and the atlas to give to them if they catch up with me."

"Who died and left you to make all the decisions?" Cara asked.

"Your father," I said softly. "I'll join you in a few days."

"And if you don't?" Cara asked.

"I promise." I knew she was thinking about the promise she'd made me at Patrice's to leave, in the van, the one she'd broken. I touched her face. I refused to cry, and she was determined to prove she was every bit as stubborn as I was. She turned her face away and I touched her hair. "I love you, little daughter."

She turned back and grabbed me, pulling me to her. "Mama, please don't."

"I'll see you soon," I whispered into her ear. Then I pulled away, her tears on my cheek, and got out of the SUV. Patrice came around to slide into my place. Cara was too upset to drive.

"Go south on I-25," I told Patrice, "and don't speed. You don't want to get stopped for any reason. You three take care of each other." I reached in the back and patted Odin's neck.

I hugged Patrice through the window and then turned my back, put up the hood on my jacket and walked around the far side of the museum, where the car couldn't go. I jaywalked across streets and headed back to the heart of downtown, my heart pounding, praying that I was doing the right thing, for Cara's sake, for all our sakes.

Chapter 15

I thought I knew what lonely felt like—all those nights, over the years, sitting on the side of the bed, watching Cara sleep, stroking her hair, wondering where the hell her father was. But once I'd shut the door to my room at the Hilton across town from the first hotel, I knew what it was like to be truly alone. Stephen wasn't coming back. Not even to bring by a bottle of scotch and drink half of it before I threw him out. That was what had happened the last time I'd seen him. The last regret I'd have to carry was not making him tell me then what was bothering him, not forcing him, finally, to be honest with me.

There wasn't much I could do for him now—except keep his daughter safe. I swore an oath to him, then and there, whether he could hear me or not, to do just that.

What I intended to do would have enraged him. I wanted proof against both the man who had killed him and the man who had ordered it done. Ackerman had gotten away with my sister Josie's death all those years ago. I wouldn't let him get away with Stephen's. And Will Donovan's. And Jayne Donovan's. A whole family destroyed.

If I'd allowed myself to think about what I was planning to do or my decision to go it alone, I would have been terrified. But I was determined to play it safe. I would be hard to find. A woman alone, operating under a new alias.

I felt certain Cara and Patrice were safe. I couldn't afford to be distracted worrying about them, and sending them to Taos would allow me to concentrate. I had a plan to put together.

I ordered room service—an outrageously expensive BLT and a bowl of vegetable soup. Then I shook out the contents of the envelope Stephen had sent me on the bed. I tapped my finger on the atlas. What secret did it hold? Why did Donovan want it? Stephen hadn't meant me to give it to him. He'd meant it for James. But that was before he was murdered.

I rolled onto my back and thought about Patrice's first husband, Peter Hirsch. Stephen hadn't mentioned Peter in...well, as long as I could remember.

When Patrice and Peter had called it quits after six years, I'd claimed Patrice in the divorce even though I'd always liked Peter. She'd moved to New York with their young son, remarried and made a new life with her new husband, an art dealer—until her son, Marc, had died. His death put too much strain on the marriage. That was when Patrice filed for divorce and moved back to Pennsylvania. Marc's death also severed her last connection to Peter. I thought Stephen had lost contact with him, as well, even though he lived in D.C. But maybe I was wrong. That showed, again, how little I knew about my husband.

Donovan knew Peter. Peter knew Stephen. Maybe he was Stephen's link to Donovan.

I needed an ally. At one time Peter had been my friend. Could

I trust him? Was that what had gotten Stephen killed—trusting Peter? Did I dare contact him? I needed more information.

The TV droned in the background. Donovan's news conference had gone forward. The trial would continue.

I fell asleep right there, lying on top of the covers, the hum of commercial TV in the background.

When I awoke it was close to nine the next morning. I showered and changed and ordered a cab from my room. I was on my way to ski country, the last place Stephen had been seen alive.

The unseasonably warm weather that had swept through last week had put a damper on the hotel's business, although there was plenty of snow in those hills. The parking lot had only a handful of cars in it. It was a Tuesday, which might explain the lack of business. Either way, it suited me well. I didn't want an audience.

The main building looked like an old lodge, but it couldn't have been built more than a few years ago. Everything, from the huge fieldstone fireplace to the plaid sofas facing the Native American inspired rugs—even the antlers over the reservation desk—had a newness about it.

The young clerk seemed excited to see me while he explained that only one of the slopes was currently open. With a bit of luck, and an expected dip in temperatures, all of them should be available by the weekend if I was staying that long. I could rent equipment in the ski shop and…

Stephen had stood here, checking in, maybe talking with this same man, less than a month ago. Alive. Vibrant.

"I'm not here to ski," I told the clerk and watched his face fall. I took a deep breath. "A few weeks ago my husband died at this resort."

He flushed a bright red. "You must be Mrs. Phelps.... Would you mind... I'll get someone right away."

I turned my back and leaned against the counter, steadying myself, while he scampered away. So Stephen had registered under the name of Phelps. I couldn't help but smile. *Mission: Impossible* had been about the only TV show he'd watched in reruns. It made me wonder what other aliases he'd traveled under. More inventive ones than my own.

"Mrs. Phelps?" I heard a voice call and turned. Definitely older. Definitely more composed. He was tall, lanky in a Jimmy Stewart sort of way, wearing brown slacks and a cardigan sweater over his shirt and tie. Based solely on looks, I'd bet ten to one he'd never had on a pair of skis in his life.

He offered his hand. "Grant Stover. So nice to meet you. I wish it were under more pleasant circumstances. If you would please come this way, I'll be glad to assist you."

He ushered me into his office and closed the door, offering me a chair, lifting the phone and ordering coffee. Then he seated himself behind the large, rustic-looking desk that also appeared newer than the distressed marks embedded in the soft wood had intended.

"First, let me assure you how sorry both my staff and I are about the death of your husband. These types of accidents happen—"

"Accidents," I repeated, more to myself than to him.

"Your husband's is the first death in my twelve years with the company and the first ever at this resort. Despite all our efforts to minimize the dangers, all sports, unfortunately, carry inherent risks," he said.

No sport had killed Stephen Larocca.

"Mrs. Phelps, I wish there was some way I could make this right for you."

"I wish there was, too," I said.

A soft knock sounded on the door, and a young woman pushed it open and placed a tray with a coffee service on the desk. He poured a cup and slid it in my direction, then poured himself one. I took a sip and clung to the mug, seeking comfort in its warmth. Being here was proving harder than I'd thought it would be.

I cleared my throat and sat up. "My husband and I were estranged, Mr. Stover, which makes his death even more difficult for me." My words were closer to the truth than I cared to think about.

"My grief counselor suggested that I come, walk through the building, the grounds, see where my husband died, retrace his final days." I dropped my gaze. I'm not a good liar. "You must think I'm morbid."

"No, of course not. How can I help you?"

"All I really want to know is how long he was here before…before he died. And who was with him. He told me he was meeting one of his brothers here, but there might have been a woman…."

"There was no woman that I know of," he assured me. "Mr. Phelps was here with his brother, and I believe there was one other man in their party, but I'll check to make sure."

"Thank you so much. I'd like the third man's physical description, if at all possible, as well as his brother's. He had several."

The ruse had worked with Frawley. I was banking on it working again.

Stover raised an eyebrow. "Surely you've spoken with his brother."

My stare bored through him. "As I said, Mr. Phelps and I were estranged. I don't speak with his family, but I'm his executor. It's all been very difficult without his family's co-operation."

"I see."

I paused, sipping my coffee, caught between the make-believe and the real.

"Who found him?" I asked in a voice barely above a whisper.

"I'm not sure," he confessed. "I'll have to check my files. Do you have other questions, as well?"

"More than I can remember at the moment. Is there any way I could see your files?"

I could see a blip of panic cross his features.

"I'm not going to sue, Mr. Stover. My husband was extremely wealthy. He was an adult who often made risky choices. No one can blame your lodge for that. Please, if you could give me copies of those files, I would appreciate it. If I have an argument, it's with the insurance company. They're loath to pay out on a double indemnity clause, but I'm certain your records will demonstrate that Mr. Phelps's death was entirely accidental and in no way due to negligence on the part of the resort."

I could tell from his look that he understood me. Both the grieving widow and the lodge would benefit from a quick resolution with the insurance company over an accidental death.

"I'll have the files copied for you right away. How long will you be staying with us, as our guest, of course?"

"Only as long as it takes you to get the information I've requested together." I had more questions for Mr. Stover, but they could wait until I had the copies of the files in my hands.

"I'll have Matthew show you to a suite, and I'll have some lunch sent up to you while you wait."

"That would be kind of you, but do you think it might be possible for me to wait in the room Mr. Phelps occupied? I'd like to see it."

Stover's eyebrow went up again. "If you wish. I believe that room is currently open. We won't begin filling up until later in the week."

"Thank you, Mr. Stover. You've been most helpful."

As Matthew, the young man who'd helped me at the counter, pushed open the door, I felt my throat constrict once again. I wanted to turn and run, but I needed to get this over with, to witness where Stephen had spent his last days.

The room was on the first floor and quite ordinary. A standard two-bed, with a TV resting on a low bureau, a small desk and twin upholstered chairs at the window.

I opened the blinds, and the view took my breath away. The mountains were magnificent, tree-studded and laced with snow against the bright blueness of the sky.

"Is there anything else I can get you?" he asked.

I shook my head, and he pulled the door shut behind him.

I forced my pulse rate to slow. I needed my wits, not my feelings, to do what I had to do. I inspected the furniture. There were no signs of struggle, no signs of blood. I bent down and sniffed the carpet. It had neither been changed nor shampooed. I pushed open the doors to the closet. It was barren except for a few hangers, an unused plastic laundry bag and an iron and ironing board hanging at the side. The bathroom sparkled. If Stephen had died in that room, there were no signs of it.

But he could have died anywhere. His neck was broken. It'd been a clean kill.

A clean kill. Had I become so distanced that I could think of Stephen's death as "a clean kill"?

Hardly.

I pulled back the bedspread and drew the pillow to my face,

searching for his scent. It wasn't there. But of course it wouldn't have been. It'd been weeks since he'd slept in that bed.

I buried my face in the down, aching for Stephen. All the emotion I'd pushed away threatened to well up and explode inside me. Then it died away again as I took a deep breath. I felt moisture gathering at the corners of my eyes. I blinked it back. I wasn't here to mourn. Any unfinished business I had with Stephen would have to wait.

I dropped the pillow back onto the bed. He could have been killed on the slopes where his body was found. But he didn't ski. So he'd been dressed, most likely, by the murderer to fit the scene. It might have been easier in this room. There were only two ways in and out: the main door and a door to the adjoining room. Whoever had killed him—if he'd indeed been killed here—had come through one of them. Who would Stephen have let in? Why hadn't he fought them—wherever he'd died?

I was looking out at the view and finishing the pasta salad and grilled vegetables that the manager had sent up, when he knocked on the door. I called for him to come in. Almost shyly he thrust a packet of papers into my hands.

"Here are copies of all the information that I thought you might want. Your husband arrived with two other gentleman, one of whom, his brother, shared this room while the other took the adjoining room. The brother was tall and dark-haired, close to your husband's age. The other gentleman was blond and a good deal younger, probably in his twenties. I'm sorry to say we don't have a copy of the sheriff's report. I'm sure you can get one by stopping past the office, Mrs. Phelps."

Phelps. The name. How had a dead Jim Phelps become a dead Stephen Larocca?

"Who called the sheriff?" I asked.

"A deputy and a coroner were already on the scene when we were notified of the death. I assume it was the brother who found him."

How had they pulled it off? Where had they gotten a uniform and a car? They couldn't withstand a real investigation, so they'd covered it up, made it appear the authorities had been notified.

"Did my husband meet with anyone else while he was here?" I asked.

"I questioned Tyler at the front desk, and he said he saw your husband with a fourth man," Mr. Stover said, "who apparently was not registered here. He said he was medium height, sixtyish, slim, very distinguished looking with white hair."

Judge Donovan. So Stephen and the two other men—Ian and James—had met with Donovan here. Why? Had that meeting precipitated Stephen's death?

"Were they seen with anyone else?"

Stover shook his head. "Is there anything else I can get you?"

I looked about the room and my stomach lurched. "Yes. A cab."

"Check again," I insisted, wanting to grab the clerk by the throat. "The message would have been for a Ms. Whitcomb. I was a guest here until yesterday."

"I'm sorry, ma'am," the clerk at the Hyatt in downtown Denver said, "but I've looked through everything we have, including all the messages in all the guests' boxes. It simply isn't here."

I turned and walked to a line of pay phones, each enclosed in its own little wooden area, nestled around the corner. I'd checked my e-mail after arriving back at my hotel. Not a word from Cara or Patrice. They should have contacted me by now. And now nothing at the Hyatt. I'm a nervous mother in the best of circumstances, which irritates the hell out of Cara, but now I felt close to panic. I'd have to risk calling their hotel. I had to know they'd made it safely to New Mexico.

The desk clerk at the Wind Whistler's Inn answered on the first ring. I asked to be connected to Evelyn Garrett's room. The phone rang twice and then a male voice answered, "Yes."

My heart stopped in midbeat. "Who is this?" I managed.

"Elizabeth, we've got to talk."

James. My blood turned to ice.

"Where are they?"

"They're safe. I've been waiting for your call."

I wanted to pound the receiver into the wall, but I forced my voice to sound calm.

"How did you find them? How could you—"

"Cara phoned Phillip late last night."

"From their room?" How could she be so stupid? How could she endanger herself and Patrice so foolishly? If I'd been with her she'd never have dared call.

"From a pay phone, using a calling card."

And still you found her. You bastard.

Of course he had. He had Cara's cell phone. Phillip's number would have shown up among her recent calls.

"Let me speak to them," I insisted.

"They're not here."

"Where are they?" I snapped. He was lucky we weren't in the same room. I would have ripped him apart.

"Someplace safe."

"Are they in New Mexico?"

"Elizabeth, you need to let me help you."

The condescending bastard. He sounded like he was talking to a five-year-old.

"Like you helped the guy at the airport?"

"You're still in Denver. I'll come get you."

I hung up the phone. What kind of equipment was he using? Or had Cara and Patrice told him where I was? Hotel telephones didn't come with caller ID.

I sat shaking so hard I couldn't stand. I should never have let them out of my sight. Suddenly the phone in front of me rang. I jumped back from it. The bastard had traced me—to a pay phone. I lifted the receiver just long enough to break the connection and then dropped it back. I wasn't three feet from the cubicle before it started ringing again. I didn't look back. I just walked out of that hotel as fast as I could.

Chapter 16

James had Cara and Patrice. How could I have let this happen? How could I have let them out of my sight for even one minute?

I lay sprawled on my hotel bed, staring at the ceiling, telling myself I could have five minutes to think, to form some kind of plan. Surely they wouldn't find me in just five minutes. My bag was packed and ready by the door. I hadn't unpacked when I checked in.

The phone startled me. Only Cara and Patrice would know what name I'd registered under. They would have had to call around to find which hotel, but they could have done that. Maybe James was lying. Maybe he'd traced them some other way. Maybe Cara and Patrice had seen him and ducked out before he got to them. Even if he'd taken them, they could have escaped. Maybe James didn't have them after all. I lifted the receiver.

"Elizabeth, listen to me." It was James.

I uttered a few oaths that had never before passed my lips. "Until I hear my daughter's voice, I have nothing to say to you."

"That's not possible. Meet me tomorrow afternoon at three at the pueblo in Taos. I want everything Stephen left with you."

"Bring Cara," I ordered.

"I can't promise you that. I want you to—"

I slammed down the phone, jumped out of bed and grabbed my bag. I ran out the door, that damned phone ringing after me.

I had no idea where I was going. Ducking out a side door of the hotel, I glanced at everyone on the street, wondering if one or more of them was working for James. Then I slipped into a coffee shop, walked through it and out the far door. I needed someplace to gather my thoughts.

My Marie Whitcomb identity had just died an untimely death. I had one more ID. If it were compromised, I'd be cut off from any source of money.

I flagged down a cabbie and told him to take me to the Denver Public Library. He dropped me in front of a huge, new building just down from the art museum. I climbed its many stairs and found a chair in the far back corner of the third floor. Surrounded by books, I pushed away my panic and forced myself to sort through my options.

Assuming Cara and Patrice were still in New Mexico, which they might not be, I couldn't go there and rescue them by force. Or by wile. James might not be alone this time, and he'd demonstrated his access to sophisticated equipment. I was no match for him with or without his equipment, and heaven only knew what he'd told Cara and Patrice. He must have convinced them to cooperate with him, that he was there only to help. Cara had leaned in his direction before. He might well have won her trust.

James wanted what Stephen had left with me.

And now he'd taken my daughter hostage.

I needed help.

The only people I trusted were in Maryland. Even if they could help, it would take too long for them to get to Colorado or to Taos.

My own daughter had trouble believing her father had been murdered. I'd kept my concerns about Stephen totally private, spoken to no one connected to my new life about my marriage. How crazy would my story sound, especially when I'd have to answer most of their questions with "I don't know"?

Of course, there was Peter. Somehow he was connected to all this. He'd loved Patrice once. Surely he'd help her if he could.

I went to the main check-out desk, requested and was given a cubicle with Internet access and booted up the machine. I found an official e-mail address for Peter fairly easily. Creating a new Hotmail account, I composed a message to him: "Need help. Elizabeth." If Peter had any idea of what was going on, that should be enough.

There was no telling how long it would take for Peter to write me back. If he wrote me back. I gave him fifteen minutes. No answer. I couldn't wait any longer.

I had no choice but to go to the police.

"You say your daughter and your friend voluntarily left Denver two days ago, driving south." The officer had a comforting demeanor. He was tall and burly and seemed sympathetic, but he'd only taken a few notes. "Do you know for sure they arrived in Taos?"

"No, that is, yes. Evelyn Garrett registered at the Wind Whistler's Inn, but, as I said, a man answered her phone when I called."

He gave me an aw-come-on-now look. "This Ms. Garrett is of age, I assume."

"Of course."

"And you entrusted the care of your daughter to her. How old is your daughter, by the way?"

"Twenty-three."

He laid down his pencil. "I understand you may be concerned about not being able to locate your friend and your loved one, but they are both of age and free to come and go as they please and to associate with whomever they please. Unless you have some reason to suspect they have been injured in some way or that they are being held against their will—"

"They *are* being held against their will," I said evenly.

"At the Wind Whistler's Inn in Taos."

"Yes."

He lifted the receiver of his phone and hit 411. "Yes, I'd like the number of the Wind Whistler's Inn in Taos, New Mexico… Go ahead and put that through, please. Thank you."

I shifted uncomfortably while he stared a hole through me. When someone came on the line, he turned his gaze toward his desk. "This is Officer Bill Owens of the Denver Police Department. I'm trying to locate a Ms. Evelyn Garrett and a Ms. Cara Whitcomb…. Yes, sir, they were traveling with a dog…. You say they checked out several hours ago…. They were alone when they did so?… I see. Did they leave a forwarding address or mention where they might be contacted?… Okay. Thank you." He hung up the phone.

Then he turned back to me. "Ms. Whitcomb, I understand a mother's concern, but what we have here are two grown women. Under the Constitution of the United States, you have no right to interfere with their movements. They need not consult you or—"

"They were driving a rental car. Maybe you could put out an APB for the license plate." I offered him a copy of the rental agreement.

He scanned the sheet. "This contract is in your name and the rental is a local."

"Yes, but they were driving this car."

He studied me, tapping his index finger against his lip. "You do know they have no legal right to be using this vehicle."

"Yes, I know."

"Tell you what. I'll contact the rental company and see what comes up."

This time he turned his back on me, punched numbers into his phone and mumbled something I couldn't make out. He hung up the phone. "That car was returned yesterday morning to a rental office in Taos."

"You see. That's what I've been trying to tell you," I insisted. "They don't have transportation because they've been abducted."

"The woman who turned in the car answers to the description you gave me of your friend, Ms. Evelyn Garrett. There has been no crime committed that I can see, Ms. Whitcomb, except, perhaps, violation of your rental contract."

And grand theft auto in Pennsylvania. And kidnapping. And murder. The lies I was tangling about me would land me in jail if I wasn't careful. It took a lot of nerve to walk into a police station and give a policeman an alias.

"Thank you." I stood, my face flushed with anger. I'd feared that going to the police would be a waste of time and it was. It had just cost me an hour and a half.

I went back to the library, walking this time, and got back on the Internet. I looked at my watch. It was close to 5:00 p.m.

I checked my new Hotmail account, saying a little prayer before I downloaded mail.

Elizabeth, I'm sorry I scared you. I would never have harmed Patrice. My only goal is to help you. I was worried about your safety then and I'm more worried now. Ian. Koalas eat eucalyptus.

My heart stopped. I sat frozen, staring at the screen. Somehow Ian had intercepted Peter's e-mail. The return address was the one that had been listed as Peter's. So Peter was involved with Ian.

Confused and frustrated, I had to restrain myself from shaking the monitor. Damn it! What was I supposed to do?

Koalas eat eucalyptus. The words leaped off the screen at me. That was the phrase Stephen and I had used with Cara when she'd started school. She'd made it up herself, a kindergarten kid's version of a spy code. She was never to leave with a stranger or even someone she knew unless we'd told her in advance. Or unless they gave her the code phrase. It meant it was safe.

But was it? How could Ian know about the phrase unless Stephen had told him?

Could I trust Ian Payne, a man I suspected of killing my husband? A man who had held Patrice at gunpoint? A man who had threatened both my own and my daughter's lives?

Or had he? The memory of the incident at Patrice's flashed through my mind. Ian could have killed me. He certainly could have killed Patrice. He hadn't used real bullets on Odin. But I couldn't get rid of the image of Ian standing there in the dark, pointing one hell of a big gun in my direction. Still, he hadn't fired. Not then and not when we were escaping.

And he hadn't been the only one with Stephen at the ski resort.

I needed to regain control, and I needed someone who was as capable as James to help me do it. Someone who had an inkling of what I was up against. Someone who, unlike the police, wouldn't tell me that women who voluntarily put themselves in the hands of a possible assassin should be allowed to do just that. I had no choice. While I had my suspicions about Ian, I knew James had killed at least one man. And now he had my precious daughter and my dear friend Patrice. Ian was already in Denver. I had to make a deal with the devil.

I hit Reply.

Ian. Can you come? Elizabeth.

Then I sent the message, sat back and stared out the window. I could only pray that either James or Ian was a good guy, a true friend of Stephen's. They both had access to high-tech equipment, and they both seemed hell-bent on finding me. If James was a good guy, Cara and Patrice were safe. If Ian was a good guy, he would help me find them.

And if he wasn't, I would be leading him straight to my child—if he didn't kill me first.

Chapter 17

I pulled on pantyhose and changed into the black crepe dress in one of the bathroom stalls of the library. This time I left off the scarf.

I fastened my gun in a holster I lashed to my thigh. My pepper spray was tucked in my purse. I felt as though I was taking a knife to a gunfight, but I didn't let myself dwell on it.

Ian's reply had been short and to the point. It had come back in just ten minutes.

Have dinner with me at The Broker. Seven o'clock. Ian.

I wondered how long he'd been in Denver. What was he doing here? Had he somehow tracked us? Or had he come to see Donovan?

I would have preferred to wear my sweatshirt and jeans, but The Broker was an upscale place, and I didn't want to arouse suspicion—which meant I'd have to lose the backpack. Ian didn't need to know I was working without a base of operations. I took a cab to the bus depot, rented a locker and left my belongings. I wasn't about to take anything with me that he might want.

I arrived at the restaurant half an hour early and took a seat at the bar, where I could watch the door while I nursed a ridiculously expensive ginger ale through a straw. At exactly seven o'clock, I felt the back of my hair flutter.

"Good evening," a voice whispered in my ear. I whirled.

"How long have you been…" I stared at him, blushing, feeling the fool. He was dressed in a black suit, white shirt and black tie, looking ridiculously handsome and every inch the gentleman.

But I knew not to be deceived by his trappings of civility. He had suggested, in none too subtle a fashion, that I was no match for him.

"Shall we?" he asked, offering his arm.

I took it, imagining how amused he must have been, sitting back there in the dark, watching me watch for him. The bastard.

The waiter showed us to a table covered in white linen. Ian helped me scoot in my chair, then seated himself and ordered wine.

"So we meet again, under more civilized circumstances this time," he said with a half smile. "I think you'll enjoy the cuisine here a bit more than the last time we dined together."

His gaze took in my face and hair, then traced the V of my neckline, before returning to my eyes. I was determined not to blush.

"You're looking lovely. I'm glad to see you're all right."

I couldn't decide if he was sincere or if this was all part of his game. I could play, too, if that was what it took.

"How's the arm?" I asked. Odin had taken a chunk of flesh, small payment for what Ian had done to Patrice.

"Coming along. You surprised me. I'll have a small scar to remind me never to underestimate you."

I didn't tell him that Cara had surprised me, too. Better to let him think she and I had planned the rescue.

The waiter placed a huge bowl of steamed shrimp and cocktail sauce between us and I wondered if Ian had ordered it.

"They serve shrimp like other restaurants offer complimentary bread," Ian explained, reading my thoughts. The waiter uncorked the wine and poured some in a glass. Ian tasted it and nodded. "I believe the lady will enjoy this one."

Then the waiter poured us each a glass and we ordered dinner, almost like normal people out for an evening enjoying each other's company.

"What made you change your mind?" he asked, peeling one of the shrimp.

"About you?" I stared him straight in his enigmatic eyes. "I haven't. James has Cara and Patrice."

The levity that had played about his features was suddenly gone. "When?" he asked, leaning in.

I could feel his breath on my cheeks, but I wouldn't draw back, regardless of how unnerving it was to have him so close to me.

"Yesterday or the day before. I sent them to New Mexico. That's where he found them."

"Damn," he cursed, shaking his handsome head. He flung the peeled shrimp to the side of the table.

I felt my own breath quicken, but I forced my words to remain steady. "My sentiments exactly."

"How do you know?"

"I phoned their hotel room and James answered. He wouldn't let me speak to Cara. I don't know if she was even there."

He studied my face. "You want my help."

I swallowed hard, aware of the sheer power of the man. "I can't do this alone."

He nodded. "It's dangerous. James is a clever man."

"You know him."

"Yes, I know him."

"And you knew Stephen."

"Yes."

I steadied myself against the table. I'd known the answer, of course, yet hearing it out loud took me aback. I was playing a very dangerous game with a very dangerous man.

"There was someone on the inside," Ian continued. "Someone Stephen trusted betrayed him."

"Someone like you?" I, too, wanted so much to trust Ian.

His expression told me he saw the conflict in my face. I tried to release the tightness I felt in my jaw. I didn't want him to sense the adrenaline that was running through me. He put his hand over mine, and I pulled back. I would not fall into his charming trap.

"Who are you working for? Who was Stephen working for?" I pushed.

"I can't tell you that."

My anger surged but I said nothing.

"I sent him back to you, Elizabeth," he said softly.

I could tell he wanted to touch me, but he knew I wouldn't tolerate it.

"Do you think I'd have done that if he wasn't my friend?"

I studied him. I could almost have believed him, if my daughter's life didn't depend on it. "Maybe. Whoever killed him would need to dispose of his body. What easier way than to have him cremated under his own name and have his ashes returned to his widow?"

"Burying it in a remote area is the first thought that comes to mind. No fuss, no bother. No questions. Do you have any idea how many people simply vanish every year?"

I wondered how many bodies he'd buried. How cold a man was he? His eyes told me not as cold as his words might lead me to believe.

"Or I could have had him cremated under the name of James Phelps without ever having involved you," Ian went on. "But I couldn't do that to you. I've watched you, worked beside you for almost three months."

I would not let myself be taken in by the velvet in his voice.

"You held Patrice at gunpoint."

"I needed her cooperation. I certainly couldn't allow her to involve the police. If there had been another way, I would have used it. I had no intention of harming her."

"You shot her dog."

"Animals can't be reasoned with. I assume he made a full recovery." He raised an eyebrow.

"You put tracking devices on my car and on Cara's."

He ignored my last comment as though he were tired of this game. "Elizabeth, you're an excellent professor. You care about your students, and they, in return, respect you. I admire your command of your subject and your dedication to your students, to your daughter. When I asked you to have coffee with me, I wasn't just—"

"Stephen didn't ski," I said, cutting him off. He didn't have to make nice with me. I wanted his help, nothing more.

"I know."

"How did he die?" I asked.

He leaned back in his chair and drew in a deep breath, never once taking his eyes from mine. "I found his body in his room."

Ian shared that room.

"There was no evidence of a break-in or of a struggle," he went on. "I assume Stephen opened the door to whoever it was that knocked."

"He trusted him or he wouldn't have turned his back," I said. "Stephen wasn't careless."

"He trusted you," I added.

He nodded. "As I trusted him."

"James was there with the two of you."

"Yes."

"If he killed Stephen, why didn't he search his body then, instead of stealing it later?"

"I'm sure he did, but a more thorough examination for an implanted microchip would have taken more time. James must have heard me coming back before he'd finished. After I discovered the body, I didn't let it out of my sight until I was certain everything was taken care of."

Ian had taken Stephen out onto the snow, dressed him in some sort of parka, strapped skis to his boots and let him freeze. What kind of man was capable of that? I forced the image out of my mind.

"I foiled your plan by canceling the cremation," I said.

"You did indeed."

All he said made sense, but I refused to let myself trust him, regardless of how much I wanted to. "I still have only your word."

"That's all I have to offer."

An honest answer.

"There was no microchip," he assured me.

"You looked, too."

No Safe Place

Again, he nodded.

"Where were you when Stephen was murdered?"

"I was…otherwise occupied."

"With the judge? Edward Donovan?"

"We met with Donovan, yes."

"Why?"

I could see him weighing what to say. For a moment I held my breath. I thought he might actually tell it all. But then his eyes clouded over.

"I don't think you—" he began.

"I don't care what you think," I spat out. "You staged Stephen's death. Then you called in someone to pose as a police officer, and someone else to play the role of coroner and sign a death certificate. Maybe Donovan helped you with that one."

I could see that I had surprised him.

"It seemed the safest and most humane choice. An investigation wouldn't have been wise."

"You told the funeral director you and Stephen were brothers."

"In many ways we were. Stephen and I have worked together for years."

I tried to rein in my own surprise. Stephen had introduced me to James but not to Ian. Why?

"How long have you known Peter Hirsch? You intercepted my e-mail to him."

"Actually, he forwarded it to me. The two of us were Stephen's friends."

"Friends or colleagues?"

"Whichever you prefer. Stephen asked me to watch over you while he was working this last case."

"Case," I echoed. A "case" involving Edward and Will

Donovan. Ian had already told me more than Stephen had in all our years of marriage.

"That's why I moved my base of operations to Maryland," Ian continued. "He was afraid for you. Once I'd met you, I understood why. You're an extraordinary combination of strength and vulnerability."

Afraid for me? Why would Stephen have been afraid for me? Why now more than before? Of course. Because Ackerman was involved. I swallowed my reaction and concentrated instead on Ian's words.

"You don't know me," I insisted, defiant that he would have the gall to try to analyze me.

"You're right. I don't, despite my best efforts. I only knew Stephen."

If his intent was to make me feel we had something in common, it backfired. I couldn't help resenting anyone who was privy to the life that Stephen hid from me.

"Tell me what the three of you were doing and what Edward Donovan has to do with all of this," I demanded.

"I'm not at all certain that would be wise."

I'd had enough. "Why? Because it might put me in more danger?" I leaned forward, no longer concerned about his nearness. "News flash—the only thing I care about in this world is already in danger. Get this straight, Ian, or whatever the hell your real name is. There will be no more lies or strategically omitted information. I *will* find my daughter, and you *will* tell me what's going on, or I'll blow off you kneecap right here and now." I nudged his leg under the table with the gun that I'd taken from my holster.

For a second he looked startled, then his features relaxed into a half smile. "You truly are an amazing woman."

I nudged his knee again.

"You don't want to make a scene," he insisted, losing his smile.

"Not unless I have to. You don't mess with a woman and her child and think you can get away with it."

Threatening the life of a man like Ian would hold little sway, but threatening his mobility—now that made him take notice. His eyes steeled. I think he was afraid I might actually be crazy enough to pull the trigger. Maybe I was.

"That damn dog should have bitten me twice," he stated, "to remind me again never to underestimate you." He saw my eyes narrow, and I saw something change in his face, a new resolve. "You've heard of Will Donovan."

I nodded.

"He's not dead."

"And you know this because…"

"Because Stephen Larocca made him disappear."

Chapter 18

For a moment I couldn't breathe. I knew it was possible. Everything I'd learned pointed to Stephen's having done exactly that, but it seemed so incredible. And now all I could think of was Edward Donovan, who had just lost his wife and whose son might still be alive. Will was the leverage Ackerman needed to influence the judge presiding over his trial. He was also why Donovan wanted information from me. Stephen had hidden Will, and Donovan had no idea where he was.

If it was true. If Will was still alive. If Cara's wish that he were alive had been right all along…

"Keep talking," I said.

Ian leaned in, his voice low, conspiratorial, seductive.

"There was a threat made against Judge Donovan."

"Because…"

"He's presiding over Nicholas Ackerman's trial."

I had deduced that much already, but I wanted Ian to confirm what I thought I knew.

The waiter placed our entrees in front of us, and I slipped the gun back into its holster. I'd ordered the oriental chicken salad. He'd ordered the prime rib. Ian cut a piece of steak and put it in his mouth. He chewed and swallowed before he went on. Impeccable manners.

"More wine?" he asked.

I shook my head, and he refilled his glass. I had no time for manners, and I needed to keep my mind clear. "Go on."

"Ackerman has created an empire in Denver. He owns an estimated third of the businesses downtown."

"That's no crime," I pointed out.

"No. But drug smuggling, money laundering, you-name-it are."

"How does he get away with it?"

"Charges are brought and dropped. The few times he's actually gone to trial, witnesses have recanted or judges and juries have been tampered with. He's up on intimidation and bribery charges. Donovan's untouchable and Ackerman knows it. Donovan sequestered the jury from the beginning. He's determined to get him this time."

"And so was Stephen," I added, more to myself than to Ian.

My mind was racing, trying to make sense of what Ian was saying. To make the father comply, put the child in danger.

"So Ackerman threatened Donovan's son, Will."

"Precisely."

"And when the son couldn't be found, the threat was redirected at the wife. Who do you work for?" I asked again, determined this time to get an answer.

I watched him stiffen. It was the question Stephen would never answer.

"Peter Hirsch."

I frowned. I knew they were connected, obviously, but could Peter actually be directing the operations?

"Peter's a federal judge," I pointed out.

"With a private agenda. Witness protection doesn't always work, you know. Sometimes it's necessary to take witnesses completely out of the system to keep them safe. They disappear before trial, then reappear to give their testimonies. If all goes well and the threat to their safety disappears, they are returned to their communities after trial."

"If not?"

"Then they're relocated for as long as it takes."

"Sometimes permanently," I said.

"Yes. But not often."

There it was, in the open at last. The secret Stephen had taken to his grave. Ian had trusted me with it. *If* he was telling me the truth.

"Who finances this?" I asked.

"Various sources. Frequently the individuals themselves, but Peter's been most fortunate in his investments."

"Will Donovan was not a witness," I said.

"Not all the people we help disappear are."

"I can't believe Peter would let Stephen…" I started, dazed.

For Stephen to be involved with anything to do with Ackerman would be risky considering how much Stephen hated him for what he did to Josie. Peter would know that.

"Peter warned off Stephen, told him to let someone else assist Donovan. This one was personal for Stephen, as you seem to know, and letting something become personal is the easiest way to get killed. Once Ackerman actually put out the hit on Donovan's son, Stephen felt he had no choice."

"Nick Ackerman ordered Will Donovan's assassination," I stated.

My sister had married a monster. My poor Josie.

I picked up my wineglass and drained it. It burned my throat and brought me back.

"Considering the venom Stephen felt for Ackerman," Ian said, "I believe he would have killed him bare-handed if he'd ever been in a room alone with him. What did Stephen have against him?"

Stephen, after all these years, you still hated him, hated him with the same all-encompassing passion that I felt for him. But you never once mentioned Nick's name to me since Josie died.

I cleared my throat. "All that matters is that Stephen offered Donovan his help."

"Yes. And the younger Donovan vanished."

Leaving his mother to grieve. *Stephen, did you once think of her? Maybe you couldn't afford to.*

"Where did he hide him?" I asked.

Ian lay down his fork. "I don't know. Only the operative directly involved in the relocation knows where the subject is hidden. Did he tell you?"

I almost choked. "No. Is that what you thought? Is that what you want from me?"

"I don't want anything from you, Elizabeth, except to know that you're safe."

That was a lie. I wouldn't soon forget that he shot Odin with a tranquilizer dart and held Patrice at gunpoint. He'd asked for the envelope at Patrice's. He knew I had it, and I knew he wanted it. The question was, would Stephen want me to give it to him?

"Then what am I? Organization business?" I asked.

"No. As I said, Stephen—"

"You're not chasing after me out of the goodness of your heart."

He brushed his napkin across his lips and then lowered it again to his lap. "Your safety has been bought and paid for, Elizabeth."

I touched my napkin to the top of my lip. I didn't want him to see the sweat I felt beading there or the blush I felt coloring my neck. "By whom?"

"By Stephen."

I swallowed my shock. "How much?" I managed.

"Is this really necessary?"

"Yes, I think it is. How much?"

"One million dollars, the usual fee."

I felt staggered. Was it actually possible Stephen had that kind of money? I knew even less than I thought I had about my husband

"How did he get the money?"

"It was an insurance policy," he said.

With Ian as the beneficiary. Another motive for murder? Ian could have killed Stephen to collect. But if he had, why was he here? Why hadn't he taken the money and left?

Because he wanted the envelope.

Another thought suddenly entered my mind: a second explanation for returning Stephen's body for burial. To collect on the policy, the insurance company would have insisted on proof of death.

"So you do this for the money," I said evenly.

He swallowed a sip of wine. "Of course. I like money and the things it can buy." He refilled my glass and raised his to me.

I had to fight to keep from throwing mine in his face. Yet there was something about his manner that made me doubt his words.

"So your mission is to make me disappear, too?"

"No. To make certain you're safe. And to avenge Stephen's death. That one I've thrown in at no charge."

"How chivalrous of you. Two for the price of one."

The steel was back in his eyes, reminding me I was dealing with no ordinary man.

"I want Ackerman. He ordered Stephen's death, but I want the operative who did this killing first, the one who belonged to our organization, the one who was turned. He's looking for Will Donovan, and he needs you to find him."

"James," I said.

He nodded.

"Why hasn't Will already surfaced? I would think once he heard of his mother's death…"

He frowned and I knew he'd already been asking himself that question. Could Will already be dead?

"That's a question we need to answer. As long as Will remains hidden, you and Cara will be safe," he assured me. "Once he's found…"

"We'll no longer be of value to James."

"Yes."

"I don't know where Will is," I said evenly. "Why do they think I do?"

"Nothing was found among Stephen's belongings. Nothing on his body."

"The autopsy—"

"It wouldn't have been an actual autopsy, although I can see why the Y-shaped incision would have been made to confuse authorities if the body was ever found. Families are rarely notified if a buried-at-sea resurfaces. An autopsy incision eliminates the possibility of death from foul play."

"All right, then, the mutilation. What was it for?"

"As I said before, to look for microfilm, computer chips, any way information might be hidden on the human body."

"But why?"

"They're looking for Stephen's code and the key to tell them where he hid Will Donovan."

"Then they know he's alive."

"Yes. They threatened him and he disappeared. They didn't kill him, ergo he ran."

"How do they know Peter's behind it?"

"Our operations aren't completely off the radar. People who need us find us."

"Why were the three of you at the ski lodge?" I asked. I knew they'd gone there to meet Donovan again, but I didn't know why.

"The threat had grown and Peter had green-lighted us to get Jayne Donovan out, despite the risks."

"You, Stephen and James."

He nodded.

"But you didn't," I went on. "She's dead."

"We waited too long. The plan was to take her the day we met with Donovan at the lodge."

"The day Stephen died."

"Yes. Stephen's death stopped our plan. We had a traitor to deal with. Jayne had yet to be informed she was to leave," he explained.

"She didn't know her son was alive when she died." I felt anger surge inside me. Another woman lied to on the pretense of safety.

"No," he said softly. I actually believed he found that painful as well.

"We have to find Will Donovan," I said.

"Yes. If we don't, they will."

"After we go for Cara and Patrice."

"Eat your food, Elizabeth."

I hadn't touched my salad.

"You're going to need all your strength to get your daughter back."

"Then you'll go with me to Taos."

"Your daughter isn't in Taos."

"How do you know that?"

"If she were, she would have insisted on speaking with you when you called the hotel. James has convinced her that he's there to protect the two of you, that I murdered her father."

Just as Ian had tried to convince me that James had killed Stephen.

"You can't be sure of that," I insisted, desperately wanting Cara somewhere I could find her, wanting her not to trust a man who could be a murderer.

"Cara compromised your identity, Elizabeth. James used it to trace where you were staying. He may have even told her you've been abducted."

"That you'd taken me?"

He nodded. "Remember she lost contact with you for two days. He can't afford to let you talk with her and plant any doubt in her mind."

"So you think she's safe?"

"For the moment. As long as she trusts him and…"

"As long as James believes I have something he needs."

"Yes."

"Where has he taken them?"

"I don't know."

"But you have an idea how to find out."

He nodded. "James wants Will Donovan. Find Donovan and you'll have something to bargain with."

One child traded for another. Was I capable of that?

"And if I say no?"

"Then we'll go to Taos. The decision is yours, Elizabeth. I told Stephen I'd watch over you, and I've done a damn poor job of it. I'd hoped to establish a relationship with you earlier, while we were both teaching, so that you would know me, trust me, but I underestimated how closed your circle of friends was. We'll work this together, however you want to do it. All I'm doing is telling you what I think is best."

But was it the truth? I would not gamble with Cara's and Patrice's lives.

"When James called me at the hotel, he asked me to meet him at the pueblo in Taos at three tomorrow afternoon," I said.

"Good. That gives us a place to begin."

"We don't have enough time to find Will first," I insisted.

Ian nodded, accepting my decision, just as he said he would.

"James will know, won't he?" I asked.

"That you contacted me? Or that I found you? He won't dismiss the possibility. You fled from him. But I doubt he would believe you'd come to me, especially if Cara and Patrice told him about our encounter in York. My main concern right now is that if you don't show at the pueblo…"

"He may harm Cara or Patrice."

His face was solemn. "I believe he will continue to woo you, to try to win you to his side. Hurting Cara or Patrice would be a major mistake. I don't think James is that stupid."

I had to believe that, or I'd never get a moment of rest.

The waiter returned and suggested dessert, which we both declined, and then left the check in a leather holder on the table. Ian scanned the figures and drew out his wallet.

"Let me," I began fishing for mine.

He slipped several bills into the folder. "I know you've been taking care of yourself for a long time, but allowing someone to assist you is not a sign of weakness. Let's start with something small, like this dinner. I'd very much enjoy treating you if you will allow me the pleasure."

I nodded. I'd just as soon Ian didn't know how much money I had with me. Besides, he played the gentleman so well I half believed it wasn't an act.

"So, where are you staying?" he asked.

"I was at the Hilton, but—"

"You've checked out. Of course. James knows you were there. There's a house, in the mountains. It's safe and I have a key."

"Are you suggesting that the two of us…"

The thought startled me. To be alone in a house with this man.

"You requested my help. It would be to your benefit to trust your instincts, to trust me, Elizabeth. You have your pistol, and, I suspect, some other means of protecting yourself. You'll have your own room with its own dead bolt as will I, just in case you decide to slit my throat in the middle of the night. Early tomorrow morning we'll head out—"

"For Taos," I said.

"For Taos," he repeated.

Chapter 19

Ian drove me to the bus station to retrieve my bag, and then we took off for the mountains. We barely spoke. My thoughts were crowding my mind, and he seemed lost in his own reverie.

The nearness of him unsettled me. I could have denied the attraction between us, but that would have been foolish. It was a factor that would color both our actions. It had already made him underestimate me. I intended not to let it make me underestimate him.

I watched him drive, making certain he kept his hands on the wheel where I could see them. He spoke mostly of teaching at Gilman, periodically glancing at me. He was trying to put me at ease. It wasn't going to happen, not with him so close.

My thoughts strayed to Taos. I wondered what Cara was doing, then shook myself out of it. I had to focus on getting there, nothing else, except, perhaps, the man beside me.

I would have preferred to drive straight through, but even

I knew I was too tired. The first moment I nodded off to sleep, I'd be at Ian's mercy. I bought most of his story—it meshed with what I already knew—so I let him take me into the mountains. If he'd wanted to kill me, I'd already be dead, attraction or no. I needed help, and no one else was standing in line to give it.

We turned onto an unpaved road that twisted through the trees. It ended in the driveway of an isolated A-frame built over a garage to keep the doors free from deep snow.

He showed me through the house. The main floor was one great room with wood floors, a huge, free-standing fireplace in the middle, a kitchen at one end with a magnificent view and a sitting area at the other with equally large windows. The two bedrooms, with walls that slanted all the way to the floor, were upstairs, each with a private bath. I inspected both, then took the room in the back, the one with key-locked windows that looked onto the snowy evergreens, the one with no balcony, the one with a good twenty-foot drop to the ground. I wasn't sure if I was keeping someone out or blocking my own escape.

I bade Ian good-night. His eyes held mine as though he wanted to say something. But he didn't. I threw the dead bolt on my door. Then I dragged the chair from the desk in front of it—not to keep anyone out, but so it would scrape across the floor if anyone came into the room. I would not be surprised.

I dared not take a shower. Instead, I sponged off and changed into my pajamas, crawled into bed with my gun, and lay there under a down comforter, watching snow flutter past the windows in the moonlight. In my mind, I replayed everything Ian had told me. Stephen, Peter, James and Ian worked together. They hid people whose lives were in danger, people the courts couldn't protect. Peter must be the contact between the "client" and the operative, and it was his money that financed the operations when the client wasn't wealthy enough to pay the fee. One million dollars. The fee that Stephen had paid Ian to protect me from Nicholas Ackerman if something went wrong.

I'd been so young when I'd married Stephen. Only nineteen. He was twenty-six. Cara had come so quickly into our lives. I was busy. But I hadn't stayed young, and I certainly hadn't stayed naive.

Now I finally had some answers, but I still drowned in questions. They ran together in my mind, melding into confusion as I sank into sleep.

The next thing I was aware of was Ian pounding on the door. My watch read five o'clock.

"Coffee's ready," he announced. "If we're going to make Taos by one, we need to be up and out of here within the hour."

He had more than coffee ready when I went downstairs five minutes later, having pulled on my jeans and sweatshirt and brushed my hair into a low ponytail. Stuffed sausages and eggs and sweet rolls. He must have gone out early this morning to get them. Either that, or this was where he'd been staying. I couldn't tell. The place was immaculate. It had been dark when we pulled in, so I couldn't see then whether there were other tire tracks in the snow.

I sat down at the small table in front of the floor-to-ceiling windows, savoring the enticing aromas. Ian brought over orange juice and joined me. I took up my fork and attacked the food, my gun tucked into the front waistband of my jeans, my pepper spray wedged, as always, into a pocket.

"Those eggs aren't going anywhere," he reminded me, sipping coffee and studying me. He had yet to lift a fork.

"Whether it takes us ten minutes or twenty to eat will make no difference, Elizabeth. Enjoy your food. Enjoy your coffee. Watch the snow fall. Part of every morning's nourishment should be for the soul."

He was either a very wise man or one who knew each day could be his last. Or the professor of philosophy he purported to be. Perhaps all three.

My heart sped up as I looked at him. Ian was the only man, other than Stephen, who had ever stirred something inside me. It was far more than his physical appearance. It was his slow confidence, his considered words, the depth of his thought, his awareness of each moment as it passed and his reluctance to waste it.

He seemed to respect my intelligence and my abilities. Feigned or genuine, he showed concern for my feelings. Under other circumstances...

I put down my fork and watched the snow silently wind its way down. So peaceful. So serene. So like the days when Cara was young and we awoke to an unexpected blanket of white that closed the schools and left us to amuse ourselves by throwing snowballs and later with puzzles, games and hot chocolate in front of the fireplace.

Cara. I wondered if it was snowing in Taos.

"Did you bother to give them an excuse—at the college? Or did you just walk away?" I asked, taking a sip of juice.

"I'm suffering from a rather unfortunate case of the shingles. Quite incapacitating. I'm not certain when I'll recover. How about you?"

"My grandmother died."

"Pity."

I shrugged. "I couldn't kill off my mother. She's still alive."

He nodded. "I've had some students with as many as eight

grandparents. The little buggers don't seem to think I'm capable of keeping score."

"Blended families make it more difficult. Why didn't you tell me who you were that day we had lunch?"

"I promised Stephen I wouldn't. He didn't want to scare you or to disrupt your life. He cared for you a great deal. I assure you he had no plans to get himself killed. He wanted to come back to you."

I dropped my gaze, ready to do anything except talk about Stephen's feelings for me. "I thought you'd be in a hurry to get out of here," I managed, picking up my fork.

"I am. Now." He joined me, relishing his food.

When we finished, I watched him wash and rinse the dishes. I dried them and stowed them in the cabinets. I was still reluctant to do anything that occupied both my hands at once, and I wasn't good at hiding it.

He wiped his hands and turned to me. "Either dive into the water or get your foot out of it." It was the first time I'd ever seen him at all impatient. "If that's a little too esoteric for you, let me put it another way. Trust me, Elizabeth, or I'll leave you someplace safe while I get on with my business."

"Finding James?"

"Finding Cara."

"I'm with you," I said. It served his purposes for me to trust him, and, for the moment, it served mine for him to think I did. Even if Stephen had trusted him, I wouldn't forget he was at the ski lodge when Stephen was killed. And most likely in Denver when Jayne Donovan died. The one thing I couldn't afford was unqualified trust.

"Good. I estimate James will give us no more than one hour past the appointed time. But, as I told you before, don't expect to find Cara there."

* * *

As we neared the city limits of Taos, Ian pulled off to the side of the road. It was close to one-fifteen.

"You do have James's cell phone number," he said.

"Yes. Do you want me to call him?"

"And alert him that we have arrived? It's better not to help the enemy, Elizabeth, except in those rare instances in which we have no choice, and then not until we have a full-fledged plan in place. The key to this game is making certain we retain options."

"This," I reminded him, "is no game. What do you suggest?"

"You're certain Patrice and Cara checked out of their rooms?"

"Yes."

"If James knows you called their hotel, he knows that you've gone to the police. He'll also know that they couldn't help you. I expect he believes you to be a hysterical woman who won't be careful what she does. It's to our advantage for him to continue to believe that."

"Will he bring others with him to meet me?"

"You're only one woman, and an untrained one at that. I suspect James has badly underestimated you. My bet is he'll come alone. He does, however, have others working with him. He won't leave Cara and Patrice alone."

"You're certain he's working for Nicholas Ackerman."

"Yes. James works for pay. He's already demonstrated he'll go with the highest bidder."

And he had my daughter. "Do you think he tapped the hotel phone lines?"

"I have no idea what he's done. There's a slim chance that Cara and Patrice may still be at the inn, registered under different names."

"You said they wouldn't be here."

"They won't, but I haven't stayed alive in this business without being thorough. I'll check it out."

He dropped me at one of the ski lodges, handed me a fifty-dollar bill and told me to try their *menudo,* which turned out to be a thick soup. I picked at my serving, fishing out something that looked suspiciously like tripe and then let the waiter take it away. I had just begun toying with the Indian pudding the waiter had recommended for dessert when Ian joined me and ordered coffee.

"I take it they weren't there."

He nodded. "Tell me about your friend Patrice."

"You held her prisoner for hours."

"During our time together, she wasn't in a particularly talkative mood. Tell me how she would react to James."

The waiter brought his coffee. Ian added cream, swirled it with his spoon and then savored it as he drank, studying my face.

"She'd be skeptical, I think. I don't think she trusts men."

He frowned. "Go on."

"She knows I don't trust him. She certainly doesn't trust you."

"Right. All I'm hoping for is, given the proper situation, she'll follow your lead. So. Are you ready?"

"To meet James? Damned straight."

He placed a hand on my arm as I started to rise from my chair. "Leave the emotion here. It could get you killed."

"I'm not worried about that," I told him.

"I know, but I am."

Chapter 20

The pueblo at Taos seemed much like an outcropping of earth, as though it had been forced up from the ground itself, sprouting windows and doors to house the wares of its earth children in a warren of rooms and passageways. As I passed by them, the inhabitants seemed, in their silence and grace, to know some profound secret that eluded me, some secret that they'd learned in the thousand years they'd dwelled there. They seemed to be a people who treasured their time on this earth, a people who were in nowhere near the rush I was.

It was a little before three. Most of the sightseers had gone. Ian had let me off at the far end of the parking area and then driven off. I had no idea where he would leave the car, but I was certain he would be watching me, following me, as I strolled through the village. The pueblo wasn't wired for electricity, so what light there was inside the buildings was dim. I stepped through a doorway and pretended to admire a pendant set in heavy sterling, resting on velvet atop a wooden counter.

"That one's more than fifty years old," an old fellow offered. He wore a long-sleeved plaid shirt and a string tie with a huge oval of silver. A white braid lay on each of his shoulders. "I can give you a good price. It would look lovely on such a lady."

I touched the stone and smiled at him, taking a subtle look through the screen door behind me. James would find me, I was sure, when he was ready.

"I was looking for pottery," I said.

The old man pointed next door, and I went out and into the next open door, emerging into a small shop that sported battery-operated neon lights and glass cases containing intricately decorated pottery. A young woman, in jeans and a peasant blouse, greeted me.

"Can I help you?" she asked.

"We're just looking," a male voice answered. I felt a hand on my waist. I jerked back and turned.

James. My breath quickened. There were only three of us in that room, and he was blocking the door.

"Good to see you, Elizabeth."

He was as blond and tanned as the last time I'd seen him, yet his eyes had changed. They were cold. They sent a chill through me.

"I wish I could say the same," I said. I unclenched my jaw and pushed away the urge to rip him apart, remembering what Ian had told me. Leave the emotion. What I needed was reason and strength.

James slipped an arm over my shoulder and bent over, pointing to a vase in the case near the door. His touch made my skin crawl.

"Where's Cara?" I whispered.

"I've put her and Patrice someplace safe."

"Where?" I hissed, as I continued browsing.

"Keep your voice down," he warned. "I'll take you to them."

"No. Bring them to me."

"That wouldn't be wise. Besides, they're no longer in the state."

"Where are they?" I repeated more quietly this time.

"Would you like to see that vase up close?" the clerk asked. "I can take it out of the case for you."

"No, thanks," James told her. He gripped my arm and pulled me toward the door. I allowed him to do it only because I didn't want that girl hurt if anything happened. Still holding my arm, he led me outside, his grip so strong I could feel my arm bruising beneath his fingers. He pulled me around the side of the building and then to the back of the mud structure.

"What do you want from me?" I demanded. I wrenched my arm from his grip, repulsed by his closeness. "You searched Stephen's belongings looking for something."

He shook his head, but I didn't pause.

"Someone mutilated his body looking for something. What is it you want?"

His eyes hardened. "The book."

The book? The pocket atlas? Is that what he meant? It must be, because he obviously knew that I had it. *Cara, why did you tell him? Did you have a choice?*

"The book wasn't in Stephen's belongings. I know he sent it to you. Where is it?" he asked, softening his tone.

I didn't get the chance to answer. Ian stepped from nowhere and slid one hand around the back of James's neck, the other across his chest. One twist and it would be all over.

Just like it had been for Stephen.

I must have paled, because Ian asked, "Did he do something to you?"

I shook my head.

"You hooked up with *him?* You've just made the biggest mistake of your life," James muttered.

"Or yours," I suggested.

I watched as Ian drew James's gun from a holster under his jacket. Ian pointed it at James's temple. I was certain, as I'm sure Ian was, he had other weapons on him.

"I thought you had more sense," James said, addressing only me.

"The lady wants to speak to her daughter," Ian told James. "I suggest you make that happen."

"My phone is in my inside pocket," James said.

Ian nodded to me, and I pulled James's jacket out, making certain I was far enough back he'd have to lunge if he tried to grab me.

"Press five," James said.

I did and brought the phone to his ear.

"Put Cara on. Two minutes, no more," he said, and I immediately brought the phone back to my own ear.

"Cara?" I choked.

"Mom?"

"Are you all right?"

"Of course."

"Where are you?"

"I'm not sure."

Her voice sounded fuzzy, like she'd just awakened from a nap.

"What do you mean you're not—"

"They flew us out of Sante Fe on a private plane. James said it'd be best if we didn't know. Are you coming? He said he would wait for you to get to Taos and then bring you here. We've been so worried."

"You sound tired." I could hear her yawn over the phone.

"Sorry about that. Yeah. All I seem to want to do is sleep."

"Is Patrice with you?"

"Yeah. She's fine. James put Odin in a kennel, but other than that, we're okay. Mom, give James the book like Dad wanted you to. He says once he gets it and takes care of what he has to do, we'll be safe and we can all go home."

"You're fine."

"Yes. I told you."

"You're eating."

"Of course. Mom, they're saying I've got to go now. Please. Just come with James. I love you."

"I love you, too," I said to a dead line.

I turned to James. "Your terms are the book for Cara and Patrice's freedom."

"No."

Ian jerked James's neck.

"Elizabeth, listen to me. Stephen wanted Cara someplace safe. That's all I'm doing, trying to help both of you. I need the book and the code to do that, but not in exchange for Cara and Patrice. Give them to me."

"You need them to locate Will Donovan," Ian stated.

Of course. The book needed a code to be understood. Ian had mentioned it earlier. That's what they'd been looking for on Stephen's body.

Ian jerked James again. "When we have Donovan, be prepared to make the trade."

"What are you talking about?" I protested. That's not what I'd agreed to.

"Name the time and the place." James turned an angry eye

toward me and shook his head. "I'll be there. With Cara and Patrice. Do you have any idea who you've—"

"We'll be in touch," Ian interrupted.

Suddenly James twisted to reach toward his boot. Ian knocked him cold with one deft punch to the side of his head with his gun. He caught him before he hit the ground.

"What the hell do you think—" I stopped myself. The old Indian with the silver stepped out the back doorway to his place. He lit a cigarette, took a deep draw and then leaned back, resting one boot against the wall. He must have heard the commotion.

"Your friend all right?" he asked, pointing at James with his cigarette.

"No, he's passed out." Ian laid James down gently, allowing his back to rest against the adobe and concealing his gun behind James's back. "Could you call 911?"

"I'll get my cell phone." The old man stomped out his cigarette and went back inside.

Ian grabbed my arm, and we took off walking fast.

"You may have killed him," I said.

"No, but I would have if his friends didn't have Cara. As long as she trusts him, she'll be all right. But if she puts up a fight, there could be trouble."

I wrenched my arm from his grip and stopped cold.

"We should follow James," I insisted. "I think Cara's been drugged. She sounded tired and she said she's sleeping a lot."

"That's good. You don't want her too suspicious."

"It's not good, damn it! I want my daughter."

He took hold of my shoulders and shook me. I was afraid I was going to burst into tears, but I was too angry to cry. I was shocked by his roughness.

"Listen to me," he said, his words measured. "We've got to find the code that goes with Stephen's book before James does."

"That's all you wanted, wasn't it?" I spat out. "You want the book and the code, just like James."

He propelled me forward. "James won't be out long enough for the ambulance to arrive. He won't harm Cara because he knows you'd die before you'd give him the book if he does. The book is going to keep Cara safe, but only if we get the key to go with it. If they locate the key first and manage to find a second copy of that book, your book won't be of any value. Do you understand?"

I nodded, although I didn't at all.

We'd arrived where he'd parked the rented BMW off the road that led to the entrance at the pueblo. He pulled open the passenger door and gently set me inside. Then he was in the driver's seat, the motor was running, and we were tearing down the road as the wail of sirens drew closer.

Chapter 21

I locked the bathroom door of the motel room where we'd stopped about three and a half hours north of Taos and took a long, hot shower, letting water run through my hair and down my face. I wanted to wash away my anger, but it had settled deep inside me, along with the heart-stopping fear I felt for Cara and Patrice. I had to put them both away. I'd be no good to anyone if I let them rule me.

My gun rested within arm's length, on the sink. I'd left the shower curtain drawn back so there was no barrier between the weapon and me, and water puddled onto the floor. I was my only true ally, and I swore not to forget it. Ian was a way to an end, nothing more.

He seemed certain we hadn't been followed, but he still wouldn't allow me out of his sight. That meant one motel room. Truth be told, I wouldn't have gotten a wink of sleep in a room of my own, wondering who might be coming through the door the moment my eyes drifted shut. It remained to be seen if I could sleep with him in the room. It wasn't that I had grown to trust him, simply that I believed he still needed me alive.

As strange as it may seem, I took comfort in knowing that Ian could easily have killed me before now, if that was what he'd intended. Even if his goal wasn't simply to protect me as he claimed, I was valuable to him, and I meant to stay that way until I used him to get Cara back.

"Damn it, Stephen. Damn you. If only you were here. If only you hadn't…" I whispered aloud.

I turned off the water and grabbed a towel, burying my face in its softness, blotting away tears as well as water. I couldn't play that game. Stephen wasn't here and never would be. Being angry with him only drained my strength. Besides, I had to shoulder half the blame for what had happened to Cara and Patrice. I'd sent them off to Taos.

And I couldn't blame Stephen entirely for getting killed. Someone had murdered him. That same someone wanted what Stephen had sent me.

If Stephen had expected me to hand everything over to James and walk away, all that changed once I realized he'd died trusting the wrong man. I wasn't about to make the same mistake.

I finished drying off and pulled on sweatpants and a sweatshirt—not clean, but clean enough—blotted up the water from the floor and wrapped my hair in a fresh towel.

I'd allowed Ian to see my anger, but I refused to again let him see my fear. He'd told me at least part of what was going on, and I was determined to make him tell me the rest, but he startled me when I joined him in our room.

He was sitting with his back to the window, the thick drapes drawn, no lights on except what shone from the bathroom. His face lay in shadow, his profile outlined by the sliver of light that escaped through the window from the porch outside. The ash at the end of his cigarette burned brightly and then faded as he inhaled and then let out the smoke. I'd never seen him smoke. It gave me an eerie feeling. This man whom nothing seemed to shake was not quite as strong as I'd thought.

I flipped on the lamps, sat down on one of the double beds and pulled my bare feet under me. I shook my hair loose from the towel, which I wrapped about my shoulders, and tried to appear casual.

"I like the wildness of your curls," he said, drawing hard on his cigarette and staring at me with eyes that were a little too intense.

"I don't," I said matter-of-factly, not at all comfortable with the way he was studying me. There was longing in his eyes, and it scared me more than anything else about him.

"Of course you don't." His voice was soft, mellow, almost gentle. "You can't control them. You like the illusion that you can influence your environment."

My skin prickled at his intimate tone. It made me acutely aware that we were locked in that room together. I wrapped one hand about my throat, hoping he couldn't see the blush I felt there. Under different circumstances, I don't know how I would have reacted. That scared me, too. I needed to pull his thoughts—and mine   back to the business that brought us together.

"What form would the code be in?" I asked.

"Each operative has his own system. When we make someone disappear, their location is recorded in some sort of code."

I felt some of my muscles ease. He was talking. His eyes had lost some of their intensity. Good.

"Why record it?" I asked. "I thought the whole idea was for your clients to vanish without a trace."

"It is. But it's essential to have a record. The codes serve as a safeguard if the operative is killed or the placement is somehow compromised."

"Does that happen often?" I asked.

"Only once before, several years ago."

When Cara was small. When Stephen took Cara and me to Disney World. When he had feared for our lives.

They had prepared, just as Stephen had prepared me, knowing someday it would happen again.

"The people you hide can come back on their own," I suggested.

"Of course. When they believe it's safe. Some don't choose to return."

"Not ever?" I asked, not bothering to hide my surprise. What could be so dear that it would keep someone from their family and friends forever?

"When someone dies in hiding, we're sometimes left with instructions to return their remains to their native soils or to let their loved ones know what happened to them."

What happened to them. As though it would make a difference after their deaths. As though learning what actually occurred during the years that were robbed from them would somehow make it all more bearable.

Maybe it would. What would I give, all these years after Josie's death, to know how she'd died, where she rested?

"Even if we find him, I won't trade Will Donovan for my daughter," I warned him.

I waited for him to react, but all he did was light another cigarette off the end of the first one. Was he that numb or did he simply not care what I thought? Probably the latter.

"Why does James think I have Stephen's code?" I asked.

"Because you do."

I blinked hard, wondering if Ian had lost his mind. True, I had the package Stephen had sent me, but that was all. And it hadn't been in there.

"They searched Stephen's body and his belongings and didn't find it," he said. "By now they've searched your home and your belongings, as well."

I cringed to think of James going through my things, but I knew Ian was right. James had found his way into my home, and he'd no doubt gone through every inch of my condo after we'd escaped from him.

"Edward Donovan doesn't have it," Ian went on. "That's why I was in Denver, to make certain Stephen hadn't mailed something or left anything with him. Will hasn't contacted his father, either. Donovan's received no correspondence of any kind from either of them. If no one else has the code, that leaves you. We all have that one person we trust. For Stephen it was you."

The irony of his words did not escape me.

"Maybe he left it with someone or in some place no one knows about," I suggested.

"Someone has to know, otherwise what's the point?"

"If you had a bottle of scotch, you'd be drinking it, wouldn't you?" I asked.

He chuckled and the smoke caught in his throat. "Is that what Stephen would do?"

"Absolutely. One good binge before he disappeared again."

"I don't plan to disappear, Elizabeth," he said with no trace of humor in his voice. "At least not without you."

He put out his cigarette, stood, and came toward me. My heart raced in my chest as he stopped beside me next to the bed. I felt dwarfed by his presence—tall, powerful—hovering over me. It put every nerve in my body on edge, but I never lost eye contact with him, as though my sheer will could be a match for his strength.

He sat down facing me—too close. Gently, almost shyly, he reached a hand toward my hair. His breathing was ragged. I could smell the tobacco on him. And now I could smell the alcohol. He must have a flask. *God,* I prayed, *just don't let him be drunk.*

He leaned in and then paused, his lips just inches from my own. I dared not move as his gaze roved my face. I flinched and he drew back. Was that hurt I saw in his eyes just before they flashed to anger?

"Damn it, Elizabeth! Do you actually find me that revolting or do you simply plan to go through life withdrawing further and further into your shell? Stephen's dead. He won't be coming back to you, but then you were living with his ghost long before he died. How long do you plan to continue?"

My cheeks burned. *The bastard. How dare he bring my feelings for Stephen into this?*

"What's really at stake here?" I demanded, letting the towel slip from my shoulders to the floor, anger flaring in my voice. "Why did Stephen die? Why did he choose to help Donovan when he'd been warned not to?"

"He did it for the same reason I'm helping you now. He did it for you, Elizabeth. He did it to stop Ackerman. That's what you want, isn't it?"

I felt as though I'd been punched in the stomach.

Ian must have moved forward, because the warmth of his breath rushed over my skin. I was aware of his body so close to mine. I was unsure of what he might do. And what I might do in response.

The back of his hand stroked my cheek. "Stephen was so

lucky to have you," he whispered, a catch in the softness of his voice.

I wanted to comfort Ian, to comfort Stephen, to make everything all right. Most of all, I wanted to believe him. I wanted so much to trust him. Where Stephen offered only silence, Ian offered explanations. And something more.

I felt his lips against my neck, my cheek, my ear.

"I can't," I whispered, closing my eyes. "I'm so sorry. I just…can't." I must have been crying because I tasted salt in my mouth.

"Of course you can." He kissed away my tears then found my mouth with his own. Tentatively at first and, when I didn't draw back, hungrily. His arms encircled me, as he lay me gently onto the bed. I drew him to me, pressing his body against mine, losing myself in his closeness. I closed my eyes again, uncertain of who I was making love to.

"Stephen." His name slipped from my lips.

Ian stiffened and then roughly drew away. "You're right. You can't."

Chapter 22

"This is all I have, all that was in the envelope Stephen mailed to me," I told Ian, as though offering him some idiotic consolation prize for what had almost passed between us.

I'd spread the two photos, the note, the atlas and the copies of the Internet articles on the bed and was studying them when he came back into the room after taking a shower. He wore only sweatpants. No shoes, no shirt, and I could see the muscles that had been hidden beneath his clothes, the arms that had knocked James cold with a single punch and that had held me so gently. I'd been kidding myself to think I'd ever been physically in command in his presence, armed or not.

He sat down on the bed, toweling his hair, a gentle crease lifting the corner of his eyes, which studied me intently. Any haze that the liquor and cigarettes may have caused was gone. If he felt any of the awkwardness I wrestled with, I didn't see it.

Briefly he examined each photo and found nothing to interest him. Then he flipped through the small pocket atlas. "The key is absolutely meaningless without knowledge of what book and which edition the reference is to. But we don't have the key."

He dropped the book, obviously disgusted.

"What if they find it before we do?" I asked.

"They'll track down Will Donovan and they'll hold him hostage until Judge Donovan finds a way to get Ackerman acquitted."

In which case Cara and Patrice would no longer be of any value to them.

And Stephen would have died for nothing.

I felt sick to my stomach.

"But only if they get the key," I insisted.

"*When* they get the key," Ian said. "That's why we have to get it first."

He picked up the note Stephen had written to me, read it, peered into my eyes and then dropped it back onto the bed. I had no idea what he might be thinking.

"Stephen wouldn't have sent the key with the book," Ian said. "Have you received any other correspondence from him? Think, Elizabeth. Did he leave anything with you the last time you saw him, no matter how insignificant?"

I searched my mind, shaking my head. "Only a bottle of scotch."

He twisted and grabbed my backpack off the floor, unzipped it and dumped its contents between us.

"Hey!" I protested, but he pawed through my clothes and personal items anyway. Then he reached for my purse. I tried to snatch it from him, but he shook it, spilling pens and lipstick, wallet and checkbooks onto the bed covers.

"Why do you have two checkbooks?" he asked, scooping them up.

"One belonged to Stephen. I found it in my condo between the sofa cushions—"

"The last time he visited," Ian finished.

I'd put it in my purse, so I'd have it with me when I saw him again. But then he'd died, and I hadn't thought to take it out.

Ian riffled through it as I scrambled off the bed to watch over his shoulder. It looked like a normal checkbook with a plastic cover, a ledger tucked into the upper flap and a pad of checks slipped into the lower. Each entry was dated with a month and a day, no year, followed by the name of the person the check was made out to, with the account number penned on the notation line.

"This is a copy of the code," Ian declared.

"How can you be so sure?"

"Because Stephen left it with you, and just look at it. It's all written in the same ink so we could recognize it when we found it. If this were an actual check ledger filled out over time, the inks, even if they were the same color, would be different. So would the handwriting. Besides, all of these entries are made out to individuals. There's not a single business in the list. The original would pass as a ledger if it wasn't scrutinized too closely, but not this one."

He was right. It was too regimented. And the dates didn't make sense. Who could have one check ledger that spanned what was looking more and more like years and years? But if this was the key to the code, how did it work?

And, if this was a copy, where was the original?

The date of the last entry, January 21, caught my eye. I grabbed the checkbook out of Ian's hand and flipped back to the checks. Number 92 was still on top, not written out, even though that same number was clearly recorded in the ledger as a check for $54.98 made out to Alan Spears. On the second line, just under the name, was an account number.

"January twenty-first was the day that Will Donovan disappeared."

Ian raised an eyebrow at me. "Well, I bloody well doubt Stephen was writing checks the day he spirited off Will." He grabbed up the pocket atlas. "Read me the account number. Include the hyphens."

"It's 238-87C2."

"First number has to be the page." He flipped through to 238. It was in the index of cities. "What's the next part again?"

"87C2."

He ran his finger down the print. "It's a reference to the map and the quadrant." He looked up at me, a smile tugging at the left side of his face. "Bingo. Will Donovan is in Cowichan Bay, British Columbia. How much would you like to bet his new name is Alan Spears?"

Chapter 23

We woke at dawn, stopped for a brief breakfast that I had trouble choking down and were at a small airport within half an hour. Money buys lots of things, and Ian had lots of money. In this case it bought the use of a private, twin-engine plane. We were the only passengers onboard. It had been idling at the airport as we drove up, and I was certain that phone call he'd made late last night from his cell phone had brought it there.

I'd discarded all my fake identification, dropping my other licenses and passports into the mail in an envelope with my Maryland address, so as not to "confuse" the authorities if we were stopped crossing the border.

The pilot filed a flight plan, and, flying low, we landed on a remote island off Seattle several hours later. Once on the ground, we took a speedboat into the tiny tree-covered islands along the border, changed to another boat in the open water and proceeded on to Vancouver Island, off the mainland of British Columbia, the crisp sea air stinging our faces.

I could see immediately why Stephen had chosen this place for Will Donovan. Water and boats were everywhere. According to the article in *The Washingtonian* magazine, Donovan was an avid sailor.

Our "ride" let us off at the dock amid the bustle of the busy, cold afternoon. Fishing boats were coming in, and the odors of fish, algae and saltwater filled my head.

Ian took my hand, pulling me across the weathered boards of the old wooden dock. We blended, as best we could, into the crowd and the noise. He wore a casual smile as his gaze searched the faces we passed. Through that smile, he whispered to me, "Don't look so sour. Make them think we're on our honeymoon."

It was obvious that tourists came up from Seattle. I decided I could do that; I could be a tourist from Seattle. Not a tourist on my honeymoon, however. "I'll smile, but keep your hands to yourself," I warned, pasting on a grin of my own. I needed my thoughts on what we were doing. Ian could be far too much of a distraction.

He didn't let go of my hand but instead drew it possessively into the crook of his arm.

We stopped at a dark little tavern one street over from the dock to get our bearings, and took a booth at the back, sitting across from each other. Ian ordered us each a pint. I started to protest that I don't drink—at least not beer— but he shushed me. Then he asked me for Will's photo. I dug it out of my pack and handed it to him.

"What are we doing here?" I asked.

"Will Donovan is in his twenties, right?"

I nodded.

"Then he'll like his ale, and this village is too small to support many of these houses. If he's here in Cowichan Bay, he'll have been in here at one time or another."

When the waiter came back, Ian showed him the photo. "Do you know this fellow? His name is Alan Spears."

"Oh, Alan. Sure. He comes in here from time to time. Haven't seen him for maybe a week now. What about him?"

"He's a friend of ours," I said, leaning forward, "actually of my daughter's. She wanted us to drop by and look him up."

"Nice sort. Likes to sail. You'll find him at his place if he's in port this week. Here, I'll make it easier for you." He drew us a crude map on a napkin. "When you see him, tell him I have some Guinness on tap that I'm certain he'd like to try."

"Of course." I tried to smile casually.

"What if Will's not there?" I asked as soon as the waiter was out of earshot. "He may have heard about his mother's death. What if he's already left for Denver?"

"He hasn't," Ian assured me. "We would have heard. If he sets foot in Denver, someone is certain to recognize him. His photo has been all over the news with his disappearance, and again with what happened to his mother."

"Wouldn't someone here have recognized him?" I asked.

"Not likely. No one's expecting him to be here. Besides, it's quite possible someone would think Alan Spears looks a bit like Will Donovan if, indeed, the Canadian news service picked up the story, but people do resemble one another."

I thought about the clerk at the ski lodge where Stephen died not recognizing Judge Donovan.

"Why hasn't Will gone back to Denver?" I asked.

"We're about to find out." He drained his glass, left money on the table and ushered me back out into the sunlight, leaving my own beer untouched.

Cowichan Bay has a feel to it a good bit like what I imagine the States must have been like in the fifties—mostly two-lane roads and small businesses populated with what seem to be friendly, wholesome people who don't expect too much from anyone who's willing to spend money there.

We rented a car and, following the map, finally found the house in an isolated little cove about three miles up from where we'd docked. The number on the post out front was 5498, the amount written on the check.

It was a modest one-story cottage built partially on pilings. The place had huge windows on the two sides overlooking the water. No boat was moored at its dock, but there was a Miata parked inside the attached garage.

Ian drew out his gun.

"Is that really necessary?" I asked.

"I hope not," he said.

He knocked on the door as I peered through the windows at the sleek wooden floors and simple furnishings. No lights were on. When I joined Ian at the door, he'd slipped the lock.

Mail had piled onto the floor below the door slot. I picked it up. Nothing personal; only advertisements addressed to "occupant." I passed the stack over to him.

"What would you say? Seven days? Eight?" I asked.

"No more than. He'd know not to be away longer than that, although I suspect he was confident that Stephen could get in touch with him if necessary."

"He doesn't know Stephen's dead," I said.

"No," he agreed.

"You're assuming he left voluntarily," I pointed out.

"That's the hope. I see no signs of struggle, and James hadn't figured out where he was last we saw him."

We walked through the main room, disturbing nothing as

we went. It was a comfortable little place, with simple, wood-framed furniture sporting canvas-covered cushions, a small fireplace, two shelving units filled with books, a stereo system, a two-way radio and a breakfast bar separating the galley-type kitchen from the main living area. The cupboards contained mostly packaged foods, the freezer mainly fish, the refrigerator beer, milk and orange juice. I checked the expiration dates. The milk had one more day left on it. Will couldn't have been gone long.

When I stepped into the only other room, the bedroom, I had to steady myself. It contained a double bed on a frame, two dressers and a bedside table. On every flat surface were photos, framed snapshots of Cara and myself, both together and individually.

I felt Ian's arm circle my shoulders. "What's wrong?"

All I could do was point. He swept past me, leaving me clinging to the doorframe.

"Damn."

"This was Stephen's place," I managed. I should have guessed. Stephen had always loved the water, always loved to sail. He'd realized his dream to someday have a cottage away from it all, a place where the world couldn't intrude.

Ian nodded, trying to shake off his own surprise a little too late. I'd already seen it. This man who was supposed to be Stephen's closest confidant didn't know about this place.

But then, neither did I. One more secret. He'd kept us here with him, if only in photos. *God. Stephen, if you loved us so much, why did you push us away?*

And why had he brought Will Donovan into his own hideaway? Was this indeed to have been his last case, as Ian had suggested? What had Stephen said the last time I'd seen him? Something about things changing. That we had something to look forward to. I'd heard that one before. I should have listened. Instead I'd thrown him out.

"So," I said, shaking off my thoughts, "if this is where the code says Will Donovan should be, why isn't he here?"

"I'd say he went sailing," Ian said. "There's no boat. The flashlights and emergency equipment are all missing." Ian slipped into the bathroom and then back out again. "His toothbrush is gone, too. He left his razor."

"Then he doesn't know about his mother," I suggested.

He nodded. "He'd have to make an effort to discover what was going on in the outside world. I suspect he was waiting for a message from Stephen."

"You say Stephen would have known how to contact him when he was on the boat."

Ian nodded.

I let out a rush of exasperated air. "So what do we do now?"

"The only thing we can do. Wait."

Chapter 24

Our wait ended the next evening, just as the sun was shooting spectacular orange rays across the horizon, lighting up the living area of Stephen's cottage through the wide windows. The tension between Ian and me had become almost unbearable. Neither of us had said a word about what had happened at the motel, and, except for a stolen glance every now and again, I could have almost believed I'd dreamed it.

I was inside reading one of Stephen's books on sailing while Ian kept watch outside. All I heard was a single tap on the window. He'd disappeared by the time I dropped my book, switched off the light, and reared up to look outside.

The whir of an outboard motor grew from the buzz of a mosquito to the roar of a chain saw, as I found my gun, slipped to the floor and crouched next to the chair. Suddenly the noise stopped, and I could hear the slap of water against the dock along with the thunk of a rope hitting wood.

I hoped it was Will. It could just as easily have been James who had somehow discovered Will's hiding place. The thought made me shudder.

My breath caught as a key twisted in the lock. I raised my gun as the door swung inward. A figure, backlit by the magnificent sunset, filled the threshold, then bent to drop a duffel onto the floor. Directly behind him, a second shadow appeared.

Ian's voice said, "Raise your hands where I can see them." Suddenly the two shadows merged and then both men came through the opening, thumping to the floor. I heard a loud groan and something metal skid across the floor. Then the shadows separated as the top one wrenched violently backward onto his feet, thudding against the wall.

I flipped on the light. "Okay, that's enough."

They both looked startled; Ian, twisting the shoulder that had been whacked against the wall; and a wild-eyed Will Donovan just gaining his footing. I'd seen enough photos of him to recognize him almost anywhere, even with longer hair and several days of stubble covering his chin. Both of his hands were raised in fists. Ian's gun lay well out of reach on the floor. Will slung his hair out of his eyes and demanded, "Who the fu—"

"Uh-uh. There's a lady present," Ian cautioned.

"Ladies don't break into people's homes and hold them at gunpoint. What the hell do you want?"

His gaze darted back and forth between the two of us, assessing his odds, and then rested on me. I saw recognition in his eyes.

"I'm Stephen Larocca's wife."

His fists relaxed slightly as he looked Ian up and down. "Where's Stephen?"

"Dead," I told him, standing up.

I'd said it enough that the word no longer stirred any emotion within me. It was simply a fact that I'd come to accept.

Will uttered a low "Damn."

I didn't lower the gun. Not yet. He was feisty, young and limber, and a good deal bigger than his photos let on. While I had no doubt Ian could handle him, Ian had already taken at least one bad blow. I needed them both in good shape.

"We're here to help you," I said.

"Good. You can help me by putting down your gun and getting the hell out of my way."

"Not so fast." Ian warned. "Show us any other weapons you have."

"Why don't you go to—" Will began.

"Do what he says," I ordered.

He motioned toward the duffel, and Ian retrieved a 9 mm Beretta, which he slipped into his own pocket, along with the one on the floor. Then he patted Will down and drew a knife from a sheath strapped to Will's calf.

"If you're so anxious to help, why the guns?" Will asked me.

I slipped mine into the waistband of my jeans. "Because I need you to listen to me. Please sit down."

He stood his ground, but Ian pushed him onto the sofa. "Do as the lady says."

"I have some bad news, Will. It's about your mother. I wish there was some other way to tell you."

He was totally alert, staring at me, daring me to say what he didn't want to hear.

"I'm so sorry, Will. She's dead."

I wished I could have told him some other way, not that there's any way to prepare someone for news like that, but there simply wasn't time. Two days had already passed since our encounter with James.

He blanched and his hand started to shake. "How?"

I wanted to touch him, this man who suddenly looked so young, but I knew not to. To him, we were part of the problem.

"We believe she was murdered," I said. He didn't need to know the details, the lies about suicide and drugs.

"Ackerman," Will uttered, fighting the anger and the grief that distorted his face.

"Yes," I said.

"When?" he asked.

"A few days ago."

"I've got to call my father."

"That wouldn't be wise," Ian said. "You have to stay in hiding. That's what your father would want."

"You don't know what the hell he would want," he spat at Ian. "How is he?" he then managed, turning toward me and running his hands through his hair.

"Worried about you," I said.

"Jesus," Will cursed. "This isn't right. If my mother was in danger, Stephen was supposed to bring her here. He promised—"

"Stephen died weeks before your mother," I explained.

"Look, I'm out of here." Will stood and reached for the duffel, pulling it onto his shoulder. "I'm going to see my father. Shoot me if you think that will somehow help you."

He might not realize it, but he wasn't going anywhere. Ian was a hell of a powerful man.

"Please," I said. "The men who may have killed your mother and my husband have my daughter."

"Your daughter?" he repeated, turning back to face me. "The one in the photos?"

He'd lain in that bed staring at Cara's face for all those weeks. He must have felt as though he knew her.

"Yes, but that's not all. They still want you," I said.

His eyes narrowed, his gaze again flitting between Ian and me. "Of course they do. That's why I intend to get them first."

"We'd like to see you do exactly that, preferably without getting yourself killed," Ian explained.

"But first we need your help," I explained. "We want to bring them down as much as you do."

"You and the goon here?" Will raised an eyebrow at Ian.

"Yeah. Me and the goon." I wondered if Ian found that term half as amusing as I did. "We need you to come back to Denver with us, voluntarily, if possible. We'll tell them we're willing to make a trade—you for my daughter and my friend Patrice."

He studied us both, his distrust of Ian now spilling in my direction. "You think I'll let you hand me over to those murderers? What are you? Nuts?"

I shook my head. "You don't actually believe we're stupid enough to think they'd let any of us walk away alive if they have a choice. We're bringing you, my daughter and Patrice out, but we may need you as bait, willing bait, I hope. And we need you where they won't find you. You're no longer safe here."

"Right. So you're taking me to them."

He had a point.

"If you stay here, they *will* find you," Ian stated. "Make no mistake about this—they intend to hold you hostage. We could also use an extra pair of hands."

"I already told you I'm not staying. Does Cara know that you're doing this?" he asked.

So he knew her name. Of course. He would have asked, and Stephen would have told him. I shook my head. "She doesn't know she's in danger. She thinks the man holding her is helping her."

"You're sure these are the same cowards who had my mother killed?"

"No," Ian broke in. "They are the same paid assassins who killed your mother."

"Terrific. So why aren't we going after Ackerman?"

Anger had settled in his jaw. It helped him fight back the tears.

"Because your father is already doing just that. For him to be successful, we have to bring in Ackerman's henchmen. First we retrieve Cara and Elizabeth's friend Patrice. Then we can take care of Ackerman," Ian assured him.

"What if I say no? What if I choose to go my own way?"

"Then you'll die," Ian said.

Wrath flared in his eyes.

"So will Cara and Patrice," I added calmly. "You trusted Stephen. You can trust me."

He seemed to consider that for a moment.

"Stephen tried to help you and your father," I reminded him. "He died trying. Help us save his daughter."

He stared at me for what seemed like forever. Then he nodded, and I breathed a sigh of relief. He was a law student. He knew about compromise. He also knew about using people.

"Who's the muscle?" he asked, nodding in Ian's direction.

"Ian worked with Stephen."

"As soon as we hit stateside, I want you to call James," Ian told me, shoving his gun into the holster strapped to his chest, "and tell him that we'll make the exchange at the Denver Mint Monday afternoon."

"Why would he agree to that?" I asked.

"No one can get a weapon into that place," Will stated, leaning against the wall. "The place has state-of-the-art security."

"Exactly."

"So what's to make this James think I'll go with him once we're all inside?" Will asked.

"Nothing," Ian agreed. "But he won't intend to meet us in the mint. He'll plan an ambush outside."

"How can you be so sure?" I asked.

"Because I trained him."

"You *trained* him?" Will repeated. "You worked together?"

"Yes. Until James threw in with Ackerman."

"James will know what you expect him to do," I pointed out.

"Yes. But what he won't know is that we plan to meet him nowhere near the mint."

"When do we leave?" I asked.

Ian didn't hesitate. "Now."

Chapter 25

Trust was in short supply. Everything I'd read about Will Donovan suggested he charmed his way through life. He wasn't used to taking orders, and I suspected he had trouble believing our agenda was necessarily to his advantage. But he gave the appearance of being on board, cooperating fully, which made me even more suspicious.

The task of watching him fell more to me than to Ian as we retraced our steps out of Canada and back to the small airfield in Seattle where the same plane stood waiting for us. Will needed to feel we'd provide the most expedient way to get back home where he could see his father and hear from someone else exactly what had gone on, where he had resources, where he could regain some control.

Once we were in the air and on our way to Denver, Ian took a seat next to the pilot, leaving Will and me alone for the first time.

"How the hell did your buddy Ian let things go so bad?" Will asked, staring out the window at the fields below, dark glasses snug over his eyes, hiding them from me. "If it got worse, Mom was supposed to get out. I never would have left if—"

"I know," I said.

He turned and looked at me, the handsome young man with the once-golden life. "I feel like a damned coward, hiding, out sailing that damned boat while my father…"

"Stephen and Ian were poised to bring your mother out. They met at a ski lodge to make final arrangements, only—"

"Someone killed Stephen."

"James." Even if I wasn't completely convinced, it was important to keep Will on board. "James was one of their operatives, and I can only assume that, once Stephen was dead, your father realized he didn't know who to trust and called off the operation. Ian had to take care of Stephen's body. Then James disappeared, and before Ian managed to convince your father your mother had to make it to safety immediately—"

"They killed her, too." Will swore under his breath. "Sorry."

"Hey, I'd be saying a whole lot worse than that if I were you." And had when I'd first heard that Stephen was dead.

"Your husband was a good man," he said. "If anyone other than you had come for me, I wouldn't have gone."

I considered that. Both his words and the situation. Was that why Ian had wanted me there?

"Yes, I believe he was," I agreed. I could, at last, say that with absolute confidence.

"He talked about you. About Cara, too."

I could see his grief and I shared it. I couldn't think about Stephen. I couldn't allow myself to grieve again, for our life together, for what could have been our life together. If I did,

I'd want to be dead, too, and I knew I wouldn't always feel like that. Ian had made me see that.

"What's going on between the two of you?" Will asked, nodding toward the cockpit.

I felt color threaten my cheeks. "What do you mean?"

"I've seen him look at you."

"Nothing's going on," I assured him. Ian hadn't so much as brushed my arm since Will had joined us.

"Good. Keep it that way. I don't want him muddling your mind."

I was too stunned by Will's audacity to reply. Yet I wondered exactly how much influence Ian had had over my thoughts. I'd remained objective. I knew I had. He was a way to get Cara and Patrice back, nothing more.

I turned to look out the window, wondering if I was only fooling myself, if I'd been able to be truly objective about anything since Stephen's death.

About a half hour or so later, Ian joined us in the back of the plane to lay out his plan.

"We'll land at a little airport just west of Boulder," he told us. "I've arranged for us to have a ride into town where we'll pick up a rental car and then drive down to Denver. My calculations put James bringing Cara and Patrice into a certain airport outside of Denver."

"How do you know that?" Will asked.

"It's the only one in the area that will accommodate the type of craft I know they'll be flying, something big enough to transport six or more people and still small enough that they won't have to take it into a major airport where security would be tighter."

"Why is it important to know where they'll land?" I asked.

"Because that's where we'll take them down—before

James has an opportunity to separate Cara and Patrice. He'll want them in two different locations before coming to meet us, so if we manage to find one, he'll still have the other to bargain with should things not go quite as he plans."

"But how do you know when they'll land?" I asked.

"I don't. But James won't risk having Cara and Patrice in the area longer than is absolutely necessary, so my best guess is no more than a few hours before the arranged meeting. The way to deal with him—and to make certain that we recover both Cara and Patrice—is to surprise them when they touch down."

How exactly he planned to do that, he wouldn't tell us. Then he again joined the pilot in the cockpit.

Will slouched in his seat, his dark glasses hiding any hint of emotion, and stared straight ahead. "He's not telling us all he knows."

"Why do you think that?" I asked.

"You say he was there when Stephen was killed?"

I nodded.

"If he knows so much about this James and how he thinks, tell me why he didn't take him out then and there? Tell me how you know which one of them did the killing? They could be working together—Ian and James. He could be delivering me to him. Then they'd have us all—you, me, Cara." Will continued to stare straight ahead, his eyes hidden, his voice low. "You can trust him if you want, but until I get a damned good reason, I won't."

I looked at the back of Ian's head and wondered if I was on a mission to save Cara and Patrice or if I had sealed our fates. The thought made me shudder.

Chapter 26

We pulled our rented SUV off the main highway some twenty or so miles from Denver and stopped just outside the gates of a flat, grassy area with no trees. The landscape was broken by two hangars, a fair-size landing pad, a handful of small twin-engine planes, a couple of cars and a fence that towered some twelve feet into the air. Ian and I watched the sky through binoculars. Only two planes landed and a third took off during the two hours we waited. Traffic in and out of the gates was almost nonexistent.

"Why did we bring Will to the airport with us?" I asked Ian. "Why not find a safe place and leave him there?"

Will lay sunning himself, out of earshot, his back against the windshield of the SUV, sunglasses again covering his eyes, his feet crossed at the ankles, his legs resting on the hood.

Ian swallowed the last bite of his PowerBar. "There are no safe places. Besides, we couldn't chance his untimely arrival

if he took it upon himself to play vigilante. He's a hothead.
No judgment whatsoever."

"He doesn't strike me that way," I stated.

"Yes, well, I've had enough like him in my classes."

"So have I. I like him. If you'd give him some credit, I
suspect he might return the favor."

Ian scanned the horizon once more.

A little blue and white Cessna whirred over our heads, and
Will raised up, shading his eyes to watch it fly in.

"Could that be them?" I asked.

Ian shook his head. "Too small."

"You do have a plan," I said hopefully, crumpling the
wrapper of my Snickers bar and stuffing it into my jeans' back
pocket. "It might help if you let me in on it."

"All in good time."

I found his evasion irritating as hell, but I knew I wouldn't
get any more out of him.

Traffic on the road was sparse. We both looked up at the
sound of a motor, and Ian swung his binoculars in the direction of the noise.

"On your feet," he called to Will, motioning both of us to
stand ready at the side of the car. Ian offered Will his pistol back.

"You trust me to use this?" Will asked.

"Only if you have to," Ian said.

Will released the cartridge, checking to see if it was actually loaded. He shoved it back into the gun and cocked it. I
wondered what was running through his mind. He'd told me
he didn't trust us. Hell, I didn't trust us, either.

"Put it out of sight," Ian ordered, and Will stuffed it into
his waistband.

Ian had changed into the black suit, black tie and white
shirt that had been waiting for him when we arrived at the

airport near Boulder. It was a strange outfit for what I suspected was about to go down. Quickly, he pulled on sunglasses, adjusted his cufflinks, and drew on a pair of thin leather driving gloves, the ones he'd worn at Patrice's. The sight of them made me cringe.

"You two wait here for my signal. When I call you over, don't say a word to anyone." Then he put his hands in his pockets and casually strode toward the gate.

Will's hand found his gun. For one heart-stopping moment, I thought he might draw it out and shoot Ian in the back. He offered me a grin. "Not yet. First we take out the other guys."

I wanted to say something to Will, but the sound of the motor had drawn closer. A black limo with darkened windows slowed to make the turn into the gate. Ian stood in its path, his hands raised in front of him, holding what looked like a badge. The car stopped. I watched as he went to the driver-side window. The glass slid down and he reached through the opening. Then the driver was out of the car, handing Ian his hat, which he drew snugly over his hair. Both of them went to the other side of the limo. Ian opened the side door and motioned for us to come as the driver climbed into the back. We piled in after him, and Ian slammed the door shut. The driver scrambled to the seat closest to the front and as far away from the two of us as he could get. Will and I sat one on each side of the door, our guns drawn.

"Don't want to get mixed up in no drug bust," the driver kept repeating, shaking his head, looking us up and down. "I got me a good job. Don't need this kind of mess. Someone calls to book a limo, we don't make no background checks. They pay their money, we provide service. I stay up front, keep my nose out of it. Not my fault what they carry back here with them."

Will opened his mouth, but I shook my head at him. No talking.

"Lord o' mercy, if you shoot up this car, there'll be hell to pay," the driver babbled.

A sudden chill swept over me. I looked at the gun I held and wondered what the hell I was doing. The thought of bullets flying with Cara and Patrice in the middle was more than I could bear. So I handled it the only way I knew how. I put it totally out of my mind. I could only get through this one step at a time. Only by following orders. And praying that Ian knew what he was doing.

The limo pulled to a stop. Seconds later the door swung open and Ian crooked his finger for the driver to get out.

"What you gonna do with me?" the man asked, climbing out between us. "You ain't gonna arrest me, are you?"

"How many employees inside?" Ian asked, putting an arm around the man's shoulders.

"Usually it's just the two—Hank, who runs the place, and Billy, who does the maintenance."

And the guy who had just landed the Cessna and one or two other pilots at the most.

"Good. You and I are going to go inside. We're going to tell them that the DEA suspects a cargo of cocaine is coming in. The three of you, plus anyone else who may be inside, are going to lock all the doors, go into the bathroom, get down and stay low until I give you the all clear. Don't come out no matter what you hear. Understand?"

"Just what you expectin' to happen?" the driver asked.

"These are just precautions, in case things go bad. Now you got it?"

"Oh, I got it all right. But watch out after my car, man."

As Ian pulled the man away, I climbed out of the car with Will following after me.

"Where do you two think you're going?" Ian snapped over his shoulder.

"I'm not going to be someplace I can't see what's going on," I insisted. I didn't like the idea of being caged in a box with only one exit.

"Get back inside, both of you," he snapped. "You'll be able to see well enough, a fair trade for them not knowing you're here. I need you to be there when they bring Cara and Patrice out. You keep them inside the limo, and like I said, keep your heads down."

Ian looked at his watch. "They should be landing in about ten minutes. I expect two men in addition to James, one for each woman. And don't, under any circumstances, leave the car." He tossed Will the keys. "If things get really bad, get her out of here, no matter what she says."

"Oh, Lord, oh, Lord, oh, Lord," the driver repeated as Ian escorted him to the office.

Ian was back in less than five minutes, leaning casually against the front passenger door with us safely inside. His arms were crossed, his gun in the crook of his elbow. I could see the barrel peeking out against his side.

We didn't have to wait long. The Lear jet flew in low, skipped to a landing, and circled the runway. Just as it came to a stop, we heard Ian's tap against the window.

"Are you still sure we're working for the right side?" Will asked.

"I'm on whatever side keeps my daughter safe," I said.

Through the dark glass I could see Ian pull his cap farther down over his face. That only left his nose and his jawline to be recognized. As careful as James would be, I somehow doubted he'd notice.

The side door of the Lear jet opened and a stair folded down. The pilot remained clearly visible at the controls in the cockpit. He must have been planning a takeoff as soon as his passengers disembarked.

My heart caught in my throat as I saw Patrice appear in the doorway with some shaved-headed man close behind. She looked fine, healthy, nothing on her wrists. I let out a sigh of relief and craned my neck for a glimpse of Cara.

James was next onto the platform, but he turned and went back inside. He reappeared in the cockpit window, talking to the pilot.

Then Cara emerged from the plane, and my heart pounded. Her foot caught on the wire mesh of the first step, tripping her, and my whole body strained forward to catch her. A man wearing a baseball cap, who was following close behind, grabbed her elbow and steadied her.

Ian reacted, too, pushing off from the side of the limo. His arms remained crossed as he came down the side and put his left hand on the back door. He must have been hiding his gun behind him because I couldn't see it.

He had called it just right. Their three to our three, not counting the pilot. Only, I suspected Ian put the odds at one to three. He had no intention of Will or me becoming involved.

Both Will and I crouched down as Patrice, Cara and their escorts approached. A good thirty feet separated the couples. No one could see us through the black of the glass until they were right upon us, at least I hoped they couldn't. The door swung open, letting in bright sunshine. I heard Patrice's voice and then saw Ian's hand helping her. I lunged for her as soon as she was inside, holding a finger to her lips. A tiny "oh" escaped from her and she frowned at me, her eyes huge. I shook my head at her.

"You all right?" the man behind called after her.

The engine of the jet was still running so it made it hard to hear.

"Fine," she managed, her eyes trained on me. Then she called out louder this time, "I tripped."

Ian had blocked the man's path and was saying something to him. Then he cleared the way, and, as the man leaned to climb inside, Ian turned behind him. Two quick thuds echoed, like the muffled sound of rivets being driven into something hard. A wheeze issued from the man's mouth, and he crumpled forward onto the floor, blood issuing from his lips.

I covered Patrice's mouth with my hand, stifling her scream, and she struggled against me as I fought my own terror.

"What the hell is going on?" she whispered loudly as soon as I let her free.

Ian, his body masking his actions from Cara and her guard, shoved the man inside. Will dragged him to the front end, leaving a bloody trail and a deepening red patch on the back of his jacket. If he wasn't dead yet, he soon would be. The placement of the wounds and the amount of blood suggested the bullets had torn right through the heart.

"The men you're with are killers," I told Patrice, tasting bile in my throat. "James may have killed Stephen. They're paid assassins."

"You're crazy," she spat back at me. "That driver is the killer. He shot Jake, and you're just sitting there letting—"

"Your Jake worked for Nicholas Ackerman," I said.

I checked Jake's neck for a pulse but felt nothing. When I looked up, Patrice's face had gone white, and she was staring out the window.

"I don't know about James, but I know that man," Patrice choked out, pointing at Ian and studying his features. "He just murdered a man in cold blood. And he almost murdered Odin."

It was true and the callousness of the act had not escaped me. Nor my own callous response. Was this what Stephen had become? Had he killed men as easily as Ian? Thinking was a luxury I could ill afford.

I motioned for Will to take a place next to Patrice. When Cara and her guard got close enough to see through the windows, they'd be expecting two shadows.

"You're Will Donovan," Patrice stated, obviously recognizing him from his photo. "You're supposed to be dead."

"Not yet, but I'm working on it."

I shushed them. My precious Cara was at the limo door.

She took one step up. I dove toward her, but she let out a loud "Mom!" before I could stop her. Suddenly she was catapulted forward, her hands thrown out in front of her to break her fall, as the door slammed shut behind her.

"Get down," I shouted, reaching behind me and pulling Patrice down with me. Cara let out a shriek, raising her blood-covered hands from the floorboard. Will vaulted toward her, slamming her down as shots rang down the side of the limo, followed by the thuds that signaled Ian's returned fire.

We were trapped, but I didn't intend to stay that way. We could hear gunfire spit from the front fender area. And then Cara's guard, still wearing his baseball cap, was quickly moving back along the limo. He tried the door, but it was locked and he couldn't pull it open. I'd lost track of Ian. Then the man was back at the front of the car. The doors were locked there, too.

Another shot rang out, more distant this time. It sounded as though it was coming from the area near the hangars, the only other area that offered any kind of cover. Ian must have removed his silencer and was trying to draw the gunman away from us so he could get a better shot.

I chanced a look through the untinted windshield. I could see Ian's arm stretched past the wheels of the blue and white Cessna. The man, the one who'd helped Cara on the stairs, was laying down a barrage of fire from his cover at the front fender. Ian would be loath to shoot back for fear of striking the limo, even if he could get off a shot in that hail of fire.

I looked toward the jet. James was making his way down the stairs. That explained the massive gunfire: cover for James. The odds against Ian were about to get much worse, and I was not about to let James kill Ian only to come finish us all off in that death trap of a limo.

"Take care of them," I told Will and then climbed over the body and onto the leather seat directly in front of the opening that led to the driver's seat. I squeezed through and fell head-first, twisting and quickly dragging my legs after me. I didn't have time to think how crazy I was. I could die trying to help Ian, or I could just wait to die.

Flipping the lock, I pushed open the driver-side door, and tumbled onto the ground on the opposite side from the gunman, pushing the door shut after me.

I scrambled to the protection of the rear tire, and, crouching on the ground, looked beneath the car. I could see the man's legs and part of the rear of his jeans as he squatted and twisted. He knew I was out.

I aimed beneath the limo and squeezed the trigger. The gun snapped back, but the bullet must have hit home. The man let out a loud curse as he jumped and then moved just enough to better shelter his body behind the front tire, making himself more vulnerable to Ian. It was just enough to break the barrage.

He could come after me, but if he did, Ian would be right on top of him—if James didn't stop Ian first. I drew farther back and heard a bullet whiz past me from under the car. Now the man in the baseball cap had two fronts to cover and a wound, however minor, in his leg. I'd bettered Ian's odds, if only a little. By now James had to be in the mix.

Will tumbled out of the driver's side door the same way I had.

"You're nuts!" he declared, crawling back to join me.

"Must be contagious," I suggested.

A second bullet whizzed beneath the limo. Will slid past me, on around to the trunk of the car. I followed, determined not to let him get killed after we'd gone to all the trouble of finding him.

The next bullet came from another direction entirely, somewhere behind us, and tore across Will's calf. James, damn it.

Will let out a loud groan and I could see blood soaking the denim of his jeans. He dropped his gun and pressed his palm against his leg, blood seeping between his fingers. For the briefest moment, I put down my gun and grabbed Will under the shoulders, tugging him back around to the side opposite the gunman, hoping the tire would offer us enough protection. I stripped off my belt.

"Just apply enough pressure to stanch the bleeding," I instructed, slipping it around his calf.

Before I could take up my gun again, I felt an arm across my shoulder and a hand slip around my throat. Breath was in my ear. I knew that aftershave.

"You don't need that," a man's voice said.

My gun skittered beneath the car as it was kicked, and I looked out of the corner of my eye to see James. He hit Will on the head with the butt of a gun, knocking him cold. Then he pressed the gun into my ribs, and now I knew the truth—

I was staring into the eyes of the man who had killed my husband and abducted my daughter and would, I had no doubt, kill us all.

Chapter 27

James crouched closer to me at the sound of more gunfire. I was repulsed at having him so near, and furious with myself for letting my gun out of my hand, if only for a few seconds.

"If you're going to shoot me, get it over with. If not, get off me," I growled.

"Listen to me, Elizabeth." He loosened his grip around my neck. "If I wanted you dead, you'd be dead. So would Donovan. Ian isn't who you think he is. Why do you think he was in Denver? He killed Jayne Donovan, just like he did Stephen."

"You're lying," I spat out.

"He only needed you to get to Will, and you led him straight to him. Ian's been using you."

Using me. The words drummed in my ears. Was that what this had all been about?

"Damn it, Elizabeth, he's working for Ackerman. I saw Ian murder Stephen."

He shook me, and my head swam. Could my instincts have been that wrong? Could James be telling the truth? I couldn't think. Could I have let Stephen's murderer touch me? Bullets cracked all around us. One of them was lying.

"You must have found the code," James insisted. "That's how you found Will. Cara told me you have the book." He pulled a copy from his pants pocket and waved it in front of me. Cara had described it, and he'd found a copy, a copy of a pocket atlas more than twenty years old.

"I need that code," James insisted.

"Why?" I asked. "You've got Will."

The gunfire continued, and I wondered just how many cartridges one man could carry in his pockets.

"Never mind. Just give it to me," James insisted.

"I don't have it with me," I lied. I was buying time. The checkbook ledger was in my back pocket. "But I can get it for you."

"What'd he put it in? An address book? On a disk? What?"

He grabbed my shoulders and wrenched me forward.

Suddenly the shooting coming from the direction of the blue and white Cessna that had landed earlier stopped, and I heard a second engine kick in.

James pulled back to look over the roof of the limo. "Shit." He raised his hand into the air and fired a single shot. I heard the Lear's engine rev. The roar grew louder. The damn thing must be coming toward us.

And so, from the sound of it, was the Cessna.

Again James jerked on my arm, pulling me almost upright. The plane was only a few feet away. The Cessna was coming at an angle perpendicular to the jet. It looked as though it might ram it if they both didn't run over the limo.

Will moaned and stirred.

"Come on," James insisted. His arm moved around my waist, brushing the checkbook that had worked its way halfway out of my back pocket. "What the…" He looked at it, then at me, and reached for it.

I twisted back and shoved the ledger back down in my jeans.

"Is that it?" he asked. "Is that Stephen's—"

"No!" I shouted over the roar. I could see a rope ladder draped from the cockpit of the jet. "What about the others?" I asked.

"There's no time. Help me get Will up."

That was when I realized exactly what he was doing. He wanted to take Will and me with him, leaving Cara and Patrice behind—at the mercy of the man he'd just called a killer.

My hand found the front pocket of my jeans, and I pulled the canister of pepper spray into my palm and let James have it. One full spray in the face. He choked, his eyes tearing and swelling shut, his face flaming red. I grabbed his gun, pushed him away hard and reached for Will, who was already on his feet, favoring his injured leg.

Ian was shooting at the jet from the window of the Cessna, as the little plane neared. But the jet was already upon us. Bullets were skidding off its side, and I was afraid one might ricochet in our direction.

I left James struggling for breath and pulled Will around the side of the limo after me. Somehow I managed to get the driver's door open, and shove Will inside. The thug in the ball cap reared up, and I shot right through the passenger-side window, shattering it. He ducked and rolled.

Half on and half off the seat, Will tossed me the keys. I cranked the engine, threw the limo into gear, and floored the gas as I swung it wide in front of the hangar, away from the Cessna and away from the jet.

"Hey, what about Ian?" Will asked, pulling himself up to

where he could grab on to the door to steady himself and see what was going on.

I didn't answer. I just got the limo back onto the road and headed straight for the gate as fast as that monster of an automobile would go.

"Cara, Patrice, get ready," I called over my shoulder, praying they were both all right back there. "As soon as we stop, I want you out of that door."

At the gate I swung a hard left, pulled right up behind the SUV and stomped on the brakes. "Out," I shouted, and then came around the front to help Will. He leaned on my shoulder as I struggled to get him over to the car. Cara came up behind and took his other arm. I opened the back door and we managed to get him inside. Then she ran around to the other side, while Patrice slipped into the front passenger seat.

I had one more thing to do before joining them. Back inside the limo, I searched frantically for a lever and then popped the hood. Then I was out and around to the front of the car where I propped up the hood and searched the engine for the distributor cap. I had no idea where it was on that motor. I grabbed at the hoses, pulling two loose and ripping off a third. Then I climbed back into the SUV, tossing the hose over my shoulder into the backseat.

"What's this?" Cara asked.

"Consider it a souvenir."

"We don't have any keys," Will pointed out.

"Not to worry," Patrice assured him as I pulled the wires down from the steering column.

Gunfire still echoed across the runway, but we could see the Lear jet turning, readying for a takeoff. I tried not to look, concentrating instead on getting the SUV started. The wires sparked and the engine turned over. I threw the thing in gear and we took off down the road.

"What if Ian manages to repair the limo and come after us?" Patrice asked.

"I doubt that will happen," I said, tossing the limo keys out the window.

"He'll have a corpse and a bloody mess in the back," Cara pointed out.

"I don't care what he'll have as long as we have a fifteen-minute head start. Just give us that," I prayed. "Who do you trust?" I asked as I glanced at Will's reflection in the rearview mirror. We were on Will's turf. He had to know someone.

I pulled the SUV off a dirt road and under a bank of trees just north of Denver. No one passing by on the main road could see us, and the trees were thick enough that we'd be difficult to spot from the air.

"We need help," I added.

"Depends on what kind of help you have in mind," Will said. "The kind we've been getting—"

I jerked on the parking brake and climbed out, slamming the door behind me, and paced up and down the side of the car, trying to shake off some of my anger. I was furious with myself. I'd let my guard down with Ian. I'd even welcomed his touch. What was I thinking? That was the problem. I hadn't been thinking. I'd let my feelings cloud my judgment. I had to think clearly. I had to get Cara, Patrice and Will to safety.

"We need a phone," I stated. "A safe one that they can't trace."

"Mom, settle down," Cara admonished, following me out of the car.

Patrice got out, too, and placed a hand on Cara's arm. "Let

her be. She got us away from the airport, which is more than you or I could have done."

"But why? James has been—"

"Filling your head with lies," I finished. "Cara, he's not trying to help us. He was ready to abandon you and Patrice at the airport. That stupid phrase we used when you were little—"

"Mom, James knew it."

"So did Ian," I said, still unable to get over my own foolishness. "Your father probably told them one night when he was swimming in his damned scotch. Ian used it on me, too. All James has ever wanted are Will, the code and the code book."

"And what does Ian want?" Cara asked.

"The same thing," I confessed.

"What does the code lead to?" Patrice asked.

"Stephen hid people whose lives had been threatened—including Will. That's where Stephen was all those days, weeks, months when he told us he was off on digs. The code and the book tell where they were all hidden. How do you think Ian and I found Will? But why they'd care about having it now, I have no idea. Most, if not all, of those people have returned to their lives."

"Oh, Lord. I described the book to him." Cara's face lost its color.

"I know," I told her, pulling her into a hug. "He has a copy. And now—thanks to me—he knows what the code looks like. He'll find the original in your dad's belongings. Unless Ian gets it first. Hell. For all I know, he copied the damn code while I was asleep, and he knows exactly what the book looks like. Double damn! How could I have been so stupid?"

"You weren't stupid," Patrice stated. "We're all here together."

I let Cara go, brushing her tears away with the back of my hand.

"Mom, I'm so sorry."

"It's all right. Patrice is right. I've got the two of you back, and we have Will. That's all that matters."

I looked at my daughter's beautiful face and felt the pressure ease in my chest. Thank God she and Patrice were all right. I wanted to grab them both and disappear just like all those others that Stephen had helped.

Stephen. He'd sacrificed so much for the safety of others. So had I, even if I hadn't realized it at the time. I pulled myself up. I'd be damned if I'd let his last sacrifice come to nothing by letting Will fall into Ackerman's hands.

"Will, where can we get a phone?" I repeated.

"Look, I've got my own mission—to help my father take down Ackerman."

"I know," I said. "The only way to do that is for you to stay hidden until this trial is over."

"We could call the authorities," Cara suggested.

"That won't work," I insisted. "Ackerman has too much influence. If there'd been a safe way to protect Will within the system, his father would have used it."

I studied Will as he weighed my words.

"Who do you want me to call?" he finally asked.

"Someone with medical knowledge," Cara suggested, eyeing Will's leg through the open window. His wound had pretty much stopped bleeding. The bullet had taken out a chunk of flesh, not too deep, missing any arteries, but infection was a real possibility, one we weren't equipped to handle. And I was seriously concerned about the blow he'd taken to his head. At the very least, he had to have one hell of a headache.

"A guy I knew in college is a paramedic here in Denver. I don't generally call in favors, but he owes me big-time. There should be a house just a little ways up this road. People out here are friendly enough. We should be able to call him from their phone."

We found a small place about a half mile up the road. We let Patrice go to the door while Cara and I made sure Will was slouched down sufficiently that his notorious face couldn't be seen in the car. Patrice told the elderly woman who greeted her that we'd been in an accident and that a young man was hurt. The woman handed her a cordless phone out the door. Patrice brought it back to the car and gave it to Will.

It took him two calls before he reached Mike Danvers, and ten more minutes to convince him he was actually who he said he was. Mike promised to be there within the hour. No ambulance. No sirens. We thanked the woman and went back down the road, stopping where we'd first pulled off.

While we waited, I pulled Cara aside.

"Tell me what happened," I said.

"Mom, I screwed up. I called Phillip. I thought it would be all right. How could it not? I used a pay phone and a calling card like you told me to."

"James must have put a tap on Phillip's phone. His number would have been in your cell phone."

She closed her eyes and shook her head. She was good at beating herself up. It ran in the family.

"How long did it take?" I asked.

Her eyes popped back open. "What do you mean?"

"Before James showed up."

"The morning after we got to Taos Patrice and I went to get a late breakfast at a fast-food drive-through. I planned to find a computer to contact you that afternoon, but when we got back to the hotel—"

"He was in your room."

"How did you know that?"

"He wouldn't risk a public confrontation. He had to have you somewhere you were sufficiently isolated so he could make you listen. What lies did he tell you to get you to cooperate?"

"I don't know that they were lies."

I could tell she wanted this conversation on an equal footing, not parent to child. She was grown; she was smart; and she was right. I didn't know better than she did, at least not about James. I'd been equally foolish to involve Ian. All I knew was that James had been prepared to leave her while he took me and Will with him. In my book, that automatically made him a bad guy.

"All he said was that they were there to keep us safe, like Dad had asked him to do. And that he was really worried about you."

Ian had used almost those exact same words.

"How did they treat you?" I asked.

"Okay. They fed us, brought in movies—"

"You sounded drugged over the phone."

"I was having trouble sleeping. I had some of my pills with me and I took them. Is that so horrible? Why are you so hell-bent on assuming James was going to harm us?"

"He restricted your movements."

"They were protecting us. For all I know, he was only trying to help you at the airport. James said Ian would kidnap me to get you to cooperate. I believed him. I still believe him."

I didn't believe anyone. I wasn't sure which of us was better off.

"Can we talk about this later? I'd like to check on Will," Cara said.

I let her go, and Patrice took her place, leaning against the side of the SUV.

"So which is it?" I asked. "Was James hiding you or holding you hostage?"

"Damned if I know," Patrice said. "But if he's harmed a hair on Odin's head, I'll have his on a platter."

I noticed her holding her side, and wincing when she thought I wasn't looking.

"When did you get hurt?" I asked.

"I'm fine."

"No, you're not." I touched her waist, and she jerked back.

"I think I may have cracked a rib when I fell into the limo," she confessed.

It was a miracle we'd come through as unscathed as we had, but Patrice's injury would have to be dealt with.

Mike found us in forty minutes, driving his own car just as Will had requested. Will was resting with his back against a tree, Cara sitting next to him, when he arrived. While we'd waited, they'd passed the time talking, Will's injured leg resting across Cara's lap.

Patrice and I had sat watching them from our perch on the front fender of the SUV. It made me wish they'd met under different circumstances. Will seemed a little infatuated with Cara, offering her a shy smile I'd never seen from him—while she was obviously reconciling her impression of him with what she knew through the media.

"Cute couple," Patrice offered, reading my mind.

I smiled at her. She was keeping it together despite her pain, especially now that she was convinced both Cara and Will were all right. She was even trying to comfort me, but I was having none of it.

Mike, wearing dark slacks and a white shirt with an emblem on his sleeve, got out of his car and went straight to his friend. "Man, you lookin' good for a corpse."

"You don't look so bad yourself—for an ugly son of a bitch."

"You keep sweet-talkin' me like that and your girlfriend here just might get jealous."

Cara blushed but she didn't move away.

"Just do your job and skip the commentary," Will ordered.

Mike pulled on latex gloves and peeled back the torn cloth matted with blood to expose the wound.

Will sucked in a breath and I noted the contortion of his jaw. He was definitely in more pain than he'd been letting on.

"What the hell you been doing?" Mike looked skeptically from one of us to the next.

"Trying to stay alive," Will offered.

The young man nodded. "You about shocked the crap out of me with that phone call. Where you been these last months, bro? You had us all convinced you were dead."

"I know. Let's keep it that way, at least for a while."

Mike took a closer look at the lot of us. I was a mess, scrapes and bruises on my arms, my jeans torn, and Cara and Patrice both had blood all over them.

"Want to introduce me to your friends?" He swabbed Will's wound.

I shook my head.

"Probably better not to," Will said.

"Any of that your own blood?" he asked at the rest of us.

We all shook our heads.

"I don't suppose you want to tell me whose it is?"

"I don't think that would be a good idea," I said.

"We need a place to crash, Mike," Will said.

"All four of you?"

"All of us."

"You know, by law, I'm obligated to report a gunshot wound." Mike applied an antibiotic ointment, and wrapped gauze around Will's leg.

Will winced from the pressure.

"What gunshot wound? I cut myself shaving."

"Your leg?"

"He's going for that smooth look," Cara insisted. "No body hair."

"Yeah, right. You girls go for that?"

"Some of us do."

"Whatever rings your bell. Seriously, you need to have a doctor take a look," Mike warned. "You probably need a shot of penicillin and a tetanus inoculation. Maybe some stronger antibiotics."

"Take a look at his head," I added. "He took a blow."

Mike changed gloves and started to run his hands over Will's scalp, but Will let out a loud "Ouch!" and shook him off. "Later. Right now what we need are some clothes, so we don't look like we've come out of a slaughterhouse."

Mike frowned at him. "You mean you didn't? If your headache gets worse—"

"I don't have a headache."

"Of course you do. If you start to have double vision, get yourself to a doctor right away. Hey, man, I'm sorry about your mother."

Will didn't answer him. His eyes seemed distant and his jaw was clenched tightly. I didn't want to know what he was thinking.

Chapter 28

Mike must have owed one heck of a debt to Will—something about alcohol poisoning at some frat party their freshman year in college—because he took us back to his patio apartment on the first floor of a large complex and was able to get us inside through the sliding glass doors without arousing too much suspicion.

We assured him we'd committed no crime, had shot no one. That last part was a little iffy. I thought I'd wounded the guy in the baseball cap, but if I had, it hadn't slowed him down much.

Mike left to find clothes to fit the lot of us from a mission that was run to help fire victims. When he got back, he also brought some over-the-counter painkillers that he administered to both Will and Patrice. We were all clean, each having taken a turn in his shower. Jake's blood mingled with our own as it washed down the drain into Denver's sewer system. I wished I could wash my confusion away as easily.

We ate take-out pizza only because Mike insisted, but we couldn't play as if we were on holiday for long. After the food, Will was getting antsy. Patrice's side was hurting more, and she'd gone into the bedroom to lie down. I was having trouble keeping my thoughts off Ian. I wondered if he was dead. Or if he was coming after us. We needed to get moving.

As Cara cleared away the trash from the pizza, Will pulled me aside and said, "I need to let my father know I'm all right."

"He knows," I assured him.

"Why do you say that?"

"Ian is in contact with your father. He spoke to him when we were in Denver. Assuming he's still alive, he'll let him know."

"Even if he's working against us."

"Yes. To blackmail your father, you have to be alive. Ian will tell him to reassure him you're all right, or to keep the pressure on. They'll take you as soon as you surface," I added.

"At least they don't need you anymore," Will said.

"That's not true. For some reason they still want Stephen's code and his key."

"From what you said, both Ian and James may already have it. You and Cara need to continue to lie low, let things play themselves out without you."

"I'm not particularly fond of the idea of hiding and waiting for someone to come after us," I said.

"Am I supposed to be hearing any of this?" Mike asked.

"No," Will and I said in unison.

"All right, then. Guess that means it's time for a beer run."

"Excellent idea," Cara agreed as she came back into the room drying her hands.

Mike grabbed his keys and took off again.

"Let me see the key," Cara said. "I wonder why James is still interested in it."

I dug Stephen's checkbook out of my back pocket and handed it to her. I explained how it worked as she flipped through it.

Will took the ledger from Cara. "Let's try one."

Cara grabbed it back and tossed him the pocket atlas. "The entry right before yours is dated November 12."

"Who's it made out to?" I asked.

"Robert Maynard."

"What's the account number?" Will asked.

"It's 226-62D5"

He looked in the index. "Charlotte Amalie, St. Thomas. Hey, I say we check it out, go down for a little interview with the guy, assuming he's still there. A little beach, a little sun and sand…"

Cara punched his arm, and he let out a loud, fake "Ow."

"I just don't get it," Cara said. "If this Robert Maynard guy has nothing to do with Ackerman, why would he care? Give me a pen."

Will tossed one over to her. She took it and worked backward through the book, jotting something as she went.

"What are you doing?" I asked.

"Figuring the years. He didn't put down complete dates, only months and days. I want to see how long Dad was hiding people." It took her a few minutes. Then she looked up. "Mom, this goes back to shortly before you and Dad were married."

"What?" I managed.

She nodded. "All the way back to July 17 of—"

"July 17," I repeated. "You're certain?"

"Absolutely. Why?"

"That's the day that Josie disappeared." *My God. Stephen, is that when all this started? Did you hide Josie?*

"Mom, are you all right? You're white as a ghost."

"Don't you see?" My voice cracked. "What if…what if…"

"Mom, are you saying Aunt Josie might still be alive?"

I swallowed hard as it all fell into place. Of course. Stephen and Peter knew how much danger Josie was in. They knew Ackerman. He'd been my brother-in-law. I'd told Stephen that Nick had been abusing Josie, and he'd witnessed his behavior firsthand. The worst part was Nick had money—or at least his family did, lots and lots of money that Nick later inherited. She'd wanted desperately to have a child, and I'd wanted desperately for her to wait. I knew that if there was ever a custody battle, money would determine the outcome. If it had ever come to that. Leaving Nick would have been like signing her own death warrant. She was his chattel, to do with as he pleased.

I was sitting bolt upright now, every nerve in my body tingling. Ackerman hadn't killed her. Stephen and Peter might have offered her their help. Stephen had hidden her. *Oh, dear God, please let me be right. Please let Josie still be alive.*

"Read me that first entry," I ordered. "Who was the check made out to?"

"Alexis Gerhart."

"And the account number."

"Um, 238-87C2."

I didn't have to look it up. I recognized the number. Josie was in British Columbia where Stephen had taken Will, where he had his cottage, the cottage he'd never taken me to, the cottage that allowed him to check on her. *Damn it, Stephen. Why didn't you trust me?* I'd been so close and never once suspected.

Why hadn't she come back?

"I've got to go back to British Columbia," I stated. "I've got to warn Josie before they go after her. For some reason Ackerman still wants her. I've got to let her know." I stood, ready to leave, then and there. I had to get to Josie in time.

"I'll get our things together," Cara said.

"No. You stay here."

"Mom, you know me better than that. I'm not about to let you go off by yourself to Canada. If you're right, James will find the original ledger in Dad's things and he already has the book. That means Ackerman will have men hot on your heels. They'll know you figured it out."

Patrice's voice came from the doorway and I looked up. "Ian may have copied the ledger, as well, and he knows what the atlas looks like. Stephen probably confided in him about Josie's disappearance. So he'll be there, too. They'll all be there, and they'll all know Josie's alias."

I felt like I was being crushed. Just as I'd finally found Josie, so had her enemies.

"You'll need my help," Will offered. "I know that area really well."

"But..." I started, swallowing hard and realizing I was outnumbered and unable to do a thing about it.

"How long will it take us to get there?" Cara asked Will.

"We can be out of here by tomorrow if we're lucky," he said.

We couldn't repeat what Ian had done. We didn't have the connections. It took us two days to make all the arrangements, days I was loath to lose.

Patrice was in too much pain from her ribs to come with us. Mike moved her in with his sister who was a practical nurse. Then Cara, Will and I hopped a flight for Seattle, bought a clunker of a car from a lot not far from the airport, drove across the border into British Columbia and took a ferry to the island, just like hundreds of people did every day. No one blinked an eye.

Fortunately Will knew the area. He'd had a couple of

months to explore, and, being the social type, had passed a lot of the time by getting to know the locals. Unfortunately, he'd never heard of Alexis Gerhart.

Ian, of course, knew about Stephen's place, making it too dangerous for us to use. So we took rooms at a little inn built on the water. Will picked up some weapons he had stashed, and, without even unpacking our bags, I tried the first most logical method of finding someone. I looked in the phone book. Her name wasn't there.

"She's probably married, which means she's no longer a Gerhart," Cara pointed out, lounging on the hotel bed, her knees bent and her shoes resting atop the bedspread.

"She never was a Gerhart," I snapped.

I stared at her. I didn't bother to tell her to take off those shoes. My mind was still reeling.

Josie. Married. She'd had a life, at least I prayed to God she had, a life I knew nothing about.

"So," Cara added, "how do you find someone whose name has changed?"

I slapped the book shut and let it drop to the floor. "You want the long method or the short one?"

"Mom, I don't think we have time for anything long."

"I start asking around. I go to the grocery store. I—"

Cara reared up on the bed. "You can't do that."

"Oh, yes I can. My sister ran off over twenty years ago. I've finally tracked her down to Cowichan Bay. Does anyone have any idea where Alexis Gerhart is? I won't need to give them my name, at least not my real one."

Will came out of the bathroom, towel drying his hair. I saw Cara's eyes take in his bare chest. It wasn't as though she needed much of a push to appreciate Will. He was charming when he wanted to be, just as she'd said he'd be. And he had that arrogance for her to work on. What more could a girl want?

"Ask Sandy Parsons, the social editor for the newspaper," he said. "She knows everyone in town. You'll find her office on the main street, between the barber shop and Cynthia's Diner."

"You look like Lexy a little around the eyes, and you have the same curly hair," Ms. Parsons observed from across her neat wooden desk, in the tiny old storefront building that served as the newspaper's editorial offices. She must have been close to sixty.

I tried to mask my surprise. Just as no one is ever prepared for someone to die no matter how long it is in coming, I wasn't really prepared for Josie to actually be alive, no matter how fervently I'd hoped I was right.

"You okay?" Ms. Parsons asked. She got up and poured me a cup of water. I took it gratefully. I forced the muscles in my throat to relax enough to accept some of the liquid.

"You have some of Lexy's mannerisms, too," she added with a clip to her consonants.

I dropped the curl I'd been twisting, put down the cup and let my hands rest in my lap.

"Lexy married Nathan Estes not too long after she came here," Ms. Parsons went on. "Six months maybe. No more than that. He's a fisherman. Owns his own boat. Their twins are great. Handsome. All grown-up now. I think John is in med school, and Stephen's working with his dad."

Sons. Twins. My nephews. One named after Stephen, the man who had saved their mother's life.

I couldn't speak. This woman whom I'd never seen before was privy to my sister's life, had seen her, interacted with her over all of these lost years. She treated that contact so casually, so unaware of how precious it was. Damn it. It wasn't fair.

"She was a real asset to the community. Helped out at school. Worked with pollution control."

"Was?" My mouth went dry.

She pursed her lips. "You don't know, then?"

Oh, God, let her say anything except what I know she's going to.

"She died about three weeks ago."

I took a sip of water, grateful to have something in my hands to steady them. "How?" I managed.

"Accident. She drowned. Took the boat out one night by herself when she should have known better. The winds were up. We did a big write-up about it." She turned and rummaged through a stack of newspapers, pulling one out and passing it over to me.

"Pity," Mrs. Parsons added. "Those boys adored their mother. So did Nathan. Don't know how they'll get along without her."

I stared at the headline. The black-and-white letters swam. I couldn't read. I could barely see. Mrs. Parsons handed me a tissue. That's when I realized I was crying.

We were too late. Ackerman's goons had gotten to her. They had killed her. But how the hell had they found her—weeks ago?

Chapter 29

About three that afternoon, we found Josie's house, a nice old Victorian in a little neighborhood at the end of town. It was authentic, not one of those new imitations. It was painted the palest blue with white trim and hinged navy blue shutters that could be closed during a storm. The large porch wrapped around the front and down one side. Lace curtains hung in the windows. On the roof was a widow's walk. Absently I wondered if Josie had stood there watching for her husband to bring in his boat. She must have made peace with the water. When we were children, she'd have nothing to do with it.

"Mom?" Cara shook my shoulder. "Aren't you going to knock?"

We were standing on the sidewalk, and I was staring.

"Are you sure you want to do this?" Will asked.

I shook my head. "It's not a matter of wanting. It's a matter of having to."

We climbed the three steps to the porch, and I rapped my knuckles on the door, which had a drape of black cloth stretched over the arch. I saw movement behind the etching on the oval glass of the door. It opened and I got my first glimpse of my sister's husband. Nathan was average in height. Muscular, not from working out but from hard work. His face was creased from the salt air and the harsh sun. I immediately saw why Josie would have liked him. He had an honest look about him, thick, close-cropped hair and a kindness about his mouth. A black band was wrapped around the upper part of his plaid sleeve. A mourning band.

"Come in, Elizabeth," he said, as though he'd been expecting me.

We followed him inside. Josie's colors hadn't changed. The dusty rose she'd loved so well dominated the sitting room he led us into. She'd blended it with a gray-blue and a cream to create a restful, welcoming room. I went to the mantel over the old fireplace. It held photos of her boys. Sailing. Fishing. Playing soccer. There was something in their faces that reminded me of Cara, and I wondered if my own sons would have looked like them if Stephen and I had had any.

Josie had had a good life.

But I hadn't been part of it.

"So you found us after all," Nathan said.

I turned and saw him offer Will his hand. I sensed this wasn't their first meeting.

"You know each other," I suggested.

"Nathan brought us in. By boat. He worked with Stephen. They never told me his name."

I nodded. So that was how they'd met. The young fisherman who'd helped Stephen and the young woman without a family, with a new name, so vulnerable, so ready to put down new roots.

Stephen had purposely kept Will from meeting Josie, protecting her to the last. But he couldn't protect her from everything, not after he was dead.

"You shouldn't be here," Nathan said, looking first at me, then at Cara and finally at Will.

"Where should we be?" I asked. "Stephen's dead." His eyes didn't flicker. "But you already know that."

"Ackerman's men have Stephen's code and the code book," I said.

"Then you need to leave before they get here."

"You can't possibly believe Josie's death was an accident." I'd raised my voice louder than I intended. "They've already been here, Nathan. Which one of them killed her—Ian Payne or James Lowell?"

"Mom." Cara touched my hand. "Ian and James didn't have the code three weeks ago when Aunt Josie died."

I heard her words, but I couldn't believe fate could be that cruel. Only men. Somehow one of them had discovered Josie's location earlier and killed her. That was the only way her death made sense. But then, why all this cat-and-mouse game with me? And why hadn't they gone after Will?

Nathan lifted his chin. "A squall kicked up. She took out the boat when she shouldn't have been on the water."

"I read the newspaper account," I said. "Josie wasn't stupid. She didn't swim, and I'm certain she'd never go out on the water alone. Why was she out there?"

"You need to leave," Nathan said, tension straining his face. "You have no business here, not anymore. Please. Just go away and leave me in peace."

I wanted to rage at him, but I didn't. He'd just lost his wife, his sons' mother. How she died didn't begin to compete with the fact that she was dead.

"I want them in my life," I insisted, holding back tears. "Your sons. I want them to know Cara."

Nathan stole a look at her. He knew her name. He had known Stephen. And he'd known Josie. He probably thought he knew me. She and I shared a lot of characteristics, stubbornness just one of them.

"Later, once things have settled down, you can come back then. But please, for now, go home. Enough people have died."

"Where is she?" I whispered.

"God's Rest. It's a little cemetery about a mile down from here. It's where my family is buried. You can go by on your way out of town."

We stopped at a flower shop, and I had the woman make up a large bouquet of cut flowers in mauves, pinks and light blue. It didn't look at all like a funeral arrangement, which was exactly what I wanted. Such a hollow token, but it was all I had to give.

Then we walked the short distance to the cemetery, passed through the huge iron gates without a word, and found the Estes family crypt, shaded by large trees.

The entrance was dark and the concrete cold. I stopped, reluctant to leave the sunshine.

"You don't have to go in there," Cara said. "We can leave the flowers out here by the door."

"Yes, I do," I insisted.

Will waited at the open doorway, keeping watch as Cara followed after me.

So this was to be Josie's final resting place, buried under an alias in her adopted country, among her husband's kin. Her vault was about shoulder high. I laid my cheek against the cold metal, forcing myself to keep from thinking what lay inside.

My fingers traced the letters on the bronze plaque. Alexis Gerhart Estes. I wanted to scratch them away. She was Josie, damn it! My poor Josie. My dear sister. Dead again, all these long years after I'd buried her in my heart.

I set the flowers on the concrete, told her I was glad I'd found her at last, and whispered to her that I loved her. My last words were a promise uttered so that Cara couldn't hear. "I'll get him," I swore. "I'll get the man who took you from me, and then it will finally be over."

That night I tossed in the bed at the inn, afraid I was keeping Cara awake, but unable to do anything about it. I would find time to mourn, but that time would have to come later. At that moment all I knew was rage.

About five in the morning I fell into a fitful sleep. I dreamed of death and black banners and funeral plaques. A shroud descended over my head. Everything went black and I choked. I couldn't breathe and woke in a fit of coughing.

Cara came to my side, calling for Will to bring some water. They forced me to drink and I finally came to my senses. We were at an inn in Cowichan Bay, British Columbia. Josie was dead, not me, and we had work to do.

We packed quickly, loaded the junker with our bags and went for one last visit to Josie's grave. Anyone looking for her now would find her already dead. I whispered once more that I loved her, as I again ran my fingers over her name on the bronze plaque. Alexis. Alexis Gerhart Es—

I jerked my hand back as if it had been burned.

Josie, dear God love you. I should have known.

It was then that I laughed, choking on my tears. Cara put an arm around me. I swiped at my cheeks and smiled at her. "C'mon. Let's get out of here."

"Are you all right?" she asked.

"I'm more than all right."

I climbed into the driver's seat of the old clunker and turned onto the road.

"Ferry's the other way," Will pointed out.

"I know."

"Then why…" Cara asked, turning to shrug at Will in the backseat.

"I intend to meet them right here. I told you before we left, this is where we'll make our stand."

"But Aunt Josie's death—"

"Doesn't change a thing," I insisted.

"I can't believe you actually want James dead," Cara said. "Mom, I stayed with that man for days. There's no way—"

"That you can see into any man's soul. You saw what he wanted you to see. When people are murdered, the killer's neighbors, friends, families all say there's no way their son or daughter or friend could have done this. Yet there lies the body. Somebody did it. Not an ogre or a boogeyman. A human."

She shivered. I knew exactly how she felt.

"Nathan's right," Will agreed. "Ian and James are headed here, if they're not here already."

Cara frowned at me. "You told Nathan that either James or Ian killed Dad. Do you really believe that?"

"We need to visit your uncle."

"My uncle," Cara repeated. "Now that's a concept to wrap my mind around."

"Won't he be out with the boat?" Will asked.

I looked over my shoulder. "He'll be home. And I don't think he'll be at all surprised to see us at his door. We're not the only ones who think it's time to put a stop to Nick Ackerman and his associates."

* * *

"Get the hell away from here," Nathan growled. "Now."

"No. Hear me out." I walked past him with Cara and Will following after me into the house.

He shut the door behind us, but he was seething, his fists clenching and unclenching at his sides, his gaze traveling back and forth through the front window, studying the wooded area across the street.

"Do you mind?" he asked, nodding Will and Cara toward the kitchen. "I need to have a few words with Elizabeth."

"Not at all," Will agreed, grabbing Cara's arm and leading her off. They'd no doubt be listening at the door.

"It's too late," I told him. "Are they watching the house?"

Nathan nodded, his gaze straying again out the window. If he was working with Stephen, he must have had some training, at least enough to spot surveillance. "Since yesterday morning."

"Then they've already seen us. They must be waiting for us to leave Cowichan Bay before they take Will and kill Cara and me. The only thing that's keeping us alive is our contact with you and their assumption that you don't know they're here. Making their move now would blow their cover. Ackerman wants Will, but he also wants Josie. Why does he still care after all these years?"

Nathan's silence bored through me.

"What's your plan?" I asked Nathan. We understood each other—Nathan and me—two stubborn people, neither willing to give an inch.

He eyed me. "Why do you think I have a plan?"

"Stephen's been dead for a month. His grave marker won' be ready for at least five more. How many years have you ha Josie's engraved?"

"Some things move faster up here."

I shook my head. "Your grief is superficial. You lived with a woman more than twenty years, she bore you children that I have no doubt you adore, but you don't even have a catch in your voice when you speak of her. What's more, you've kept your boys away when you would need each other more now than you ever have in your lives."

"What are you suggesting?"

"For years I've been afraid the danger in Stephen's life would engulf Cara and me, and I've been preparing for it. Josie knew exactly what her danger was. You both knew what you were up against even if I didn't. I know she's alive. You should have waited to put the marker up. No one dead a few weeks has her name on her grave. Where is she?"

He opened his mouth to tell me what I knew would be a lie, but then he closed it.

"No, don't," I said. "It's better if I don't know."

"Walk away, Elizabeth. Take your daughter and run."

"We have nowhere to run. There is no safe place for us." And I had too much invested. I'd lost Stephen and I'd lost more than twenty years with Josie. Will had lost his mother and might yet lose his life. I was staying. One way or another it would end here.

"Stephen lived knowing Ackerman was working his evil for years," I told Nathan. "I want to sleep when I lie in bed at night, not wonder when he might show back up in my life. I can't get Stephen back, but I can damn well get Josie. I'm in, like it or not." I leaned back against the wall. If he wanted me gone, he'd have to physically throw me out.

"How can you possibly help?" he asked.

"Do you know either Ian or James personally?"

"No. I got out of the organization shortly after Lexy and I married. I helped Stephen with Will Donovan only because he was bringing him here and because Ackerman was behind the threat, but that's it. Lexy had had enough."

"Well, I've had dealings with them both. Stephen trusted them, and that's why he died," I added. "I wouldn't turn my back on either one. Ian seems to be working alone with Peter Hirsch's support unless he's picked up an accomplice since I last saw him. James had one man with him at last count, but he's probably recruited another one or two. I can help you. I can identify them both."

He clenched his jaws. "Lexy won't—"

"Need to know. Faking her death was a wise move, but it isn't going to fool either James or Ian, not if I figured it out. I know you have a contingency plan. So tell me how you're going to take them down. They will kill us if we leave now, Nathan. I won't let that happen to my daughter."

"Lexy never wanted you involved."

I was having enough trouble dealing with Nathan calling Josie Lexy. "Stephen chose not to tell me—"

"Not Stephen. Lexy. She wouldn't let Stephen tell you. Lexy knew that if you knew she was alive, you'd insist on seeing her. She refused to risk it, for both your sake and the boys'."

I found a chair and sank into it. My knees were too weak to hold me up. Stephen wanted me to know.

"Surely she didn't expect to live her whole life and never see me again," I insisted.

"She had a fit when Stephen bought that place up here. Said he planned to retire and bring you here to live once he'd settled things, once Ackerman was out of the way."

All this time I'd blamed Stephen for how screwed up our lives were. And he'd taken it. Never once letting on that it was at least partially misplaced. I pushed back my anger. Telling or not telling me hadn't been his choice. Or mine.

Damn it, Josie! Who were you to make all the decisions!

Yet Stephen had planned to make it right...after he'd dealt with Nick Ackerman once and for all. So many secrets wedged between us.

"How did you know about Stephen's death? And that they might be coming after her?" I asked.

"When I didn't hear from Stephen after two weeks, I checked on the Web. I found his obituary in the *Washington Post*. That's when I opened the envelope he'd sent us."

Of course. He would have left a warning, in case he failed. Why had I thought I'd be the only one to receive an envelope?

"It said to put our plan in motion, that there was a possibility the secret of Lexy's location would be compromised."

So Stephen had helped Nathan with his plan to keep Josie safe.

"You arranged for Josie to die in an accident at sea," I said.

"I hoped they would accept Josie's death," he said. "And now *you're* here, creating more problems."

"Don't try to pull that on me, Nathan. For the first time in all these years, I know what I'm a part of. These are my enemies every bit as much as they are yours. I'm not the problem. I'm the cavalry." I found myself unexpectedly on my feet.

He smiled.

Damn. How many times had I heard Josie say something similar when we were kids? How many times had she said something like that to him?

"I plan to lead them straight to her," he said.

The shock must have shown on my face. "You can't be serious."

He leaned toward me. "They're watching the house, waiting for me to make a supply run. She's been in hiding for weeks now. They'll assume I'm providing her with fresh provisions."

"You're not?"

"No. She's far from here and she's stocked with enough shelf-stable food to last a year."

"You're going to lead them into a trap."

"Yes."

I was certain Josie knew nothing of his plan. She would never have let Nathan go through with it, not alone. Josie was no coward.

"You'll need help taking them down," I said.

"No. I don't want anyone else hurt. This is my battle."

"And mine. If you don't have help, they'll kill you, no matter how well trained you are. I've seen these men in action."

"You need to go," Nathan repeated.

"You're not going to get rid of me. Understand? I've lost too much in life to lose Cara, and I will not lose Josie again. Or let her lose you. When is it going down?"

He paused, studying me. I wasn't moving and he knew it.

"Look, Nathan, I can be a liability or an asset. Take your choice, but you're not getting rid of me."

I could see the resolve soften in his face. And something else take its place. Maybe relief.

"Tomorrow night," he said. "I'll leave the house shortly after 2:00 a.m. I'll be carrying two grocery bags. I'll load the boat with them, and then I'll head up the channel about eleven miles. There's an old marine research facility on one of the small islands. It's completely isolated. It's been abandoned for about six years."

"So if there's gunfire…"

He nodded. There would be no unnecessary casualties.

"You know this place?"

"Every inch. I spent twelve years of my life working there."

My surprise must have been obvious.

"What? You don't think a fisherman goes to prep school and college? Marine biology, Stanford University." He shook his head at me. "Priorities change. My current research is private, financed by my fishing. I live the life I want to live. At least, I have up until now."

My sister had chosen well. So had I. I just wish I had realized how well before Stephen died. Yet, he had made a major miscalculation by not trusting me. Ultimately his deceit had destroyed our marriage and each of us in turn. He should have told me. Josie need never have known.

I pushed Stephen to the back of my mind. I had to stay focused. Josie's life was still in danger, as was mine and Cara's and Will's. And now Nathan's.

"Let me take the supplies," I suggested. "That will free you up to follow behind them."

"Can Will go with you?"

"I don't know. He has other business to—"

"I'm in," Will announced, coming into the sitting room.

"Me, too." Cara was right behind him.

I looked at my daughter and my heart leaped to my throat.

"What about Cara?" I asked Nathan. "We can't leave her here alone. They might try to grab her again. But if we take her with us—"

"I'll take her with me," Nathan said. "She can drop me near the dock on the island and then conceal the boat where the trees and bushes overgrow the water's edge. We'll need it to escape, and she can make sure that happens."

He turned to Cara. "I'll leave the radio with you. If things go bad for us, you alert the authorities and get the hell out. If by some miracle some of us survive, you'll need to bring the boat to pick us up at the shore. Agreed?"

Cara nodded. I could tell she was none too happy to be left out of the fight, but it was necessary for her safety and my sanity.

"I've already compromised the lock on the fence that surrounds the compound," Nathan assured us. "When we get to the island, you'll see the lights in the building where Lexy is 'staying.' That's where, God willing, this will all play out."

Chapter 30

Nathan spread a layout of the compound on the kitchen table plus the floor plans of all the buildings.

"I've rigged the two main buildings and the Quonset huts that served as labs with explosives, and set live charges at the wharfs. The place has been abandoned for years and is scheduled for demolition. The plan is to lure them onto the island by making them believe Lexy's hiding there and I'm taking supplies to her."

Josie, I corrected in my mind.

"I'll strand them," Nathan continued, "and then systematically take them out one at a time on my terms. A body here and there in the rubble and the only thought will be they were somewhere they shouldn't have been when the explosions went off."

"To do that you'll have to be able to track their movements," I said, "know where they are at all times. Will and I can help with that."

"I can help, too," Cara added.

"We'll need you to stay with the boat throughout this operation," Nathan told Cara firmly. "Once they land, I'm blowing up their boat—and the one Elizabeth and Will go in on. That will leave only one functioning boat, the one you're to guard. The last thing we need is to find ourselves with no escape route and have to explain to the authorities what they'll find on that island."

He didn't add that Cara might have to defend the boat from James or Ian. That was understood and something I couldn't afford to think about.

"What are you using to trigger the explosions?" Will asked.

"Remote controls, trip wires and deadfall devices," Nathan explained.

"What if they find you?" I asked.

"I'll blast us out of the water and let God sort us out. No one is getting to Lexy."

"Josie has no idea what you're planning, does she?" I asked. "If she did—"

"You've done what you had to do, Elizabeth, and I'll do what I have to do," Nathan said.

He'd like to survive this, but he'd go down protecting Josie and his sons if that was what it took. He'd stepped right into the same trap as Stephen.

"We can't afford to lose you," I insisted. "This won't be the only battle."

"No, but it's the one we're fighting now," he reminded me.

"When it's over, Ackerman will still be alive," I reminded him. "You don't know Nick. You've never stared into those cold eyes. Losing men won't bother him. Money will just buy more."

"Then we'll take them out, too."

"It's going to be dark as hell out there," Will reminded him. "How are we going to be able to see them?"

"We have night-vision glasses, and spotlights are mounted in two areas—the water tower and ringing the roofs of each of the brick buildings." Nathan located each of them for us on the map. "When we were doing sensitive work for the government, state-of-the-art security was installed."

"State-of-the-art from the Stone Age," Will pointed out. "That was what? Twenty years ago? Motion detection and what else? Sirens? Any of it still work?"

Nathan shrugged.

"Great. A security system with no security," Cara said. "Now that ought to scare the bad guys."

"What exactly does work?" I asked, sending Cara a behave-yourself look.

"The lights do, at least they did a few weeks ago. I checked the day I confirmed Stephen's death."

"You say you plan to entice them to where the charges are set by turning on lights in the buildings by remote," Will said.

"Yes. They'll come to check it out."

"Hate to tell you," Cara said, "but I suspect these guys learn a hell of a lot faster than lab rats. After that first big boom, they'll be on to your little game with the lights."

I shook my head. "Cara's right. It won't work past the first blast. I like Will's plan using him and me to lead them into the buildings. They'll think we're setting the devices."

"I don't like it. It's too risky," Nathan said.

"Where are the trip wires?" I added

"At the entrances to the Quonset huts," Nathan said.

"Okay. That means you've got two dead. Think that will do it?" Will asked.

Will had made his point. Nathan's plan was too simplistic, but then, he'd put it together when he thought he'd be in this fight alone and hadn't expected to survive.

"James has allies," I reminded him. "And then there's Ian. He may have men with him, too."

"You'll need Will and me as human lures," I insisted. "Without us, it won't work. You can't be all over that island by yourself. You need to be able to set off the explosives."

I could tell Nathan was frustrated, but he was past arguing. "If you go in, turn on the lights, and let them see you there. I'll set the charge, but I won't be able to make sure you're clear of the area unless I get a visual on you. You don't show and that sucker still goes up in under four minutes."

"I can live with that," Will agreed. "You?"

I'd learned to live with a lot of things I never thought I could. I nodded.

"Then it's agreed. We take them all out," Nathan said. "To-night."

We left soon after the strategy session and made our way back to where we were staying. I reasoned Will, Cara and I would be safe only because anyone watching wouldn't want to tip their hand to Nathan with Will's kidnapping or a couple of dead bodies in a very public place. For some reason, Ackerman seemed to want Josie almost as much as he wanted Will. If we were lucky, that would be his downfall.

We made our final preparations, changing our clothes and gathering supplies.

Close to one-thirty in the morning, we drove back to Nathan's place. Will was itching for a fight, so antsy he could hardly sit still.

"Calm down," I warned, pulling the car into the driveway. We were all dressed in black, with stocking caps and gloves in pouches at our waists.

We slipped into the dark house. Nathan had left the door

unlocked. He met us just inside and handed Will and me each a paper grocery sack. No one said a word, but Nathan did lean over to give me a kiss on the cheek. "For luck," he whispered, and I saw just a glimpse of the gentleness that had won Josie's heart. Cara's hand squeezed my arm and then she disappeared into the dark behind Nathan. We'd already said everything we needed to say to each other. She knew exactly how much I loved her.

Will and I were quickly back outside, down the steps and at the car. We laid the bags on the backseat. Then I threw the transmission into Reverse and swung backward onto the road.

The boat, a small outboard with the keys in the switch, was where Nathan had promised it would be, the second slip from the end of the dock. We climbed in, each carrying a bag, and drew on our caps and gloves. Holding a penlight in my mouth, I examined the map that Nathan had left by the front seat. Red lines and circles told us exactly where to go. It was a good ruse to give James or Ian time to catch up, not that I thought either would need it. In the hours following our confrontation with Nathan, I'd used the maps Nathan had given us to memorize every turn, every bend of the water around those islands, every placement of every building.

Will cranked the engine and we were off, speeding into the darkness.

The island was lush with vegetation, shutting out the moonlight that shimmered on the water and wrapping most everything beyond the water's edge in twisted, menacing shadows. My heart picked up a staccato beat. I felt as though I'd entered a surreal world, and the opening I'd come through was rapidly sealing behind me.

We tied the boat to the small pier. The only sounds were water lapping against the dock and insects heckling us from the woods.

Through the trees I could make out artificial light off to my left, coming from windows some two hundred yards away. It shone like a beacon, leading us toward the compound. If I were looking for Josie's hideout on that island, that was where I would go.

We stopped at the gate of the wrought-iron fence that rose some twelve feet into the air with spikes on the top of the rails.

Neither Will nor I spoke a word. I glanced over my shoulder and saw nothing. They were out there, somewhere in the water, just beyond sight and hearing. My skin prickled knowing they were watching us, waiting for us to get enough ahead of them before they docked.

The pier was the only safe place to tie their boat. The inlet was too treacherous otherwise, so they had no choice but to wait until we cleared the area—at least, that was Nathan's reasoning.

My pistol lay heavy against my hip, an uncomfortable reminder that I might actually have to shoot someone. I shoved the thought to the back of my mind and prayed that I'd have the strength to do whatever I had to do.

My pepper spray, as always, was wedged in my right pocket, not that I expected to get close enough to anyone to use it. If I did, our plan would have gone terribly wrong. James would know that I had it. This time I wouldn't catch him off guard, assuming he didn't simply shoot me dead if he got the chance.

Will was armed with a .45. I suspected there was a knife in his boot. Unlike me, he was itching for this fight, but neither of us was trained like the men we were up against. We had only two things going for us: a personal investment, which was sometimes, God willing, worth more than training; and an unshakeable determination.

In the clearing just beyond us, the yellowy brightness of

the moon bathed the abandoned facility in a strange light. We pushed against the gate and it opened, just as Nathan had assured us it would. Vines had grown up and over the fence, threatening to reclaim the whole area, but those on the gate, cut from their roots, crumpled in my gloves. We stepped through.

There were only two brick buildings, yet the compound seemed massive, with half a dozen Quonset-type huts off to the right. The bricks of the large buildings had been brought from the mainland. Expensive but worth it to anyone stranded here in the middle of a storm.

Nathan had also warned us about the pools covered by tarps. Three large tanks, some twenty feet long by fifteen feet wide and designed to hold large marine specimens, lay directly in front of the brick buildings, invisible in the dark. Despite the tarps, they would be filled with water from the rains.

The location of those tanks was etched in my mind. One wrong step meant, at the very least, a broken leg or ankle. For me, it would mean much more. Unlike Cara, who took after her father and swam like a fish, I shared Josie's terror of water even in daylight, even in the calm of a public swimming pool. I shook off my thoughts and strove to get my bearings.

The dormitory lay, as Nathan had said it would, to the left as we headed forward. That was where the light was coming from. It had been burning for weeks now, running off a generator ever since Nathan had confirmed that Stephen had died and Josie's secret might have been exposed.

For a moment I wondered if we'd all been playing the fool, having grown so paranoid that we were convinced Ackerman's men had been able to follow us to Cowichan Bay. I didn't have long to think.

Will touched my arm as we detected the whir of an outboard faintly in the distance. It took every ounce of my will-power not to turn around. The noise stopped. The boat must be drifting toward shore.

We forced ourselves to maintain a steady gait, so whoever was out there could follow us to the dorm. Inside the main door we dumped the grocery bags. We had very little time. We ripped off our gloves, and, with Will holding his penlight under his chin, we attached flare guns to our belts, along with large flashlights. He cut the light and we pulled on night-vision goggles. The black turned to an eerie blue-green.

Silently we headed toward the light source itself, a room near the front. In the hall, we gave each other a quick hug for luck and took off in opposite directions down the dark corridor. My hand was on the knob to the outside door when I heard the first explosion. It came from the area of the dock and it rocked the building, rattling the windows. I slipped outside and dashed for the trees as the second explosion erupted.

The men were on the island.

Fire spread its brightness as it devoured the dock. Both our own boat and the one behind it were engulfed in orange flames. I tore off my goggles to watch the glow. Instinctively, I ducked as a third explosion boomed as fire reached the boat's engine, soared upward and skated across the water on gas from the outboard.

If whoever was on that boat was still alive, they now knew this was no simple supply drop. With the explosions, Nathan had drawn his line in the sand.

Leaning over to catch my breath, I felt the bile rise in my throat. When I raised my head, I searched the flames. I could see no movement, not in what was left of the boats, not on the pier. Where were they? *Who* were they?

I'd heard no screams. If someone had died or been injured

or set on fire, I'd have at least heard a splash, seen something. But there was nothing now that the explosions had stopped, only silence and fire. I shook off my thoughts. If I wanted to stay alive, I had to move. I had my own tasks to perform.

I slipped my goggles back on and headed into the darkness, to the fence. Nathan had promised me an opening. Three yards farther up, there it was, a broken spike that gave against my hand. I lifted it and shimmied through. On the other side, I followed the fence, staying under the cover of the dense vegetation that surrounded the compound.

My objective was the water tower in the back of the main buildings. It was a steel structure that rose some sixty feet into the air from a concrete base, designed to catch rainwater and filter it down to the buildings below. Nathan had given me a simple task: flip a switch on the foot of the back leg of the tower. That meant crossing into the clearing, drawing attention to myself. I found a second opening in the fence and slipped back through.

I surveyed the area and caught a flicker of movement near the back of the dormitory. Whoever was out there was now out of sight. Neither Will nor Nathan should have been in that area.

I didn't give myself another moment to think. I took off for the base of the tower as fast as I could run. A bullet skidded off the structure and I dove forward, hugging the ground. Damn it. That was no friend in the shadows, but at least the shot had located him for me.

The box was at the base of the leg, some sort of generator. I crawled forward and flipped the switch outlined with fluorescent tape, hit the ground again and closed my eyes, covering them with my hands. The brightness shone right through my eyelids, as the tower lit up with huge spotlights that illuminated the back side of the buildings.

I grabbed off the night vision glasses and heard a loud moan. Then another. They must have been wearing goggles also. The light would have left them temporarily blinded. Four shots spit from somewhere above me. Good. Will was in place. When I opened my eyes, I saw a figure sprawled on the ground, and a second at the other end of the dormitory.

Will dropped down next to me from above.

"Good going," I told him.

"I aim to please," he said.

"You did not just say that," I protested.

He shrugged. "Actually, I can't believe I hit one. I'm not that good a shot."

Damn. He was right. When I looked back, one of the figures was gone, the other struggling on the ground.

"Hot damn. Get out of here," Will whispered. "They know where we are."

I rolled as a shot ricocheted off steel. Then I dashed for the safety of the trees. Will disappeared in the opposite direction, as a second shot whizzed past. Someone was hot after me.

Frantically, I fumbled for the opening in the fence that I'd come through earlier. Prying it up, I slipped through and dove into the thick vegetation pushing against the fence. I could hear my pursuer fumbling after me as I began putting distance between us. I headed right. He, whoever he was, was supposed to follow me, but I'd hoped to lead, not be chased. My heart was pounding as I slipped back through a large hole in the fence at the side of the main building and sprinted toward the side steps that still lay in darkness. I made it to the door and pushed it open. Heading straight ahead, I came down the hall toward the large room in the front that served as the compound's cafeteria. Nothing stirred the darkness inside as I cautiously opened the door and crept across the tiled floor.

Slipping behind the serving counter, I located the toggle switch resting on a shelf under the serving line and flipped it. Fluorescent light filled the room. I checked my watch. Now all I had to do was get the hell out in the next four minutes—before Nathan blew up the place. Piece of cake.

I reached for the door behind me, which was supposed to lead through the pantry to the loading dock outside. The knob turned in my hand. The inward thrust sent me careening into the stainless steel counter, knocking the breath out of me. I stared up at the man towering over me.

Chapter 31

"Get up," a gruff voice ordered. But I could barely move. The pain shooting up and down my arm pinned me to the cafeteria floor.

I stared up into Ian's solemn eyes and cursed my earlier stupidity.

A part of me had prayed that he wouldn't be the one to show. I'd hoped James was the one in league with the devil. Even now, looking into those icy blue eyes, I felt there was something softer behind them. My reasoning told me there wasn't.

Ian, too, was dressed all in black. I saw no blood, so he hadn't been the man Will had hit near the back of the dormitory. That must have been one of his men.

As I struggled to regain my footing, I felt his hand grasp my injured arm and practically lift me off the floor, sending spasms all the way to my shoulder. I stifled the cry in my throat. My gun was in my pouch, but there was no way I could get to it.

"Hold it right there." James had burst through the door leading in from the hallway, his gun drawn and pointing straight at the two of us.

So they were both here, and I was right in the middle of them.

Holding my arm in a death grip, Ian trained his gun on James. James had blood on his sleeve. Had he been at the water tower, the one who had shot at me as I fled?

I did the only thing I could think of to do. My teeth sank into Ian's index finger. He cursed, and his grip loosened just enough that I was able to pull free and roll to the end of the counter. He dared not take his gun off James, and that was all that saved me. As I rolled I ripped the flare gun from my belt. When I came up, Ian was at the other end of the counter. The three of us stared at one another with our guns drawn, mine pointing at Ian's head.

James smiled. "Good work, Elizabeth. Now back up and ease your way over to me."

My gun turned in James's direction.

"She's not the fool you think she is," Ian warned.

I swung it back toward Ian. "Where's Will?"

He was supposed to meet me at the loading dock, the way Ian had come in. We were to padlock that way out and then the other two exits to give Nathan time to blow the place. If Ian had harmed him…

"I don't know."

"Tell me where Josie is so we can get her safely out of here," James ordered.

I opened my mouth.

"Don't say a word," Ian warned before I could say anything.

"Which one of you did it?" I demanded. "Which one of you killed Stephen?" I stared at Ian, then James. Their faces gave nothing away. My hand tightened around the grip of the flare

gun. How long did I have before Nathan blew us all to hell?
Three minutes? Less?

Before I died I wanted to know, so I could personally kill
the bastard who had murdered Stephen.

"Would you believe me if I denied it?" Ian asked.

I shook my head. "What happened at the ski lodge?"

"We took rooms and met with Edward Donovan," Ian began.
"He knew his wife was in danger. Ackerman was ready to make
good on his threat. I was the one designated to bring her out."

"She was to leave on a flight in a private jet out of Denver
the next morning with me," James broke in.

I trained the flare gun on Ian. If it went off, it'd make one
hell of a hole. "I saw you murder Jake."

"I had no choice."

"That's right. You know Ian's a murderer," James stated.

For a moment, I thought Ian might actually shoot James
right then, as angry as he was. If he did, I could take him down
at the same time. But it really didn't matter. If I managed to
keep them in that room for another two minutes, they'd both
be dead. And so would I.

"Stephen trusted you," Ian told James. "I trusted you. How
much did Ackerman pay you to turn?"

"Enough!" My gun returned to James. "Who died at
Reagan National Airport?"

"I don't—" James began.

"Say that one more time, and I'll shoot you." I edged backward toward the window. If they took their eyes off me for
half a second, I might be able to shoot out the window and
dive through it before the whole room exploded.

"Leo Ryan," James stated.

Ian added, "My backup."

"He tried to kill me at the airport," James insisted.

"He flew in from California to meet me." Ian's words were clipped, precise, his anger again under control. "James ambushed him. He was already in the area. He drove in from Denver. He was there when you buried Stephen. He stole his body."

"Where were you when Stephen died?" I demanded of Ian, trying to push the confusion out of my mind.

"Escorting Donovan back to Denver."

"And you?" I motioned toward James.

"At the airport, making flight arrangements to take Jayne Donovan out."

Which one was lying? My head hurt. I had nothing to go on, nothing more than gut instinct to help me sort it out. That wasn't enough. I was at the window, but I had less than a minute left.

A volley of shots sounded outside. Will, Nathan and the others were still at war.

The window shattered behind me. I threw myself flat on the floor as shards rained down. For a moment I was convinced the whole building had exploded. Someone inside was already on the move, so I did the only thing I could. I rolled onto my back and shot straight up. The flare took out the lights and part of the ceiling in a spectacular burst of energy as it went through to the floor above, leaving us in darkness.

Another explosion, this one close outside, boomed, lighting up the night and rattling the walls.

I heard a woman scream, then a splash. I vaulted over the shards that littered the floor and out through the window. The scream had sounded just like Cara. What was she doing on the island, away from the boat?

One of the tanks lay outside the window. The impact must

have thrust her into it. Once in the pool, she would tangle in the tarp and risk drowning even though she was a good swimmer.

Someone rolled through the window after me, nearly knocking me flat. He shoved me down, thrust his gun into my hands, and dove into the pool. I heard the whap of his body connect with the tarp, as the room we'd exited thundered into a fire ball.

I was surrounded by fire with the cafeteria in flames behind me and the blaze from the Quonset raging to one side. Heat radiated in waves and flames licked high into the night air while shards of metal littered the ground, reflections of orange dancing across them. Yet I could see little past the immediate glow of the fire.

The pool remained a huge black hole in which someone struggled against what looked like a giant black jellyfish billowing the length of the pool. Then the man disappeared, sucked into the shadows beneath it. I saw no sign of Cara.

Flat on my belly, I lay down the gun and reached out to draw back the heavy plastic, tugging with all the strength in my one good arm. But it remained securely in place. Only the two ends waved loosely. Once under the water, whoever was in that pool would be disoriented, trapped, and unable to come up for breath.

A shot rang out and I rolled onto my back, fumbling for the gun that had been thrust into my hands, but I couldn't find it. A flare burst in the air. Will or Nathan must have sent it up. It left me exposed, easy pickings for anyone trying to take me out. I continued to roll as a bullet slammed into the concrete rim of the pool, and suddenly I, too, was in the water, on top of the tarp. It swayed and bucked from the enormous struggle taking place beneath it. Another bullet tore into the tarp as the light from the flare faded. Once again we were lit only by the heat from the fires. Another shot came from behind me, as I fumbled at my pouch. My gun slipped out and fell into the water as I finally managed to extract the automatic knife from inside. I pushed the button and tore into the tarp with wild, long strokes. Water gushed upward.

A gloved hand reached through the opening and grabbed my arm, pulling me down hard, but the fabric held. A head, gasping and choking, emerged. The man let go of my hand only long enough to force my fingers around a slender wrist I pulled with all of my might and another face emerged. Somehow I got my arm across Cara's chest and under her arms, well aware that the tarp would only hold if all my body weight was spread out evenly. I dared not move or try to bring her farther out of the water.

I closed my eyes, gunshots popping. My arms ached. I didn't have much strength left, and my grip was weakening. Without warning, the strained threads of the tarp parted. The last sound I heard was a rip as water rushed over me.

I swallowed water as I sank into darkness, but hell if I was going to let my daughter drown in some specimen tank. I kicked fiercely. Her arm circled my neck as I felt myself buoyed upward, splitting the water, only to be washed over once more. We came up again, gasping for precious air. Her arm went slack, but I hugged Cara to me and kicked upward with the last ounce of strength in my body. We rocked forward and my hand hit concrete. Someone grabbed me under the arms. I struggled against him as I felt my daughter slipping from me.

"Hey, hey. It's all right. We've got her." It was Will's voice. So he was still alive. *Thank God.*

He pulled me up far enough that I was able to grasp the thick vegetation and drag myself the rest of the way out of the pool. The fires from the cafeteria and the Quonset hut still blazed.

A light shone in my eyes. I cursed and blinked them shut.

"You need to sit up," he told me.

My ears rang and I felt wet, not just outside, but inside as well. I managed one word, "Cara."

"She's going to be all right." Again it was Will's voice. "She's with James."

"James?"

"He's helping her. She took in a good amount of water, but you got to her in time."

So it had been James who had come through the window after me, James who dove in to save Cara. A part of me had been sure it was Ian.

"Where's Ian?" I asked, pushing myself upright. Just breathing was an effort.

"I don't know."

I turned enough to look at the fire that still raged inside the building. He couldn't have survived that inferno, not if he were still inside. I ached for the man I'd thought he was, even as his betrayal stung my soul.

So he had killed Stephen and he would have killed me, as well. I'd let him seduce me into trusting him once and that had been a mistake. So why was a part of me now grieving?

I shoved thoughts of Ian from my mind. This fight might not yet be over.

"Have you seen Nathan?" I asked.

Will shook his head.

"What happened to you?" I asked. "You were supposed to meet me at the loading dock." I eased back down on the ground, not caring that I was lying in mud. All my strength was gone.

"I got distracted by the guy I wounded near the water tower. He took me on as a personal project."

"Did you kill him?" I asked.

"No, but I had him on the defensive. He made it to the first Quonset hut."

"So he was the one who tripped the explosive." My voice had gone hoarse. That made two. "Where's the other one?"

"Cara took him out. It looked like he had you in his sights," Will said. "He was aiming through the cafeteria window. She shot him as he pulled the trigger. It was his stray bullet that shattered the glass."

"How do you know?" I asked.

"I watched it happen as I came around the building," Will stated. "I saw the lights come on in the cafeteria and heard voices. I ducked out of sight, thinking you might need me, but I had that slight problem with the creep who was trying to kill me."

So Cara had taken out the last of Ian's men. Or were they James's?

James had put himself at risk to save Cara. And he'd given me his gun.

Someone knelt beside my head. I raised up on my elbows, and James laid Cara next to me like a father whose child had fallen asleep on the sofa.

"Have you seen Ian?" I asked again.

"He didn't make it out of the cafeteria."

So it was over. Stephen's murder had been avenged, and we were safe. It made me feel sick.

James brushed Cara's cheek with the back of his hand and then patted my arm before he drew away.

And then he was gone.

"Cara," I said, reaching for her.

"I'm here."

"If you'd just listened to Nathan and stayed with the boat—" I started.

"Save it, Mom." Her voice was faint and wispy. She cleared her throat, choked a little, and I wondered exactly how much water she'd swallowed. "You could simply say thank-you, you know," she added.

She had saved my life.

"Thank you," I whispered.

Chapter 32

As disgusting as that mud was, I would gratefully have lain in it and slept for the next several hours, but that was not going to happen. I pushed myself into a seated position about the time that Nathan appeared.

"What was with that flare?" I demanded. "You could have gotten me killed."

"The lights on the roof of the building weren't working and I had to locate you. We'll talk later. Right now we need to move it," he commanded. He was wearing a wet suit and held a rifle with a strap. "The authorities will be here any minute. Half the coast must have heard the explosions and seen the fires. We'll be lucky to make it out of here before they show."

"I thought you said this place was scheduled for demolition."

"It is. But people don't like explosions in the middle of the night. They'll report it."

I forced myself onto my feet. "Cara. She can't—"

"It's all right," Will said. "I've got her."

He lifted her amid her protests and hefted her over his shoulder. Whatever her injuries, her mouth worked perfectly well. The four of us headed toward the water as quickly as we could manage, considering the darkness and the vegetation.

"I kept waiting for you to blow up the cafeteria with me in it," I whispered to Nathan. Vines pulled at our feet.

"I considered it. I saw you go in, but I never saw you come out, not until you rolled through that broken window. I gave you a few seconds to clear before I set off the charge."

"You were pretty adamant about the four-minute rule when we made our plans."

"Yeah, well, you don't have to live with Lexy. I knew that if through some miracle I survived all this, she'd kill me if I blew up her sister."

I stumbled and he steadied me.

"Where were you?" I asked.

"By that time, on the roof of the dormitory."

"James is helping us," I told Nathan, realizing he might not know that, smarting again at how wrong I'd been.

"He was the one who pulled Cara out of the pool? Sort of figured whoever did that was on our side."

"How do we get out of here?" Will asked, shifting Cara against his back. She was mumbling something, but none of us could hear her, which was just as well.

I heard a loud smack, followed by Will's "Ow!" and realized Cara had somehow found enough energy to slap his rear, about the only part of his body she could whack considering how he was carrying her.

"One more pop and I'll drop you headfirst," he warned. "Or retaliate in kind."

I could barely force myself forward, yet the "kids" were playing.

"Why do we need anyone else to beat up on us when we've got each other?" I asked.

Cara reared up and then collapsed. "You try being treated like a sack of flour. It's hard to breathe hanging upside down."

We passed through the gates of the compound and were almost to the edge of the cove. Nathan shushed them, and I immediately realized why. There was motion ahead. Moonlight shone on someone standing near the water's edge.

Nathan pulled up his rifle. I no longer had a weapon. James had retrieved his before he left, and mine lay at the bottom of the pool. Cara was also unarmed. Will set her down and I put my arm around her to keep her upright as Will and Nathan went forward together.

The figure straightened. As he stood, I caught my breath. He didn't raise any weapon, only his voice. "They're all accounted for—my man and the three that came with Ian—all dead." It was James.

Just as I'd figured: James had checked and then come to the water to wait for us.

I helped Cara forward. She was more in control now, putting on a better show than she needed to, and really glad to be off of Will's shoulder.

"Will you be all right?" I asked.

"Perfect," she said.

I shook my head at her, and I joined the men at the water. A splash split the water as Nathan dove in. Within minutes he was back with the boat, its outboard motor humming loudly.

"Move it," he commanded. "We're pushing our luck as it is."

We had to wade out chest deep as the dock was in ruins. The water was so cold that my teeth chattered too hard to speak. James pulled himself into the boat, followed by Will. The two of them helped Cara and me aboard, and Nathan spun the boat around and out toward open water.

"We can't just leave the bodies here," I insisted, thinking of Ian. He'd brought Stephen home to me, just as he'd said. It didn't seem right to leave him—or the others—on that abandoned island.

"We can't very well take them with us," James said. "Even if they are identified, they'll never be linked to any of us."

"Yes, but—"

"Let it go, Mom." Cara heaved a sigh. "Even you don't have to micromanage a shoot-out."

Cara was right.

James was right, too. I had more worries than the authorities finding corpses on a small, abandoned island that had been ravaged by fire. I sank back against the side of the boat, shivering, and not just from the cold.

The five of us—Nathan, Will, Cara, James and I—took our soaked bodies back to Nathan's place, taking turns in his shower. He clothed Cara and me in Josie's too-big jeans and sweaters. They helped, but we were both still chilled to the bone. He offered Will and James some of his own clothes, but James had a bag in the back of his SUV down near the dock. Nathan's clothes wouldn't have fit him anyway.

Nathan gathered our old things into a large plastic trash bag, tied it and stuffed it behind some boxes in the back of his garage. He'd have to dispose of them later. We had something else we had to do first, and I wasn't about to put it off another moment.

"You're not going with us?" Cara asked James as he gathered his gear at the front door.

His gaze met mine. James had risked his life to save Cara, but I didn't want him to know where Josie was, and I'm sure he knew it.

"It's better if I don't," he said. "I'm headed back to Washington to report to Peter Hirsch. He needs to know that Ian is dead. I'll be back here in two days to help in any way I can until Ackerman's trial is over." He hefted his bag onto his shoulder and withdrew his gun from his jacket pocket.

"You keep this," he said, pressing it into my hand. "Promise me you'll carry it with you at all times, in case Ackerman somehow gets wind of where you've gone. Promise me."

I nodded and accepted the gun.

"Good. Two days. Here," he repeated.

Cara hugged him. Will and Nathan shook his hand. I was grateful to him, but distrust dies hard.

He left and, ten minutes later, we took off, as well.

As we drove some hundred miles up the coast, I watched through the windshield of Nathan's Hummer as the sun sparkled across the water and then began its rise into the sky. The ocean was starkly serene and somehow hauntingly lonely. Victory, knowing that people had died—especially Ian—offered an isolation and a coldness that I hadn't expected. If I'd only trusted James from the beginning, perhaps things would have been different.

I'd cared for Ian, even if I'd never allowed myself to trust him completely. I found myself irrationally mourning him, mourning the quiet strength and the ready philosophy of the dedicated teacher, not the cold-blooded traitor who had crept up behind Stephen and snapped his neck. Intellectually I knew it must be true, but I still couldn't accept that I'd been so thoroughly duped.

Ian had offered me answers, and maybe that was why I'd

been so taken in by him. No, it was more than that. He'd made me feel an equal partner, so unlike Stephen who had kept even Josie's existence a secret from me.

Cara stirred in the backseat, made a noise and snuggled down next to Will with her head on his shoulder.

"You're awfully quiet," Nathan said, glancing over at me and then back into the rearview mirror. We weren't being followed. There'd been no cars on the roads in any direction for the past hour.

"I'm fine," I assured him, not at all certain how my voice was going to sound when I spoke. I didn't want him worrying about me. And I didn't want him guessing what I'd been thinking about. "How much longer before we get there?"

"Forty-five minutes. Maybe less."

"It's not over," I said.

"Not yet," Nathan agreed. "Not until Ackerman is in prison for good."

I settled back and allowed my eyes to drift shut. I'd think about Ackerman later. And Ian. I had someone else to concentrate on for the moment.

Josie was alive. And she was about to get one hell of a surprise.

Chapter 33

The house was a small, white, two-room cottage with a porch facing the inlet and a slanted tin roof. As we entered, we were met by the scent of something tealike and lemony, like what my mother used to make for my sister and me when we were sick. It was coming from a pot on the gas stove under the gingham-curtained window.

The front door had been left open, allowing air to sweep straight through and out the back door. That was where I walked and, through the screen, caught my first glimpse of Josie in half a lifetime. Her back was to me as she hung bed linens on a line, but I caught her profile and then her face as she moved easily in the early morning, unaware of my presence, clothespins in her mouth, positioning a sheet. The blueness of the water was full behind her, against the greenness of the grass that rolled almost to the water's edge. The breeze picked up stray strands that escaped from the clasp that held her hair up off the back of her neck.

She took my breath away. I'd foolishly expected Josie to be given back to me as she'd been taken from me, a slim and vivacious young woman with rich brown hair cascading in ringlets down her back. Instead, the years had etched fine lines around her eyes, filled out her cheeks and added the slightest droop to her jaw. Her hair was blond now, no doubt fighting some gray, and she'd added some weight at her waist and in her thighs.

My eyes stung. She was beautiful. She looked a little like our mother. God. Our mother. She'd be frantic with worry, wondering why she couldn't get in touch with me or Cara. But before long, she, too, would finally have our Josie back.

I pushed against the screen, and she looked up as the springs creaked. The end of the sheet she'd been holding dipped to the ground, the one corner pinned to the line keeping it high enough to flap in the salty breeze.

She stared at me, standing there in her doorway, and then her face crumpled. I, too, must have looked much as our mother had the last time she'd seen her.

"Don't you go crying on me," I insisted as I went toward her. I could feel tears welling in my own eyes. "You've got a hell of a lot of explaining to do."

She grabbed me and buried her head against my shoulder, her tears soaking into my sweater, her arms so tight around me I could barely breathe. I held on to her, too, with all my strength, fearing that if I let go, for even a moment, she might evaporate out of my arms.

Josie passed the sugar bowl as we sat together at the small table. She was beaming, just like I was. I studied every little nuance to her movements. I couldn't take my eyes off her. She radiated life.

Nathan, Will and Cara had all gone outside onto the porch to give us time alone.

I passed the sugar back to her. The tea was naturally sweet.

"Since when did you stop putting sugar in everything you drink?" she asked.

"Since I hit forty. And you can stop with Mom's diversionary tactics. I asked you a question—why did you run? You were never one to back away from a fight."

Her eyes held mine. "It wasn't me I was worried about."

I could feel my brow crease. "Who, then?"

She looked at me as though I was dense. How many times had I seen that expression growing up? I never thought I'd see it again.

"You've been to my house, haven't you?" She pushed the tray of biscuits and jam in my direction.

I searched my memory, and suddenly I knew what she was saying. The photos of her sons sitting on the mantel. They'd reminded me of Cara, but they'd also reminded me of someone else I couldn't quite place. I should have guessed. Of course. The answer had been right in front of me.

"John and Stephen—they're Nick Ackerman's sons."

She nodded. "I was three months pregnant when I left.

"How long had the abuse been going on?" I asked, feeling the muscles in my jaw tighten. How blind could I have been?

"It began a month or two after we were married."

I felt my throat tighten. My sister had been in trouble, and I hadn't helped, despite any suspicions I'd had. "You never let on."

"Foolishly, I thought I could make him stop." She forced her mouth into a smile. "I wasn't so smart back then. When I discovered I was pregnant—"

"You knew you had to get out."

"Don't think less of me, Elizabeth." Her eyes pleaded with me to understand, and I did. I shook my head, unable to speak. I could fault her for staying with Nick, but never for protecting her children. I would do anything for Cara. I'd expect her to do no less for my nephews.

"It wasn't just me anymore," she continued. "Nick threatened to take the children away—assuming I didn't miscarry from his abuse—as soon as they were born, if I left him. With his family's money, I had no doubt he would do just that. I couldn't let an abuser raise my children."

"Why didn't you tell me?" I asked, stifling the betrayal I felt. "I would have helped you, Josie."

"I tried to the night Nick knocked me down the stairs. You weren't home. I called Stephen's apartment frantically looking for you."

"You spoke with Stephen?"

"Yes, but Peter answered the phone. They were still rooming together back then. You'd gone over to Mom and Dad's. Stephen was making spaghetti sauce."

I'd forgotten how Stephen liked to cook. It'd been years since he'd made it for me.

"Peter could tell I was shaken up. Stephen got on the extension and they made me repeat exactly what Nick had said and done. Peter kept me on the phone while Stephen came to get me. I spent that night at their apartment."

"You should have been in a hospital." And Nick should have been in jail, the bastard.

"I was only bruised," she insisted.

I reached across the table and covered her hand with my own.

"Stephen wanted to go after him," Josie continued, "but Peter said no, that harming Nick would only ruin all of ou lives and threats would do no good. He made me an offer. He said he had the money and the know-how to make me disappear. They'd both been trained in intelligence in the service. He said he knew people. They could provide me with a new identity and a place where I'd be safe. Peter warned me not to wait. But the condition, at least to begin with, would be that no one would know where I was."

"And you agreed? Just like that?"

She shook her head. "I couldn't believe what he was saying. I couldn't imagine giving you up, giving up Mom and Dad, my friends, my degree, my future."

"But they knew Nick."

"You have to understand that I had no choice. Either Stephen would go after Nick or I'd have to flee, because I knew Nick would hurt me or my children. I couldn't ruin Stephen's life, your life together—Elizabeth, you loved him so much—because I'd been so stupid as to get involved with Nick."

I shook my head again. In her mind she'd been protecting both Stephen and me. What she didn't realize was she'd created the first wedge of deceit that would ultimately drive Stephen and me apart.

No, Stephen, you and I did that on our own. You should have known never to lie to me.

"If Nick had been your husband, would you have risked Cara?" Josie asked.

Nick would never have been my husband, but she knew I'd never risk my daughter.

"Stephen and Peter could have done it together," I insisted. "They knew how to dispose of Nick's—"

"Listen to yourself," Josie interrupted. "You've lost your reason. That's what I was feeling. Stephen wasn't a killer.

You knew him better than anyone. He was a trained soldier, but this was different. He would have done it, but I couldn't let him, not when there was any other way out. Peter kept talking to us, telling us that taking another person's life would change Stephen."

Hiding Josie had changed him. Letting Nick live had ultimately killed him.

"Surely you could have gone to the authorities," I suggested.

"With what? There were no marks on my body that couldn't be explained away, no documented history of physical abuse. Nothing but a threat I couldn't substantiate, and Peter's utter conviction I had less than twenty-four hours to act."

A chill swept over me, and, despite the warmth of the cottage and the tea, I shook with cold. Nick had always scared me. He had charmed Josie, but looking into those eyes that never seemed to smile, I had seen the lack. His subsequent acts had borne out all our fears.

Josie closed her eyes and I could see the guilt etched in her face. "Stephen and Peter had warned me several times to stay away from Nick before I married him." She opened her eyes and squeezed my hand. "But, Elizabeth, he seemed like the perfect man. He was well educated, handsome, so charming and so rich. I never saw his dark side. Not until after we married.

"I made the best decision I could," she insisted, her voice strong. She'd had a lot of years to weigh her choice, a lot of years to examine all that had happened. "We all did."

"So that's how Peter's organization was born," I stated.

"Yes. I was the first. A short while later, Peter was interning in the D.A.'s office. A rapist was acquitted and began stalking the woman he'd raped. She was his third victim, but the jury wasn't allowed to hear that he'd been charged before. Peter offered her their help. They hid her and Peter put a tail on the man. They anonymously called the police as he broke into another woman's apartment. He was caught before he harmed the fourth woman. Once he was convicted, she went back to her family.

"Another case followed, this one with an informer whose testimony was ultimately blocked from trial. He wasn't eligible for witness protection. They hid him, and, as far as I know, he's never come back. Word got around on the underground, and people sought Peter out."

"How do you know all this?"

"I helped them for a while, with the ones they brought into Canada. They sometimes came through here before going on to their permanent destinations."

"You actually became part of the network?"

"Only for a short time."

"So you stayed in touch with Stephen all these years."

"He would come visit me to bring me news about you and Cara, and to give me photos. I watched my niece grow into a lovely young woman. About a year ago he bought a place in Cowichan Bay.

"I'd never intended to stay away forever," Josie added. "I thought it would only be for a few months, maybe a year or two at the most, but then the boys were born. Nick moved back to Denver. He was already rich but everything he touched turned to gold. He became more and more powerful. I followed the growth of his political influence. I knew him, Elizabeth. If he'd ever gotten the chance after what I'd done to him, he would have killed me."

"It wasn't what you'd done to him, it was what he'd done to you," I reminded her. "And then there was Nathan."

"Yes." She smiled.

"You gave up your education, your career goals."

"No. I did my graduate work at the university here. Peter provided a transcript of my undergraduate work in my new name."

"Forged?"

"It was my work. I'd attended every one of those courses, earned those grades. I teach as an adjunct professor. There was a time when I considered moving back, under my new name, but—"

"There's no way you could have risked anything happening to your children."

"If Nick had tried to take them from me, if he had touched one hair on either of my babies' heads…"

But her babies weren't babies anymore. A lifetime had passed between us. It was almost too much to bear. I felt tears spilling from my eyes. She put an arm around me.

"Elizabeth, it's all right. You're safe now. We're all safe."

"No, we're not," I managed. "Ackerman is still after Will, and when his men don't come back, he'll know you're still alive."

Chapter 34

"You can't go back to Cowichan Bay tonight," Josie insisted.

She drew a long wooden spoon from an empty coffee can on the counter and stirred what she called her can-can stew, which was made entirely from shelf-stable meats and vegetables. She scooped up a taste and offered it to me. It was amazingly good, thanks to the dried herbs and garlic she'd added.

"See? Not so bad after all."

"I remember you vowing never to learn to cook," I said.

"I also vowed never to do dishes, mop floors or make my bed, once I was able to escape Mom's tyranny."

"Right. You couldn't waste your valuable time on trivial tasks."

"What was I? Twelve?"

"Closer to eleven."

"Yes, well, reality set in. I discovered that once I dropped something or failed to put it away in my own apartment, it stayed right there, waiting for me to pick it up. Whatever the item, it would outwait me.

"And as far as cooking was concerned, I soon found that Lean Cuisine offered only so many options. It got worse when the boys were born. They came out of the womb hungry. Once they started playing hockey, I couldn't make enough food to keep them full."

"You miss them," I said.

"With every breath I take." She turned the burner down and flipped on the stove, but I saw her smile slip from her face before she put it back on and turned to me. "They're all grown-up now. I'll see them soon, and lucky you will get to meet them. Now that Ian's dead—"

"Nick will send someone else."

"So you keep reminding me. James will help."

"Yes," I agreed. "There's James."

"But first you've got to get some rest. None of you got any sleep last night. Look at Cara. The girl still hasn't gotten her color back."

I stopped beating my muffin batter and took an appraising look at Cara. Her color wasn't great, but it was a heck of a lot better than it'd been a few hours ago.

"I'm fine," Cara insisted, sitting next to Will on the little couch. "I'm also over twenty-one and legally responsible for making my own decisions concerning my health. I'm not sick unless I say I'm sick."

"And saying makes it so, I suppose," I said.

"Just feed her," Will said. "Her stomach is growling so loud I can barely hear you over it."

Cara threw him a dirty look. "He's lobbying on his own behalf. I'm not even hungry."

I filled the muffin tin. "You're right. She needs rest. We all do. I'd like us in decent shape before we meet back up with James tomorrow."

"What's worrying you?" Josie asked.

"What do you mean?"

"You're frowning. Is there something about James—"

"No," I cut her off. "We've got planning to do, and you've only got two beds. You can't put all of us up without some of us sleeping on the floor."

"Not to worry." Nathan came up behind Josie and put his arms around her waist. "There's a bed-and-breakfast about ten miles up the road. I can drop you and the kids off there."

"No," I said louder than I had intended. "Not me. I know the two of you could use some time alone together, but Josie and I have a lot of years to make up for. I want to stay here tonight. You take Cara and Will. They'll rest more comfortably there."

And I'd rest more comfortably knowing they were there.

Josie rinsed the Dutch oven and handed it to me to dry. The sun had gone down and darkness was settling around the outside of the cabin. Nathan, Cara and Will had been gone almost an hour. As I listened to Josie chatter, I kept one ear on the road outside. Nathan should have already been back.

Tinny music played "Clair de Lune," startling us both.

"My cell," Josie said, quickly grabbing my dish towel and wiping her hands. "It hasn't rung since I got here. Nathan insisted we only use it for emergencies."

She lifted the phone from an end table. "Hello?" She smiled at me and covered the mouthpiece with her hand. "It's all right. It's Nathan. When he got in the Hummer to come home, he discovered he'd picked up a nail in his back tire. It's flat and so is the spare. He's trying to find someone to fix it, but the B and B is pretty much out in the middle of nowhere."

Josie seemed relieved. I was anything but.

"How long's it been since he found it?" I asked.

She said something to Nathan and then reported, "Fifteen minutes."

"Get off the phone. Now," I said.

"Later, baby," she said and hung up.

I should never have left that island without seeing Ian's dead body for myself.

"What's wrong?" she asked.

"You know what's wrong. The flat tire is no accident. It's Ian. He's found us."

"Oh, God, no." Josie hit the lights, and the cabin swam in darkness. I pulled James's gun from my waistband. Moonlight through the window glinted off metal in Josie's hand. It looked small enough to be a derringer. I hadn't known she had it on her.

"Do you think he's already here?" she asked.

"Yeah. He's had plenty of time to get back from the B and B. I think he's been watching us through the window."

The phone rang again.

"Turn it off," I commanded. She hit a button and slipped it into her pocket.

"Both doors are locked and bolted. All the windows have alarms."

"You had everything open this morning when we came in."

"When you came in, only one person knew I was here. Nathan. That's not true anymore."

Seemed paranoia ran in the family.

"What's your guess as to how many are out there?" she asked.

"Only one person was unaccounted for."

"Good. That means we outnumber him."

"Have you got anything bigger than that pop gun?" I asked.

"Yeah. In here."

She led me into the bedroom and drew something about eighteen inches long from under the bed. I couldn't see it well in the dark, but I was betting it was a sawed-off shotgun.

"We might do better if we separated," I suggested.

"Not a good idea."

I didn't argue. She knew the lay of the land a whole better than I did.

Josie threw back the rug next to the bed, fumbling over the hardwood. In seconds she raised a trap door.

"Go, go," she insisted.

I heard the back door burst open as I ducked through. I landed roughly on my rump in the soft, moist earth of the cabin's crawl space, the stagnant odor of dirt that had lain here undisturbed for years filling my head.

Josie scrambled after me. She pulled the lid down and I heard it click into place.

"As soon as he gets the lights on, he'll know where we went," I whispered.

"He won't get the lights on," she promised. I heard a snip and saw a spark. Josie was prepared right down to the electrical shears waiting on the other side of the trap door.

"Go forward," she urged, "toward the lattice. He's sure to have a flashlight."

I wished we had one, too, but we didn't. Or Josie couldn't find it in the dark. Either way, we couldn't risk light escaping up through the boards in the floor.

My shoulder hit a cinder block support as I crawled toward specks of light. I bit my tongue to keep from curs-

ing. I would gladly have rolled on my back and shot straight
up through the floor, but if I'd missed, our pursuer would
know exactly where we were. We had less freedom of
movement than he did and no idea what weapons he might
have.

At the lattice, I swung my legs in front of me and kicked
hard, splintering it outward. Josie crawled through after me
and we struggled to our feet.

The grass was silvery in the moonlight, but most everything else was coated in amorphous darkness.

"Where to now?" I asked.

She pointed toward the woods, and we both took off running. I looked over my shoulder and realized why Josie had
taken us out that way. No windows on that side of the house.
Whoever was inside would have to come outside to see which
way we'd gone. And if we made it to the trees before he
cleared the porch, he wouldn't know.

Hidden by the night, we paused at the edge of the woods,
holding our breaths. A figure emerged from the back of the
house. Tall, shrouded in black, all I knew was that he was
armed and he was surveying the yard with a spotlight, his gun
following his every turn. The light went out and he stepped
back, enveloping himself in the house's shadow. I couldn't
imagine what he was doing, but then I saw it, a tiny, blinking
red light, the only bit of color amid all that darkness.

"C'mon. If we can make it half a mile through these
woods, there's a cabin where we can borrow a car," Josie
whispered.

"No, wait," I insisted. "What's he holding?"

Her breathing steadied as she grew still and watched.

"I don't know, but the hell if he isn't coming our way."

She was right. The man had stepped out of the shadow and

was rapidly heading straight for us, his flashlight once again on, and this time, aimed in our direction.

"He's got some kind of homing device." Frantically, I went over in my head what we were wearing. How could he possibly...

"Move it, Liz, we don't have time."

She grabbed my arm and I spun to follow after her. She knew these woods, which was fortunate because a flashlight would have given away our position.

He was gaining on us at an unnatural rate. I could hear him tearing through the brush behind us. We'd never make it. I spun and shot, ducked down and shot again. Still he came, and now his flashlight was trained on me. I froze and aimed once more directly at that yellow target. The gun fired and snapped backward, but instead of the light going out, a bullet flew past my head. I ducked and flung the gun at him. I'd wasted seconds that I didn't have to waste, exactly as he'd planned. I'd lost Josie in the confusion. I hoped she had enough sense to go on without me. The flashlight had me pegged like a bug wriggling on a straight pin.

"If you want your sister alive, don't give me any trouble."

"What'd you do? Put a tracking device under the pistol grip?" I asked James as he lowered the light and roughly pulled me to my feet.

"Right on the first try, Elizabeth. After we got back to your brother-in-law's, I loaded blanks in the chamber. But I guess you figured that out, too."

His grip was so strong, his arm circling me in front of him, that I could barely breathe. "You make even one unexpected move in the direction of that pepper spray in your pocket and I'll blow your head off," he whispered in my ear, snuggling the gun barrel under my chin.

"Let her go." It was Josie. Damn. Why hadn't she gotten out of there? Her shotgun offered her only two options: kill us both or kill no one.

"Gutsy, but not so bright as you," James whispered, and swung his gun in the direction of her voice. The hammer drew back and a male voice called out, "Relax."

I didn't think. I simply let out all my breath and went slack, slipping just enough in James's grip that when the bullet tore through his shoulder and snapped back his torso, I was already in a controlled fall to the ground. James crumpled behind me, as I dove for the gun that slipped from his hand.

Josie screamed, "Elizabeth!" and ran toward me. In the dark she couldn't tell which one of us had been hit.

"I'm all right." I grabbed for her, but she'd already swung the shotgun toward the shooter and stood in front of me, protecting me from the faceless intruder.

He stepped forward and I spun James's flashlight in his direction.

"Jesus," he swore, ripping the night vision goggles off his head. "You're the most damnably aggravating woman I've ever known. I endure being bitten by a dog and run down by a van, I engineer Patrice and Cara's rescue and you leave me to be killed at the airport, I cover your back on that godforsaken island that has more dynamite than mosquitoes, you blind me with that accursed flashlight, and now your sister is prepared to blast me to kingdom come after I've saved both your lives."

"You know this man?" Josie asked.

I pushed the nose of her shotgun toward the ground. "Meet Ian Payne. He was Stephen's friend."

"Your friend," Ian corrected. "I'm Elizabeth's friend."

Chapter 35

"Rule one— never assume. No body, no definitive proof of death. Remember that," Ian lectured.

"Consider it filed for future reference." I took the steaming mug of Constant Comment that Josie handed me and passed it over to Ian. "How'd you get off the island?"

"My boat was in the bushes on the other side of the island where I'd left it when I came in."

"When the cafeteria exploded, I thought you'd been killed," I confessed. I felt a twinge in my chest, an echo of the pain I'd felt at the time. My original instincts had been right. If only I'd trusted them.

"Hardly. The blast knocked me out of the main room and into the pantry. There was no way I could get out through the fire to where you were, so I made my way through the side of the building and onto the loading dock. A bit overenthusiastic, that husband of yours. Likes his dynamite," he called to Josie at the sink and then turned back to me. "By then Nathan had joined you out front."

"Why didn't you show yourself?" Josie asked, bringing another cup for me and one for herself as she joined us at the table.

"Elizabeth had obviously embraced James as the one who was there to help her, thus labeling me Stephen's killer. If I'd made my presence known, I would have gotten my bloody head shot off."

I heard James stir in the bedroom. Ian had done some pretty inventive things with duct tape after Josie had dressed his wound. It wouldn't do for James to die on us. We needed him alive.

"James saved Cara," I said. Ian had told me James was clever. He knew exactly where my weakness lay.

"He still needed you to lead him to Josie. He knew you'd trust him if he pulled her out of that pool. He had access to Will and would soon have Josie, as well."

"He gave me his gun to cinch the deal," I said.

"The one with the homing device in it," Josie added. "But I don't think you ever completely trusted him."

"Half trusted. My instincts always leaned toward you," I told Ian.

"Hah!" Ian retorted. "That wasn't instinct. That was your pride. If James had been Stephen's ally, you'd have to rationalize running from him in the first place and causing all sorts of grief to Cara and Patrice as well as yourself, not to mention our little…" He cocked his head. "You know, in the motel."

Josie let out a shocked, "What?"

I felt my face color. "We had a moment, literally only a moment," I insisted.

"Yes, well, call it what you will."

"Then you won't mind filling me in," Josie said.

"Later, perhaps, when we have something to actually report," he said.

Josie bailed me out, but I knew she'd get me eventually. "So you left the island and followed them back to the house."

"Yes," Ian said. "When I saw you separate from James, I knew he had something else up his sleeve, so I watched him. 'd used a device on Cara's car to track you when you and Cara went to Patrice's. He was certain you wouldn't fall for something quite that obvious again."

"I was stupid to fall for it the first time. Nathan swept the Hummer for bugs before we got in it."

"Exactly. You say it was in the gun he gave you."

"Under the pistol grips," I said. I felt like a fool and he knew it.

He shook his head. "You have to trust someone sometime."

"Even if it gets you killed like it did Stephen?" I asked.

He looked at me with solemn eyes.

"Yes. Even then. It's what makes us human."

Josie had called Nathan on her cell phone to let him know what had happened and that Ian was alive and with us.

The owners of the B and B had contacted a friend who repaired bicycles. After trying several different patches, he was able to get the tire sufficiently inflated for Nathan to operate the Hummer. James had driven the nail in only far enough to let the air out. Fortunately, no structural damage had been done to the tire itself. He hadn't dared give himself away by slashing it.

We'd finished our tea and begun our plans when Nathan, understandably agitated and suspicious, arrived at the cabin an hour later, bringing Cara and Will with him. After Cara had a long, silent moment with James, she and Will went outside and sat on the porch, leaving us at the table. James was lucky we didn't leave him alone with her.

"Ackerman will never be convicted of Stephen's murder," Ian said, "not with the cover-up I did on Stephen's death."

"It was necessary," Nathan insisted. "If you hadn't, you would have blown the whole operation. Jayne Donovan was still alive at the time, and the plan would have gone forward if possible."

"Donovan believed you to be innocent of Stephen's murder," I said.

"Yes. He aided in the cover-up, another reason none of this can ever come out. He would face disbarment. He refused, however, to allow Jayne to leave at that point, knowing the organization had been infiltrated."

"Did she know Will was safe?" I asked.

Ian nodded. "She was told when the plan to take her out was finalized."

Somehow that gave me comfort.

"So what do you suggest we do now?" Nathan asked.

"Oh, I suspect James can be convinced to help us convict Ackerman in the murder of Jayne Donovan," Ian said, glancing at the door open to the bedroom.

I could see James's legs struggling against his bonds. He had to be uncomfortable as hell, but I didn't feel sorry for him.

"Where do you think he stashed them?" Nathan asked Ian.

Josie and I exchanged puzzled looks. They knew James's modus operandi. She and I could only guess at it.

"He'll have recordings of the conversations he held with Ackerman about killing Stephen and Jayne Donovan," Ian explained. "Never trust a crook. They don't trust each other. They're always up for a little blackmail if things go wrong."

"My money says they're digital," Nathan stated.

"Could be. Oh, hell. I'm in no mood to search the continent. I say we make it simple."

Nathan winked at Ian. "Hey, man, let's go for it. I'm tired. He either gives it to us or he doesn't. If we have to look for it on our own, we don't need to be worrying about what he's doing in the meantime. We've got a lot of wooded land surrounding this place. Nobody's going to come here looking for a body, and if they do, they're sure not going to find anything if we bury it six feet down."

James's legs stilled. I didn't know if Ian and Nathan were serious or not. All that mattered was that James thought they were.

"If he cooperates, he might even buy his way out of the death penalty," I suggested. "He's a young guy. Who knows? He could live long enough to see daylight someday."

I walked over to the doorway and stared into the eyes of the man who had caused me so much grief.

"I won't save you," I told James, "if that's what you're counting on. Cara would never have been on that island if it hadn't been for you. Once that tape comes off your mouth, you've got half an hour to tell us everything you know."

Chapter 36

It's true what they say. The sky over Greece is a color unlike anywhere else in the world. The contrast with the white stone of the buildings made it even more breathtaking as I stared out at the blue of the sea and let the warm wind blow my hair about my face. What had surprised me most about my first experience on the islands was that I'd expected to feel drawn into the past, into the glorious history of the place. Instead, I felt as though I'd never before existed so much in the present.

Ian slipped an arm around my shoulder and I let myself relax into the joy of his touch. We had three more days before my conference began in Athens, and I wanted nothing more than to spend them with Ian under the Grecian sun.

"I just got off the phone with Will," he said. "Ackerman has been found guilty of jury tampering and bribery. Judge Donovan imposed the maximum sentence. And the grand jury has indicted him on first-degree murder and conspiracy to commit murder, as well as several lesser crimes. If he miraculously manages to avoid the death penalty when this is all over, he'll still take his last breath in prison."

"Good," I said. All I wanted was an ending, to know that Nicholas Ackerman would never harm anyone else ever again.

"Will also said he'd see you in a couple weeks."

He was meeting up with Cara and me in Manhattan. Patrice's pottery would be on exhibit by then in one of the finer galleries, and she wanted me to see it. Odin didn't much care for the city, but they'd be back in Pennsylvania before long.

"He'll only be able to stay a day or two. He filed a multimillion-dollar wrongful death suit against Ackerman half an hour after the verdict came in."

I turned to face Ian, and his arms encircled the waist of my sundress. He looked different. Younger. The burden he'd carried around his eyes and jaw was gone.

"What's Will need with that money?" I asked.

"Nothing. He filed it at Peter's suggestion. His intent is to tie up Nick's assets, to cripple his network financially and give his law team one more headache. Then the boys—Josie's sons—can come into their father's money if they wish to pursue it once Ackerman's convicted of murder."

I suspected no amount of money would tempt them to trade their Estes heritage for Ackerman's. That the world would never know who their father was would be Ackerman's final defeat.

I smiled. The system would finally put an end to the man of my nightmares.

"Speaking of money, you should be in a fairly good position to retire," I said.

"How so?"

"The million dollars Stephen left you with his insurance policy. Surely you didn't spend all of it chasing after me."

Ian laughed out loud. "Oh, that. I thought you might forget that little detail. Elizabeth, I'm afraid I haven't been totally honest with you."

I stiffened. Could this man who, I believed, had given me the one gift that Stephen had denied me—honesty—be about to take it from me?

"There was no insurance policy."

"But you said—"

"What made sense to you at the time. Stephen did ask me to watch over you when Peter positioned me in the D.C. area after the Donovan operation began. I've been half in love with you since the first day I saw you in the halls at Gilman. I could hardly have told you that, now, could I, especially when my kneecap was at stake. I'm afraid it was thoroughly unprofessional of me. I'm incredibly ashamed."

Laughter bubbled up from somewhere deep inside of me. I didn't know where our relationship would take us, but, for the first time since I could remember, I had no fear, not of the future, not of anything. Ian had given that to me. I had my life back. I was free.

* * * * *

At Silhouette Bombshell, the excitement never stops,
and the compelling heroines never give up
till they get their men, good and bad.
Every month we bring you four innovative
stories that will keep you riveted!
Turn the page for a sneak peek at one
of next month's compelling reads:

PAST SINS
by Debra Webb

Available June 2006
at your favorite retail outlet.

For ten seconds Olivia couldn't breathe.

This was impossible.

She told herself to take a breath. Instinctively she reached up and fingered the necklace that served as a constant reminder of all she wanted to forget.

"Is everything all right, Olivia?"

Her gaze shot to the dining room, where her boyfriend, Jeffrey, stared at her, concern marring the smooth features of his intelligent face.

She swallowed. "I have to take this call."

Before he could give her a disappointed look for allowing the intrusion during dinner—during their time—she escaped out the front door.

This was not a call forwarded from her office number or her home number of any other number represented by some part of her present life.

This was the past calling. An old cell number she'd once used as a lifeline…a number she'd tried three years to forget but could never bring herself to let go.

By the fifth ring she had reached the edge of her driveway. She flipped open the phone, her heart pounding. "Yes." It was a miracle her voice didn't quaver.

"Sheara?"

The earth shook beneath her, or maybe it was her rigid frame doing the shaking. She tried to steady herself but the name kept reverberating through her like the aftershocks of a major quake.

This wasn't possible.

She licked her lips. "Yes."

"I have a problem that requires your special brand of attention. You were highly recommended." He cleared his throat. "I would like to arrange a meeting as soon as possible."

Olivia blinked, glanced around the neighborhood to ensure she hadn't attracted any unnecessary attention. It wasn't dark yet, but the temperature had dropped significantly, making her shiver.

Or maybe it was the call that had sent that bone-cold chill rushing through her veins.

Sheara didn't exist anymore. How the hell had this guy gotten her old number? This wasn't supposed to happen. She'd kept that number for one reason only….

"Ah…Sheara? Are you there?" The caller cleared his throat again. "Maybe I have the wrong number."

"No." She said the word more sharply than she'd intended. "You have the right number." What the hell did she do now? She was a psychologist, for Christ's sake. She didn't do *this* anymore.

Sheara was dead.

She'd been dead for three years.

She bit back the need to ask how he'd gotten her number. "Where would you like to meet?"

There was only one way to find out who this guy was and how he'd gotten her old number. Meet him. Right now. Tonight. This couldn't wait. Her heart rate climbed with each new realization.

"The location is your choice…right? That's what I was told."

Olivia squeezed her eyes shut and forced herself to take another breath. He was right. She had to focus. "What's your location? And I'll need a name." She tried to block the sound of her heart thundering, pumping blood so fast it roared in her ears. What was she doing? This could be a trap. But why? She'd been out of the business for three damned years. The woman she used to be was dead.

His hesitation told her he wasn't too keen on the idea of giving his name or his location. "Ned…Soderbaum. Chicago."

It was seven-thirty now. Approximately a three-hour flight. Assuming he could get one in the next hour, midnight would be the earliest meeting time.

"If you can get a flight—"

"My company has…I own a jet."

Well, okay then. Flight scheduling wouldn't be a problem. Where to meet? It wouldn't be a good idea to have him come to Hollywood. Wait. What was she worried about? This was Los Angeles County, including Los Angeles, Beverly Hills and dozens of other mass-population centers. There was an endless supply of anonymous places to meet, and far too many people to make her easy to single out.

"The pier at Santa Monica. Midnight."

More hesitation. "How will I know you?"

"What will you be wearing?" she countered.

"Business suit…ah…navy."

And you'll stand out like an American tourist on a nude beach in the south of France, she wanted to say. "Won't work,

Mr. Soderbaum. You want to look like a local. Wear khaki shorts, a white T-shirt and a red baseball cap. I'll find you." At that time of night the pier would be pretty much deserted.

"I guess I can do that."

"Don't forget the sneakers and the retainer fee."

"I'm…I'm not sure on that last part. I didn't get a clear idea of your fee."

She blinked, suddenly uncertain what to say to that. She remembered well the going rate three years ago, but that would have changed now.

"Ten now, fifteen later. Nothing larger than a twenty."

Olivia didn't wait for his acknowledgment. She closed her phone, ending the call.

She stared at the compact device for an endless moment. What had just happened here? Confusion cluttered her thinking process. Too many questions filled her head. No answers.

She stared at her brick home with its clean, crisp coat of white paint…her silver Audi…Jeffrey's blue Saturn…the lush, colorful landscape all around her. This was her life. She and Jeffrey were supposed to be having dinner. Then they would watch a little television and go to bed. Maybe they would have sex, maybe they wouldn't. And tomorrow everything started over again. Work. Home. Sleep. Uncomplicated. Safe.

Her gaze dropped to the phone in her hand.

Until thirty seconds ago.

HOTEL
MARCHAND

Four sisters.
A family legacy.
And someone is out to destroy it.

A captivating new limited continuity, launching June 2006

The most beautiful hotel in New Orleans,
and someone is out to destroy it. But mystery,
danger and some surprising family revelations
and discoveries won't stop the Marchand sisters
from protecting their birthright…
and finding love along the way.

HOTEL MARCHAND

This riveting new saga begins with

In the Dark

by national bestselling author

JUDITH ARNOLD

The party at Hotel Marchand is in full swing when the lights suddenly go out. What does head of security Mac Jensen do first? He's torn between two jobs—protecting the guests at the hotel and keeping the woman he loves safe.

A woman to protect. A hotel to secure. And no idea who's determined to harm them.

On Sale June 2006

Page-turning drama…

Exotic, glamorous locations…

Intense emotion and passionate seduction…

Sheikhs, princes and billionaire tycoons…

This summer, may we suggest:

THE SHEIKH'S DISOBEDIENT BRIDE

by Jane Porter

On sale June.

AT THE GREEK TYCOON'S BIDDING

by Cathy Williams

On sale July.

THE ITALIAN MILLIONAIRE'S VIRGIN WIFE

On sale August.

With new titles to choose from every month, discover a world of romance in our books written by internationally bestselling authors.

Silhouette® BOMBSHELL™

COMING NEXT MONTH

#93 DAUGHTER OF THE FLAMES—Nancy Holder
The Gifted

The nightmares, the feeling of being followed, her father's hospitalization…something wasn't right in Isabella DeMarco's life. Then a mysterious stranger clued her in to her shocking family legacy of fighting the forces of evil in the world, and it all made sense. But her newfound supernatural gift felt like a curse, especially when she found herself up against a formidable vampire hell-bent on bringing Izzy down in flames….

#94 EXCLUSIVE—Katherine Garbera
Athena Force

Investigative reporting was in TV anchorwoman Tory Patton's blood, and when her colleague and fellow Athena Academy grad was taken hostage in the Middle East, even Tory's own pregnancy wouldn't stop her from taking the life-or-death assignment to save her friend. But the kidnappers weren't who they seemed…and suddenly this international crisis loomed closer to the academy than anyone could ever guess.

#95 THE FIREBIRD DECEPTION—Cate Dermody
The Strongbox Chronicles

In CIA agent Alisha MacAleer's world, betrayal was the name of the game. So when she set out to recover the firebird combat drone and return it to its rightful owner, it came as little surprise that her ex-fiancé had beaten her to the punch and taken the drone right out from under her nose. Between her ex's games and the deadly threat of a secret society bent on her destruction, how could she not take this assignment *very* personally?

#96 PAST SINS—Debra Webb

With a new boyfriend, a new career—an entirely new life—in Los Angeles, Olivia Mills thought she could finally relax. But one telephone call from her past changed all that. Now to protect the ones she loved, she raced back east to track down the top secret forces at work against her, confront the irresistible man who'd abandoned her in her hour of greatest need…and face the consequences of her former life as a hired assassin.

SBCNM0506